MAYAN SHADOWS

THE CRYSTALS OF AHRUM, BOOK 1

CRAIG A. HART

S.J. VARENGO

ALSO BY CRAIG A. HART

The Shelby Alexander Thriller Series

Serenity

Serenity Stalked

Serenity Avenged

Serenity Submerged

Serenity Engulfed

Serenity Betrayed

Serenity Reborn

Serenity Possessed

The Maxwell Barnes Adventure Thriller Series

Mayan Shadows

The SpyCo Novella Series

Assignment: Athens

Assignment: Paris

Assignment: Istanbul

Assignment: Sydney

Assignment: Alaska

Assignment: Dublin

Assignment: London

The Cleanup Crew Thriller Series

The Demon of Denver

The Simon Wolfe Mystery Series

Night at Key West

Collections

The Shelby Alexander Collection, Books 1-4

Assignment: Adventure, SpyCo Books 1-3

Assignment: Danger, SpyCo Books 4-6

A Cleanup Crew Collection, Books 1-4

ALSO BY S.J. VARENGO

The Cleanup Crew Thriller Series

The Beauty of Bucharest

The Count of Carolina

The Terror of Tijuana

The Demon of Denver

The Maxwell Barnes Adventure Thriller Series

Mayan Shadows

The Cerah of Quadar Fantasy Series

A Dark Clock

Many Hidden Rooms

A Single Candle

The Shelby Alexander Thriller Series

Serenity Reborn

Serenity Possessed

The SpyCo Novella Series

Assignment: Paris

Assignment: Istanbul

Assignment: Sydney

Assignment: Dublin

Assignment: London

Collections

Assignment: Adventure, SpyCo Books 1-3

Assignment: Danger, SpyCo Books 4-6

A Cleanup Crew Collection, Books 1-4

Standalone Novels

Jelly Jars

PROLOGUE

Yucatán Peninsula, 16th century, Spanish Conquest

The scent wafted on a fetid jungle breeze that did nothing to refresh.

Danger has a smell.

The thought invaded Francisco Estrada de León's mind like a psychological parasite, even as his nostrils flared at the scent.

He sat atop his horse at the crest of a small hill and overlooked his straggling army. The peninsular sun beat down on the procession, reflecting off the steel and iron tips of lances and halberds in blinding, sparkling flashes of light, and causing the helmets and cuirasses of the soldiers to gleam and glow.

The main body of the army—if such a small group could be called such—was crossing an open area, a clearing, allowing Estrada to see most of his force *in toto*, and the sight both worried and filled him with pride. They were roughly half the number of their original landing strength, having lost men to battle, fever, and fatigue. Yet they were hardy troops, hardened like iron in the irate kilns of adversity.

Estrada glanced at his officers, the others also on horseback, to determine if they too had the scent of danger in their nostrils. But they all appeared oblivious, and more intent on swatting away bugs and complaining about the heat inside their armor.

With a feeling of intense isolation rearing up, *again*, Estrada settled more firmly into his blistering saddle. He'd yet to meet another soldier who could smell such a thing. It was a gift—nay, a curse—that had beleaguered him since his days as a young cavalryman. He'd always known when a battle would play out poorly, although he did not always know exactly what that meant. Sometimes it had meant complete and utter defeat. On occasion it meant that, although victorious, he lost someone close to his heart. At other times, it meant they won the battle but did so at much too large a cost—a Pyrrhic victory of the classic order.

This uncertainty, along with the sheer manner of the revelation, had prevented Estrada from ever sharing his ability with anyone. It would have sounded ridiculous, and impossible to prove, given its ambiguity, so he labored on, alone in the oppressive knowledge, but at least not chained up as a lunatic.

Estrada's mouth thinned and twisted; on the eve of this battle, there was danger—real danger—on the air.

The line of soldiers, mostly single file, moved across the large clearing toward the tree line. They now numbered one hundred and fifty-three souls.

There were ten officers, including Estrada, and twenty cavalrymen most of whom were *jinetes*—a lightly armored and lightning-fast version of the heavy cavalry that Estrada would have preferred to use. Upon arrival, the numbers had favored the shock cavalry, but one disastrous battle in the thickest part of the jungle had seen their numbers decimated as they became caught in the overgrowth and vines, dragged from their horses and beaten to death by natives with heavy *macuahuitl* clubs.

Since then, Estrada had opted to feature his *jinetes* while in thick jungle, as they were much more agile and trained for fast, tactical strikes, rather than the blunt trauma of the shock cavalry, which were better used on open plains. And *jinetes* still proved highly effective. Years after the initial encounter with the Europeans, the natives remained unaccustomed to horses and regarded them as nearly paranormal. This alone gave cavalry—light or otherwise—a distinct advantage. Add to that their speed, and the fact that their weapons were centuries more advanced, and it was, most often, no contest at all.

So, it was not his dwindling numbers that most worried Estrada. They had faced overwhelming numerical odds since their arrival on this cursed peninsula, and still their losses had mostly been inflicted due to the conquistadors' unfamiliarity with the land and their opponents' tactics and frightening abilities in close range situations. More recently, as experience had been gained and tactics altered, their casualties per battle had decreased by a significant percentage. Yes, they faced potential thousands, but Estrada was confident in their martial superiority. He had worked out his battlefield strategy against the natives almost to a science, and he played it out now in his mind.

Their single cannon—one left of the original three they'd brought, and which they had since named Rosita—would open the conflict with a blast into the main force of the enemy, followed by a volley from a dozen crossbowmen. This, if history was any guide, would serve to scatter the native line, allowing the *jinetes* to swoop in and out with the speed of some sort of deadly hummingbirds, slashing and thrusting with grace *and* twelve-foot lances.

The line of infantry would be formed and slowly advance, pressing the enemy back until they turned to run, at which point the entire cavalry would have a field day mopping up their isolated and fleeing opponents. It was a simple enough strategy—and one that could be repeated over the course of a single conflict—because at the same time it was one that *had* worked over and over as Estrada had marched his men deeper into Mayan territory.

In truth, the only real change the natives had made to counter such an obviously effective strategy was attempting to battle exclusively in the thick of the jungle, which maximized both their fleetness of foot and knowledge of the terrain.

It was Estrada's job to keep that from ever happening, and so far, he had succeeded—save for that initial horrific experience during which the cavalry had been slaughtered. But he prided himself on learning from his mistakes, and since then he'd employed advance scouts, and lookouts to act also as surveyors, finding the open areas and thereby planning their route, keeping his army's time in the heaviest jungle to a minimum—and never, ever, setting up camp there.

The few times a native force had slipped past the loose cordon of lookouts around the moving army and attacked their flanks, Estrada's response was to make for the next clearing as quickly as possible, setting up a defensive line there until he could mount a counterattack. So far, this had worked, and they had managed to move through the unavoidable areas of thickest jungle with few losses.

Estrada turned at the sounds of hooves to see an officer riding up the hill, his horse bathed in sweat and laboring.

"Capitán General," the man called out, "Capitán General!"

Estrada straightened in the saddle and raised his chin in both recognition and permission to approach. The officer was Colón, a *coroneles* who Estrada had known since childhood, as they had grown up in the same town of Badajoz. During their earlier years, theirs had been a volatile relationship—sometimes friend, sometimes enemy, and always competitor. But once Estrada had begun rising in the ranks—and certainly since his appointment as Capitán General of the current expedition—it became clear who was going to be in control of that particular equation. For his part, Coroneles Colón now seemed generally content with his rank and status, even though Estrada occasionally caught a glimpse of irritation or resentment. He had, in fact, been against bringing the other man along, but had agreed after a secret visit from the man's aging mother, who considered this New World conquest to be the last chance at greatness for her son. Estrada admitted that the wisdom of his decision was yet to be determined.

Estrada focused on the man. "Approach, Coroneles Colón," he said. "What has you and your mount in such a state?"

Colón had brought his horse to a walk and slowly came forward. "I have just received word from an advance scout," he gasped desperately, as if he'd been the one carrying the horse and not the other way around. "He reports seeing the city of Ahrum not more than three miles ahead."

"And what of the terrain between here and there?"

Colón paused in speaking to gather both his breath and his wits, and Estrada had to force himself to repress an expression of disdain. There was a reason this man had never attained higher rank. He was missing something deep inside his gut, something that separated men from boys, a soldier from a farmer in armor. It would be, Estrada thought grimly, probably the best thing for his legacy to die here in conquest. At least then his family could make an appeal to the crown for a title and stipend. Whether or not they would be granted such a luxury was quite another thing, but at least they could lay claim and use that to bolster their own status.

"The terrain?" Estrada prompted.

Colón nodded. "Ah, yes—the terrain. It is mostly jungle, divided by a river that is moderate in both size and current. Both manageable. The city itself sits upon a hill surrounded by open area, which appears to be used for agriculture."

Estrada frowned. The report was both good and bad news. The open area around the city was good, but the stretch of jungle—and a damn river—between here and there was not so good. Getting Rosita across water was always an arduous task. Doing so this close to a populated settlement, well—it was likely they would be spotted before arrival, which significantly increased the odds of premature strikes on their flanks, if not a full-on assault. If they were attacked during a river crossing ... well, that would simply be a worse-case scenario. He would have to double or triple the scouts to prevent any nasty surprises.

"Very well," he said, dismissing Colón with a flick of his hand. "You may return to your place in the line."

Again, Estrada thought he caught a flash of resentment in the coroneles' eyes, but he chose, as he always did, to ignore it. Their close upbringing and shared hometown were not insignificant, and sometimes it helped to keep potential enemies even closer than known friends. If there was one thing Estrada did not need at this point in the expedition, it was dissension in the ranks.

His nostrils flared once more with the tickling scent of danger.

1

Yucatán Peninsula, Present Day

Maxwell Barnes rolled over in his sleeping bag and tried to go back to sleep, but the scent of coffee had begun its siren song not too long before and had only grown more alluring as the minutes ticked past.

"Dude, it's, like, perfect outside," Axel rumbled, his impossibly low voice like auditory molasses in Barnes' ears. "Get your butt out of that bag before it gets any hotter, and I might be persuaded to fry up the rest of this bacon before it goes bad."

Max's eyes popped open. If there was a man on earth who could resist the twin temptations of coffee and bacon, Barnes had no desire to meet him, as that man was clearly a sociopath of the most depraved order. In fact, the only thing that could even approach the allure of coffee and bacon, was a set of twins of another variety—but women, along with their wonderful anatomies, were distressingly scarce in the field.

Today, coffee and bacon would have to suffice.

He rolled again, this time back in the opposite direction, and managed to focus his eyes on his friend, whose broad back was hunched over the fire pit. He reached down, grabbed the zipper of the bag and, through sheer exercise of an iron will, forced it down enough to slide his bare legs out.

As he completed this heroic act, the loud *chick-burr* of a scarlet tanager sounded overhead, somewhere in the tree canopy, and it sounded to Barnes' surly ears exactly like a sarcastic cheer. He glared upward and fantasized briefly about tanagers tasting like bacon.

"Would you like that, *chac yuyum*?" he yelled, using the Mayan name for the bird, just to show it who was boss. "Bacon and you, together in my belly?"

Axel, who'd been busily tending the fire, froze for a few seconds, and then slowly turned, still crouched, to look back at Barnes. "I know you're always grouchy in the morning—but that was just ... *mean*."

Barnes struggled to his feet, stopped to consider this, then gave a curt nod. "You know what, Ax? You're right." He looked back up at the bird. "Sorry, *chac yuyum*, I didn't mean to give bacon top billing. I meant to say, 'you and bacon, together in my belly.'"

Axel let out a chuff of laughter and turned back to the fire, shaking his head. "Well, get your pants on before you scare off the rest of the wildlife with those skinny gams. Bacon, delicious and bird-free, will be ready in a flash."

At the mention of clothing, Barnes flicked a finger at Axel's bare upper body. "Aren't the bugs eating you alive?"

"It's not bad over here by the fire," Axel said, "and I'm waiting for my shirt to dry out." He cast his eyes upward to indicate the garment in question, hanging from a low vine a few feet over the fire.

Barnes whistled. "Did you ... finally wash that thing?"

Axel's broad face, bronzed by sun, flushed darkly. "I ... er ... thought it was time."

"Way past time, buddy, but I'll give you credit for getting there eventually. You going to be okay?"

"It'll be tough, but I'll make it," Axel said, setting his face in a resolute grimace.

There was something about the expression that felt off to Barnes. Then it came to him and he checked his wristwatch, which included the days of the month. "Oookay, martyr. Now I get it. You washed your shirt because we're headed back to civilization tomorrow, and you're hoping to see Rosita."

Axel dropped the act and grinned. "Yeah. Her perfume wore off long ago anyway. Now I can get a refresh."

"You're such a romantic, Ax." Barnes shook his head, as he reached down to pick up his pants, taking care to shake out any jungle squatters that might have settled there before stepping into them. He scrunched up his face. "I thought you said it was perfect out here. I feel like I'm wearing a wet blanket."

"I lied to get you moving," Ax admitted, without shame. "Besides, you would have been boiled out of that bag soon anyway."

Barnes growled. "Speaking of getting me moving, I think I was promised coffee and bacon."

"And bird."

"I've pardoned the bird. Let's just stick with the staples for now."

Chick-burr, the tanager said, making it clear that any pardons received from this odd, earth-trodding creature were unwelcome and unneeded. Its wet dropping on Max's shoulder a moment later was clearly a premeditated exclamation point.

As was the case almost every time Barnes moved from wilderness to city, thinking about it now filled him with a mixed cocktail of emotions. To be sure a nicely mixed cocktail would be delightful. Even a nice Mexican beer (or ten) would do a great deal to cut through the bits of the jungle that one carries back *inside* of him. One can scrub the tree gum and pollen from clothes and skin and hair, but it's harder to purge the film that sticks to the mouth and throat and guts.

"That's where the Dos Equis comes in," he said aloud.

"Dang it, man," Ax said. "How many times have I got to tell you that walking through the jungle talking to yourself about beer is just weird. This is why I have a *girl* waiting for me, and you have ... what? What's waiting for you, Barnes?"

"Beer."

It was not quite two full days' walk back to La Libertad, a city of almost eighty thousand, from the north of Lago Peten Itza. They'd set up camp within an hour of the lake itself, and if they humped nonstop, they could have stumbled into La Libertad just before midnight, of no use to themselves or, importantly in Axel's case, anyone else.

They hadn't been six weeks in the jungle for fun and relaxation, although both men found both of those in great quantities whenever they worked together, even in the rank 80s and 90s, the temperature range that the weather in Guatemala never seemed capable of breaking, except for about fifteen minutes in January. They were on an assignment. That's what Max chose to call it. It sounded better than what it actually was, which was a shopping trip for Myron Crabtree.

He spit.

Even though he'd not spoken the man's name, he still felt like he needed to clear it from his mouth. Then he shook his head. At that moment, the trail on which they moved was wide enough for them to walk side by side, so Axel saw the whole process as it happened, and he smiled.

"You're thinking about Crabtree. You always spit when you think about him and then shake your head. I've never asked, because we're dudes and officially I can't give a shit, but I gotta know the thought choo-choo you ride on every time he pops into your head. I get the spitting his name out of your mouth part."

Barnes laughed easily. He and Axel were almost exactly the same age and had known each other since they were kids. They had grown up together, brothers in every regard other than shared DNA. When they'd been sixteen, Max had stopped growing. Axel, however, seemed to grow another quarter inch every month until he topped out at 6'7" and a zero-fat 310 pounds. Extremely odd for his racial mix, but it made him a good guy to have around.

Still, sometimes he knew Barnes *too* well.

"The head shake is always me reminding myself that he's not *that* bad."

"Yeah, not that bad as crazy billionaires go."

"His checks never bounce."

"On that we agree. And there should be one of those waiting for us when we reach La Lib, *sí?*"

"*Sí!*" he replied enthusiastically. "And we both know what's waiting for you."

"We know *who's* waiting for me. You talk like Rosita is a possession. She's a living, vibrant woman, you rat!"

Barnes laughed giving his friend a shove.

"You know your problem, Maxwell Barnes? You've been

working for Crabtree so long now you're starting to think like him. You can't just buy every pretty thing you see."

"You know what your problem is, Axel Morales? You're a walking solar eclipse. You're too big."

Axel's smile was more than bright enough to compensate for any sunlight he obscured.

"That's what she said."

Axel's reservations about Crabtree were not that different from his own. After all, he did have to keep *reminding* himself that the man was not that bad. His fondness for, nay, his *obsession* with Meso-American artifacts was the stuff of legend, and that also happened to be Max's area of expertise. Win-win, at least from his and Axel's perspective.

The fact is that the arrangement was a win for Myron Crabtree as well because Max knew more about the Mayan culture and its associated artifacts than just about anyone on the planet. From a practical point of view, he knew the difference between treasure hunting and archaeological research. His heart constantly yearned for the latter, but his wallet often drew him to the more lucrative, but far uglier former.

"To the dark side," he said aloud.

"Dark side? You still going on about the eclipse thing? Because I'm not shading you from the sun at all, and if I was, I gotta think you'd be thanking me."

"No, I was still thinking about Crabtree. He is nominally funding the research, and, in theory, if we find Ahrum, he'll make sure everyone knows that he was the sponsor. But in the meantime, that means finding him trinkets."

"Yes, but that also means we were able to buy enough provisions on his dime to look for clues for six weeks this time. I mean, you didn't find anything but—"

Just then Barnes stopped in his tracks and reflexively held up his hand. Axel had been looking elsewhere and took another step before noticing that his partner had stopped and was looking at the bark of a tree which grew beside the ancient footpath which they were traversing.

Axel had seen him look at a lot of trees over the years.

What Max was looking for, as had his father years before, were discrete markings in the tree bark, some of them hundreds of years old, others on younger trees. Oftentimes, it was little more than a scratch against the grain to show a traveler that he had not strayed, and sometimes there was ...

"An arrow."

"Are you sure? The last time it wasn't even a mark. It was a bug."

"Look, Ax! It's an arrow!

Axel walked to where Barnes was gesturing almost comically, tracing the mark from one end to the pointed other. It was very clearly an arrow, and from the depth of it as well as the thickness of the mango tree on which it was carved, he estimated it was extremely old. But he was not about to let Max off that easily. He began to squint his eyes and tilt his head at various angles, at one point stroking his chin thoughtfully.

Eventually, Barnes realized he was being put on, and he gave Axel another playful shove.

"You see it, right, wise guy?"

"Dude, that right there is an arrow! Pretty old one from the looks."

"It's indicating northwest. Ahrum?"

Axel smiled and put his huge hand on Max's shoulder. Ahrum was the legendary last city of the Maya. Accent on *legendary*. Myths and rumors, little more. There was precious little concrete evidence. Max's father, Anderson Barnes, had seen only one seemingly legitimate item and had told both Max and Axel about it many times. It had been far from the Yucatán; in Morocco, the senior Barnes had said. It was the corner of a map—nothing more. There was a story attached to it, leading back here. To Yucatán, to Guatemala. To Ahrum.

But he'd spent his last years looking in vain. Axel also loved the man like a father and his belief in *him* never wavered, but he'd lost faith in the stories.

Max had not. And that's why he was smiling at him now. That's why he'd touched his shoulder.

"Maybe. Could also have been directions to a guy who sold good smoked fish too."

"For the sign to have been maintained this long, it would have to be some pretty great fish."

"Like I said, maybe."

Max could hear the hesitation in his voice. He pointed a finger at his friend.

"We built time in."

"I know, I know. We *always* build time in. But we never build in as much as you're going to want to spend going in the direction of that arrow, which I might add, takes us off the trail."

"You hate trails!"

"Not when I'm trying to get back to Rosita, Maxy! Then I *love* trails. Sheesh. How heartless are you?"

"You know better than anyone, probably."

"You have an excessively big heart, Maxwell Barnes. We budgeted four hours for rabbit holes. Two hours following that vector, if we don't see another mark, two hours back since we're closer to La Libertad now than we will be after a hundred-twenty excruciating minutes heading north when my sweet Rosita is to our... our... what direction is it again?"

"South," he said.

"South is correct. Two hours, *hermano,* then we tag the GPS coordinates, and we walk back. Or I drag you back."

Max spit into the palm of his hand and held it out. Axel smiled and repeated the ritual, grabbing Barnes' offering and once more creating the emblem of agreement they'd employed since childhood.

"Two hours," Max said.

TRUE TO HIS WORD, two hours later, after one questionable scratch that Max finally decided looked like it had been caused by a bird's beak, they came to a stop.

"Wait, look at that," Max said, pointing. It was a clear line, cutting across the grain of the tree's bark. The sort that Professor Barnes had always said were meant to indicate the sojourner was not lost.

Axel stepped to the tree. "It's another one of those stick bugs."

Max stepped closer and saw the creature move one of its legs slightly.

"Crap! You're right." He looked at his watch, sighed, then opened its GPS function, putting a pin at this location. "Alright, but we're coming back as soon as we get some free time."

"We're not going to get six weeks again for a while if you don't find Crabtree something pretty to put on his mantle. Which you're going to have to do in La Lib."

"Rosita did get me a line on some top-notch pottery—late 600s."

Axel shot him a sharp look. "And how would you know that?"

"We text each other late at night when you're sleeping."

"Now I know you're lying," Axel growled. "Unless you brought your own cell tower into the rainforest."

"Come on, Big Ax. Let's get you home to your woman."

Barnes double checked to make sure the GPS marker had taken. The global positioning satellite did not rely on cellular data, making the tool usable even where cell phones were little more than stylish, shiny bricks. Once certain he could get back here, he turned and began walking in the direction they'd come, two hours earlier.

Almost as soon as they'd left, the walking stick bug on the tree felt safe enough to wander off, revealing as he moved a very intentionally carved arrow, which pointed in a slightly different vector.

2

It was late when Barnes and Ax dragged into the city of La Libertad. Even so, there was activity around the bars they passed, which somehow made Barnes even thirstier than he already was. While beer is a poor option for countering dehydration, especially in the jungle, they were now in something more closely resembling civilization, and his throat was very, very dry.

"Hey, Ax—let's stop in for a drink."

The big man heaved a sigh that caused his massive shoulder muscles to ripple with irritation.

"I can drink at Rosita's."

Max huffed. "And how does that help me?"

"You can have a drink."

"And then get immediately kicked out when you two want to get busy, which I suspect will be approximately thirty seconds after we arrive?"

Axel grinned lasciviously. "Ten. I texted her. She's already mostly—"

"Stop!" Barnes shook his head violently. "Don't put thoughts in my head. I don't have a girl waiting, remember?"

"We'll throw a beer down to you."

"Nothing doing. Listen, you go on to see the woman of your dreams. Drink all you want ... of whatever you want. I'm stopping in at one of these bars for mine."

Axel frowned and hesitated. "Sure you can take care of yourself? It can get dangerous in these cities at night, you know." His tone was ever so slightly condescending, causing Max to bristle.

"Pretty sure I can find my way around without getting kidnapped or killed. I'm no babe in the woods, you know."

His friend shrugged. "You do way better in the woods, truth be told. Okay. But don't make me drag your body out of a dumpster tomorrow morning."

"Aw, you're worried about me!"

"Nope. I just don't want to come away with garbage stank or fill out any paperwork."

Max rolled his eyes. "Go on. Get out of here."

"Whatever you say," Axel said, starting to move away. "Give me a call if you need anything." He was shaking his head "no" as he said the words, causing Max to smile. He paused. "But for real, it better be important. Like, dumpster-level important."

"I wouldn't dream of interrupting anything, young stallion."

Axel grinned and drifted off into the darkness, leaving Barnes to marvel once again at how such a large man could move so quietly and vanish so quickly.

He shook his head and then turned his attention to the bar closest to him. Imaginatively named *La Taberna de la Libertad*, the bar featured a flickering Dos Equis sign and an open door, painted blue. Sad paint was chipped and peeling, and the two windows sported bars over the glass, but these details were of no concern to

Max. The sign promising beer was commanding his full attention, and was beyond sufficient to draw him in.

Down the street a bit, he saw a small man, dressed in what appeared to be vaguely Mayan garb. From this distance, and in the dim light, it was hard to tell. Max was far too jungle-weary to take much more notice than that, although from the few Spanish words he was able to pick out of the man's ramblings, he sounded like a prophet of old, warning that the end was near.

"Nope, not interested," Max muttered.

He began to turn to enter the bar, but then caught sight of sudden movement somewhere in his peripheral vision. His head swiveled, and he saw that the strange figure in the distance was being set upon by a group of shadowy assailants.

Against his better judgment, he adjusted his trajectory so that he was moving toward the struggle. While the visibility was poor, provided only by a limp circle of light from an old streetlamp—probably from late in the Liberal Revolution—not much light is required to recognize when someone is getting the crap beat out of them.

Ultimately, though, it was not sight but rather sound that caused him to act, as whoever was getting their clock cleaned was now screaming. The attackers did not relent, and the screams were actually growing weaker now.

Not a good sign.

"*¡Oye! ¡Policía!*" he shouted, trying to make his voice carry the authority he clearly didn't have. He picked up his pace, as a chorus of Spanish curses in the cracking voices of adolescent boys came dancing down toward him. But their defiance was fleeting and, immediately after cursing him roundly, they ran off into the darkness.

The immediate danger having been averted, Max walked

toward the crumpled man, who was attempting to crawl further into the lighted area. Seeing the movement was sufficient to increase the pace of Max's approach, as he'd been dragging his feet a little at the thought of coming upon a body, rather than ... whatever this less dead thing turned out to be.

"*Hola*," Max called.

"*¿Qué?*" came the reply, in a weak but definitely the same male voice he'd heard earlier.

Knowing his Spanish to be sketchy, Max assumed that he'd misspoken. Approaching, he turned on his phone's flashlight and passed it over the man's battered features. The victim was clutching his ribs, which had no doubt felt many boot tips before the thugs ran away. Max could see that the man—or boy, as he looked to be no older than his late-teens—had the clearly defined facial features that identified someone with Mayan blood flowing in their veins. Curiously, Max also saw that he was dressed *not* in any traditional garb but rather exactly like ... an American skateboarder, right down to the baggy cargo shorts, a hooded bulk-knit top, and a well-worn pair of Vans on his feet.

"Oh, Dude," the young man said, in the accent and vocal characteristics of a Lord of Dogtown. With his eyes closed, Max could have easily thought he was in California, not Guatemala. "I thought I was toast, brah. That was a pretty good idea calling for the police. You're a thinker, you are."

"Are you okay?" Max asked. While certainly concerned about the young man's physical condition, he was also now harboring doubts about his mental state as well.

The man began to laugh. "Yah! No worries. They were a bunch of ams."

"Ams?" Max asked, reaching a hand down to help him up.

"Amateurs, posers. You know, brah!" he said, grinning through his obvious pain.

Max returned a smile as the young man grabbed him by the wrist and painfully hoisted himself vertical.

"Name's Bembe," he said, converting the hand-up to a handshake.

"Max Barnes."

Bembe tried to take a step, and his leg seemed to buckle under his slight weight. Max heard some distinct and very unpleasant crunching sounds from the general area of the right knee as the young man nearly went down. Max grabbed his arm.

"You're not as okay as you think you are. Is there a clinic around here somewhere?"

"Prolly, dude, but it wouldn't be open now. Besides, I'll be fine in a minute." Further crunching, further stumbling, and a loud shout of pain caused Max to doubt the prognosis.

"I really think you should—"

"Brah! Relax. You kids are so impatient."

Max wasn't quite sure what to make of that, and even less sure of what he saw next. He watched as Bembe put his hand against the bricks, as Max had done when first walking down the alley and closed his eyes. He lowered his head and took a series of three very deep breaths, holding each for several seconds before exhaling. The night was hot, but his breath came out as steam like on a serious winter's day in New England. After the third exhalation, Bembe seemed to not breathe at all for nearly half-a-minute, and Max was just about to check to see if he'd died leaning against the wall.

Instead, with a huge smile, Bembe turned and did a perfect pirouette on his right leg, which a moment earlier had seemed on the verge of snapping into two pieces, then did an impressively high leap before coming down firmly on both feet. The adopted pose reminded Max of what had initially drawn his attention to the man.

"So, what were you doing over here, anyway? Preaching?"

"Nah, I wasn't preaching. It was more of a ... a job posting!"

"Okaaay," Max said, drawing the word out. "Now, my Spanish isn't as good as one might expect, given the amount of time I've spent in this neck of the woods, but it sounded kind of 'The end is nigh-ish' to me."

Bembe smiled again, and there was something about the expression that Max both liked and wanted to hide from. "Like, your Spanish is good enough to know what I was saying, brah. You thirsty? We could go get a drink."

The paranoid part of Max's mind began a drumbeat of warning, but there was something about this teenaged Mayan skate punk that he couldn't resist.

"Wouldn't mind, I guess."

"Yeah, you wouldn't!" Bembe exclaimed, again jumping ridiculously high in the air while executing a full 540, a move that would have been impressive on a skateboard and defied physics altogether without one. "Follow me, Max Barnes. I have beer and an epic tale for you."

Max shook his head as the young man trotted off, looking behind to beckon. Against his better judgment he broke into a trot behind the bouncing Mayan.

THERE ARE many common elements in most population centers of South and Central America. One of these similarities tends to be the presence of makeshift communities of the homeless, and in places with an ethnic diversity like this part of Guatemala, with its lingering Mayan bloodlines, the tents and lean-tos often congregate along those cultural lines.

Thus, when Bembe led Max through a rather uncomfortable and twisty series of alleys and narrow streets—none of which gave any indication that the government was investing public funds in lightbulbs or paving—and they ended up squeezing through a fence into a small group of people with similarly native looking features, Max was only slightly taken aback.

Seeing this many Mayan faces in one place tickled something in his professional brain, but Bembe was not making introductions. He was skipping through the huddled, mostly sleeping people toward a corner formed by a wall and a wooden barrier, where a tarp covered the area beneath. Into this, Bembe went now, holding up the plastic tarp for Max.

Max had never thought of himself as a big guy—but then, he'd grown up with Axel. Tonight though, just about every place Bembe wanted to take him required a bend or squat, and the plastic shelter was no exception. Possibly the worst; almost a crawl. Once inside, however, Max saw the place was oddly comfortable. A canvas camp chair sat behind a wooden crate that served as a table. An old mattress, which looked lumpy as hell but relatively clean, was where Bembe plunked down, offering the chair to Max with the gracious flourish of one hand. As the American took the offered seat, Bembe opened a cooler, which Max saw had a brick inside of it.

Paranoia was starting to reawaken.

But Bembe was opening it with a grin. "I keep a brick in it so that it's heavier, and when people open it to rip me off, they get all snarked up. 'Dude—it's a brick!' Ya know. Then they don't even move it to see this ..."

He pushed the cooler aside, revealing a piece of plywood cut to be just slightly smaller than the bottom of the red rectangular container. This he also slid aside. Max was beginning to shift his worrying away from the brick and onto whatever Bembe was about to extract from the hole beneath it.

He needn't have.

Two inexplicably cold bottles of Dos Equis and just about the coolest skateboard Max had ever seen were the only things excavated. He handed Max one of the beers and the board.

"Check my deck."

"It's ... amazing."

The skateboard appeared extremely well-constructed, but what really made it stand out was the design embossed upon it. Max knew what he was seeing. It was a detail from the Dresden Codex, one of four existing Mayan books, captured during the Spanish conquest of the area.

While Max had never bothered to spend much time building up his proficiency in Spanish, he'd studied the Mayan texts extensively under his father's tutelage, and he pointed to several of the pictogram images.

"Lots of talk about the gods," Max said, running his finger on the board's gritty surface. "And ... a crystal?"

Bembe said nothing, so Max continued. "Chaac ... Jaguar ... Itzamma ..." He stopped reading and looked at Bembe, who was grinning broadly and taking a long slug from the sweating beer.

"What is this?"

"The hell, brah! It's a skateboard."

The grin, the same that had won Max over and made the hair on his neck stand up simultaneously, did not flicker now. It beamed full power.

"Nah, I'm messing with you. I'll tell you. I'll tell you. You should have seen your face, brah." The young Mayan's ensuing giggle attack reminded Max of the butt-kicking from earlier, and the word "concussion" formed in his mind. But after a moment, Bembe regained his composure and said, "You comfy? It's a long story."

Max finally got around to opening the beer and nodded.

"Comfy."

"Okay, cool. So, a long time ago there was no Spanish spoken in this land. In that regard, you'd have been okay, because it's not like you'd have understood if it had been."

Max lifted the beer in a gesture of *touché.*

"Back then everybody looked like me. Well, not quite as good looking as me, but you get the idea, right?"

Max nodded.

"So, my people had a pretty decent relationship with the gods, as long as we, ya know, gave them what they required, and in return they used to look out for us. Give us a heads-up if a big storm was coming, if the crops were in trouble. That sort of thing."

Max noticed that he spoke very familiarly about his distant ancestors. It was cool, he thought, that a people could have such a strong social bond that they were able to speak across the centuries as if they'd been weeks instead.

"Sometimes the messages *blew,* though, brah. Like the one on the deck." He pointed to the skateboard, balanced now on Max's knees. In a gesture that showed more trust than Max realized he was feeling, he handed it back to Bembe.

"The crystal?" Max said.

"The crystal, brah." Bembe paused, then said slowly, "I truly do despise that crystal."

Max came up short. From one sentence to the next, Bembe had

sounded like two very different people, but before he could wrap his head around it, the grinning Bembe returned.

"Well, you know. The stuff it represents. See the gods got all ... what was it you said, 'the end is nigh-ish.' I understand now they were letting us know that the Spanish were coming, and the end *was* darn well nigh after all. But you get it, don't ya, brah? Who could know? Half the time we couldn't figure out what the gods were even talking about. My personal opinion is they liked messing with us, is all.

"But the shaman class, the true protectors of the people, more or less figured out that, whatever was about to happen, it was going to be bad, and the preservation of our people depended on getting the power of three of the mightiest gods into one main crystal." He made three jabbing points at the skateboard, pointing out the images that represented the gods that Max had read earlier.

"It was a very big deal," Bembe said. "They got to work on the project right away, sending the novice shaman out into the jungle to collect the arcane plants and rare earths needed to complete the ceremony. It was a lot of sweaty work. A real pain in the hacky sack if you get me. And when everything had been collected and prepared according to the ancient texts and traditions, the high shaman gathered to conduct the ceremony. For the most part, the novices were sent away at that point, except for one, left behind to run for any last-minute needs of the elder priests, who—let me tell you, brah—were a lazy bunch of men when it came to getting stuff. 'Oh, no! Where's the topaz dagger? Who took my curare?' Ugh."

Max laughed at the depth of detail Bembe was putting into this. Whatever else he was—prophet, skate punk—he was a first division storyteller.

"Sorry, brah. Getting off track. It's just those guys ... ANYWAY! Ritual commences. Now, the novices that got told to Casper Flip their way out knew before anyone in the pyramid that—"

"Pyramid?" Max asked, sitting up straight.

Bembe waved his hand in a "chill-out" manner.

"Not important. Getting to the good part."

"Bembe, that's very important. That's what I—"

"Okay, okay. I'll circle back around to it. Don't mess with my steezy. The novices leave and find out that the whole city is under attack. All these light skinned dudes with beards and pretty sticks that kill you when they go off, show up on the doorstep, so to speak. So things got real, and they got that way fast, with people dropping like flies. But at that point, the only thing remaining to complete the whole crystal thing was a small blood sacrifice to each god."

Max's eyes widened, but Bembe repeated the chill-out gesture.

"Just a little one. No one even got their heart cut out!" he said dismissively, but with a hint of deceit, causing Max to wonder if that was *exactly* what had happened. "Horado was the eldest of the elders. It was his spilt blood that would seal the gods within the crystal, one cut for each god. He drew the topaz dagger across his hand, and the blood dripped on the first crystal – you saw the names, Max. The first was *Chaac* which contained the power of the storm and would let the holder call down lightning from the sky. Then Ek Balam—"

"The Black Jaguar," Max said, almost to himself.

"That's the one. Horado made a cut on his hand for that one, too, letting the blood drip onto the crystal, trapping in it the power of fire, the power to make war."

"Whoa," Max said.

"Right? Freakin' cool!" Bembe took another drink from his beer, then after a deep breath, he continued.

"Then there was the big one. The one that would contain Itzamná. Now, I'm gonna be honest with you, Max. It's hard to keep track of all of our gods, and I never came close to learning them all. But everybody knew Itzamná. Some scholars eventually came to believe all the other gods were just manifestations of him. That he was the *only* god. Would have been fine with me. One name is way easier to remember than over a hundo.

"Problem was that before Horado could lift his hand above it, one of the Spaniard's musket balls shot right through his head. And although plenty of his blood got on the crystal for Itzamná, it wasn't the *ritual* blood. The blood of sacrifice from his hand. Without the willful act of sacrifice, it didn't work. Game over.

"One by one, the other elders were cut down as well. By sword or by shot, they fell. Any one of them could have completed the ritual, and the gods would have been pleased with their sacrifice. But before any could even find the topaz dagger, which had fallen to the stone floor when Horado had been killed, they joined him in the beyond."

"So, if that was to be the end of Mayan civilization, how are there still Mayans here? How are you here?"

Bembe grinned again, the full two-faced number, and again Max shivered a little.

"Remember the one novice? The one that had to go find Horado's dagger and his potions and his stinking loincloth? Well, he saw the knife on the floor and while the Spaniards were busy running around grabbing up gold and making sure the elders were really dead, he snatched the knife and made the cut—"

As he said this, he pantomimed drawing a blade across his

palm, and in the warm light of the battery powered camp lantern on the table, Max thought he saw a jagged scar there.

Bembe continued, "The new guy wasn't sure if it would work. I mean, he hadn't finished his training. He hadn't learned all the names. But he was a shaman, and his blood was willfully spilled, so they might have considered the ritual completed and sealed the crystal. We'll never know."

By this point, Max was nearly hypnotized by the young man's story. He was lost in his voice. It seemed as though a mist had formed before his eyes, and he could almost see the things Bembe was describing, as if he was looking across the centuries.

"Because at that moment," Bembe said, "none other than Francisco Estrada de León, the *grand conquistador de España*, fired his weapon at the novice."

Max gasped involuntarily, and Bembe chuckled as he once more patted his hand downward, urging him to relax.

"Luckily he was a lousy shot! Well, lucky for the kid, ya know, because it only caught him in the shoulder and not the head! Even so, the shock and force knocked him backward, where he hit his head on the side of the stone wall. And then everything went black!"

Bembe brought his hands together and then made the exact explosion sound Max remembered using when he and Axel used to throw mud at each other and pretend they were grenades. At the same time, Bembe's hands mimicked the expanding detonation.

Bembe continued. "When the novice regained consciousness, he was lying in the jungle to the side of a path that was trampled by many feet. His hands were bound behind his back, but he was completely alone. He figured that he'd been taken prisoner but then abandoned when he was found to have a bad fever. You tend to spike one during the apocalypse. But he was dead weight, I guess, and his captors didn't want to be bothered. And, let me tell you, he felt awful, brah. He thought he was gonna die, but he managed to get out of his bonds and make a fire. Then he gathered some ingredients to make a strong tea. With his last ounce of strength, he downed the mixture—which tasted horrible—and fell into a deep sleep. When he woke up, the fever was gone, and he was so hungry and thirsty he thought he was going to go stark raving mad."

For a moment, Bembe seemed lost in his thoughts. Then, as if remembering Max was there, he slapped his hands on his thighs, breaking the spell. Max's vision cleared, and the misty images of the long dead shaman faded.

"Anyway, that's pretty much the story!"

"And?" Max asked.

"And what, brah?"

"Uh ... the crystal. What happened to the crystal?"

"Oh, right! Well, nobody really knows the answer to that. Maybe the Spanish took it, maybe it's right where it was when Horado fell. But you're right on track with me, brah, because that's where the job offer comes in. They say that if the crystal can be discovered, and the proper ritual is performed to open it up, the power of the three gods would cause the Mayan to rise again and cast the Spanish from our ancestral lands."

"Assuming the ritual was actually completed," Max said.

Bembe shrugged. "Well, yeah, brah, assuming that. But why be such a downer about it?" He gave Max another treatment of his patented grin. "So, anyway, I'm in the market for a guy who likes to find stuff. Know anyone like that?"

Max suddenly found himself exhausted. It had happened

almost instantly. He shook his head as he stood and handed his empty beer bottle to Bembe.

"Good luck finding someone." Max opened the tarp and started to walk out. "Sounds like a fool's errand to me."

"That sounds like your father talking!" Bembe said with a laugh. Max assumed he meant it sounded conservative and staid, and smiled as he continued out of the lean-to. "Imagine if Anderson had known that the crystal might still be right in Ahrum."

Max's heart jumped into his throat. Bembe had spoken his father's name ... and the name of the lost city for which the professor had spent his life looking.

"What did you say?" Max said, snapping back around to the enclosure.

Instead of answering, Bembe leaned down and felt around in the cavity from which he'd produced both the beers and the skateboard. Max was practically vibrating with impatience, but he forced himself to wait until Bembe found what he sought and pulled it out.

The skater stood and held out his hand, which now grasped a manila envelope. He shook it slightly, indicating that he wanted Max to take it.

Max did so and, as Bembe watched carefully, pinched the metal clasps open and then turned up the flap of the envelope. Peering inside, Max saw a single piece of paper, one that appeared yellowed with age and torn along two sides. He reached in and carefully drew the paper out.

He recognized it immediately. The untorn edges were decorated with Mayan symbols and a heavy double border—it looked exactly like the map that Max's father had tried to use to find the lost city of Ahrum—a copy.

No, Max realized with a jolt, *not a copy.*

Max shivered as he realized that this was an additional piece of that same map. And there, in the middle, was the drawn icon of a Mayan pyramid with the word AHRUM printed underneath. Unlike his father's torn section, this showed the actual location which, if pieced together with his father's in order to gain geographical context, might actually allow them to locate the city.

Max felt like letting out a gigantic whoop of exultation but restrained himself just in time. Instead, he looked up and said,

"Where did you get—?"

But the lean-to was empty. Bembe was nowhere to be seen.

3

Upon leaving Bembe's lean-to, Max's first inclination was to find a *hostal* and fall immediately asleep. His time in the jungle, and then the crazy, surprisingly emotional journey of Bembe's tale, had absolutely drained him. But now, that same tale preyed upon his mind. His body was unanimous in its vote for sleep; his mind, however, was staging a filibuster.

Heading back in the direction from which he'd followed the eccentric skater punk, he recalled the bar that had been in his immediate future, prior to rescuing Bembe from the street thugs, and decided that another beer might help calm his thoughts.

Before long, he was walking up to the blue door with chipped paint, which was propped open with a cement block, (a tip from *Modern Tavern Décor*? *Cantina Beautiful*?) and he stepped inside. He took a moment to get his bearings. The walls were painted in a light, avocado green and two ceiling fans slowly rotated. On the bar, a box fan rattled loudly, but the noise blended nicely with the chatter of Spanish being spoken by the clientele. Mostly locals, the current drinkers paid him little notice. La Libertad was no stranger to tourists *or* beer-drinkers. It was, by all accounts, Guatemala's gateway to all things Maya. It featured a few nice restaurants, an impressive outdoor market and other ... establishments with less reputable tags. Even so, Max knew he appeared a bit worse for wear than the average tourist, given his time in the trees, and appreciated the simple, local hospitality of not staring at his dirty, bedraggled condition in disgust.

As he approached the bar, however, the proprietor did cast a look over him from top to bottom and gave a single quirked brow.

"Dos Equis," Max said, sliding money onto the bar.

The man looked at the money, as if making sure it wasn't as filthy as Max looked, then took it and shoved it into a cashbox.

"Keep the change," Max muttered in English.

If the bartender understood the words, they were ignored, and he simply yanked a beer from the cooler, popped the top, and slid it over to Max, who grabbed it eagerly.

"Gracias," he said, turning away and surveying the room for an empty table. There were plenty to choose from. He moved to a corner at the back of the establishment, where a table sat at an angle. Taking the inside chair, this allowed him a clear view of both the front entrance and the employee's door at the back. He was not expecting trouble, but old habits die hard, and this was one habit Barnes had no intention of breaking. Paranoia had saved his life on more than one occasion. He smiled as he remembered someone from his past, Henri Absil, who'd been a spy during the Cold War. Barnes was too young to have been around when Absil was plying his craft, but the two had become friends in the spy's later life.

"Max," the old Frenchman had said, his cigarette voice low and nostalgic, "if you look for danger in every corner, eventually it will be there."

Max had, at one time, thought that espionage would be his career, but the harsh discipline required to be the best turned out to be anathema to his preferred lifestyle. Not to mention that a spy's life was 99% tedious repetition and 1% abject terror. The tedium percentage was much, much too high.

Max had discovered he could find excitement and travel at a far better ratio by following a passion he'd picked up from his father, Professor Anderson Barnes—that of archaeology. His father, of course, had been content to operate under the watchful eyes of a university's oversight. Not so for Max. And he'd proven skillful and resourceful enough to find opportunities in the field as an independent archaeologist, something that caused no small amount of friction between the two men.

He took a sip of his beer. It was not ice cold, but neither room temperature, so he figured he'd be able to choke it down. And then the next beer would be easier. And soon it would seem like nectar, no matter what its temperature might be.

At that thought, something caught his eye from the opposite corner, and he thought that the temperature might just be rising after all. It was a beautiful, raven-haired señorita, her dark eyes fixed directly on his blue ones. She approached, a Negra Modelo held lightly in her delicate hand. Her hips swayed a bit as she approached, not enough to be overtly provocative, but enough to draw the eye—which they certainly did in this case. Drawn and shackled. Max dragged his gaze up from her hourglass figure and forced himself to look at her face, not that it was a chore to do so. Her lips were slightly parted and, as he watched, a pink tongue flicked out to wet them.

Her approach was so deliberate that Max almost felt as if he should rise to greet her, but was worried about embarrassing himself. So, instead, he remained seated, deciding that she'd have to be satisfied with a welcoming smile. He'd been told—mostly by women, to his satisfaction—that his was a dazzling smile, and he put it to good use in this case. She smiled in return, revealing perfect teeth.

Who is this woman? he wondered. His reliable paranoia chimed in from the back of his mind, competing with his masculine pride for attention.

Get rid of her, Paranoia said. *Stranger danger.*

FEMALE stranger, Pride said, totally ignoring the "danger" part.

She wants something from you, Paranoia warned.

Yeah, and it's something you want to give her, Pride comforted.

Before the debate was settled, the woman had pulled out a chair and settled gracefully into it. She looked into Max's face, still smiling, and lightly tapped the red-painted nails of one hand against her beer bottle.

"You are not a local," she said, in very good English, while still retaining plenty of the accent that always got Max's blood racing. "You are a tourist?"

Max had to pause for a moment to gather his thoughts. It had been a while since a woman had taken away his ability to even think.

"Uh, no—no, not a tourist." He paused again. "Not a local either—I mean, obviously. Ha!" He took sudden refuge by drinking from his beer.

Get it together, Pride said. *You got this.*

Get rid of her, Paranoia pouted, knowing it was losing ground. *Or she'll get you!*

"What brings you to La Libertad? Business?"

Her pronunciation of "business," which was more like "busy-ness," made Max happy to be alive.

"No, well, yes—not the town actually. I'm just here after a dig."

"A ... dig?"

Again, that sexy pronunciation: deeg. Max sighed inwardly.

"Yes. I'm an archaeologist."

Her eyes widened. "Oh! You are Indiana Jones."

Max grinned so broadly he thought his face might crack and, as he did so, Paranoia grunted out a curse and slinked into the dark recesses of his mind to lick its wounds, readying itself to fight another day. Now in total control, Pride wasted no time setting up shop, rearranging the furniture and painting the walls some bright, conceited color.

"Well, it's not quite *that* exciting and dangerous," Max said, his tone leaving open the possibility that it might be *exactly* that exciting and dangerous. "But I do get around quite a bit."

"And you must find so many fascinating things," the woman said.

Max nodded slowly, dipped his head slightly to suggest a remnant of humility. "It's very rewarding." Then he raised his head to look directly at her again. "What's your name, beautiful?"

Wow, Pride said, rolling its eyes. *That was really lame. What are you, some stupid intern on leave from the lab?*

Lame or not, it seemed to hit home with the living work of art sitting across the table, because she flashed Max an impossibly bright smile and leaned forward, which allowed her blouse to dip low, revealing some absolutely stunning landscape.

"I am Margarita." She drank from her Modelo. "And now you will tell me of your most exciting travels."

"Don't you want to know my name?"

She laughed lightly, the sound like distant chapel bells. "I already know your name ... Indy."

My work is done here, Pride said with great satisfaction. *You can take it from here, cowboy.*

4

Max groaned and tried to shut his eyes, only to realize they were already shut. *Then how was it still so bright in here?* It was as if his eyelids had holes in them. His head pounded and his limbs felt heavy. It had been a while since he'd experienced a hangover this intense, and he figured it probably had something to do with the fact that he'd been low on hydration even before drinking the alcohol, thanks to his trip out of the jungle, and because he hadn't done his due diligence in loading up on water before going to bed. This was partially because of the fact that he hadn't had bottled water handy—and there was no way he was going to risk the tap water, partially because his mind had been too preoccupied with the insane events surrounding Bembe and his story, but mostly because he had been far too distracted by Margarita to give any thought to preventative care.

Even as he lay on his bunk in the *hostal*, he wondered if he'd imagined the whole thing. A Mayan skater punk named Bembe? An ancient ceremony involving ritual blood and a supernatural crystal? Crazy! And what about Margarita? Had she been just a dream? If this was what it was coming to, maybe he should swear off Mexican beer as well as the sketchy water supply. Or as Margarita's gorgeous face hovered in his memory, maybe he should give in and just live off the stuff exclusively.

Then something speared through the fog in his brain and reached the one synapse that remained in operating condition.

Bembe had mentioned his father.

"That sounds like your father talking!" he'd said. *"Imagine if Anderson had known that the crystal might still be right in Ahrum."*

Max cracked open one eyelid and immediately regretted it. The sun was streaming in through a window that some builder had thoughtlessly placed so as to direct a beam of light directly into Max's face.

Rude! he thought.

Summoning every ounce of willpower, he forced his eye to remain open until it slowly—very slowly—began to feel less like someone was driving an icepick directly into it. Only then did he experiment with the other eye: same stabbing pain, same heroic effort, same slowly-abating agony.

"Okay," he said. "Eyes open. Now the real battle: sitting up."

"¡Cierra el pico!" a voice hissed, and it was only then that Max realized he'd spoken aloud.

"Perdone," Max muttered, although he wasn't sorry at all. He glanced over and saw the speaker, a small man who looked in even worse shape than Max felt. The man glared at him with red-rimmed eyes, and Max felt some kinship with him, despite the obvious hostility. Drinkers, and those who are suffering the after-effects of a night (or day or week) of debauchery, have a special bond, even if they are far more willing to demonstrate that bond during the *act* of tying one tightly on. Once the drinking is over

and the suffering has begun, they tend to prefer less companionship and more solitude ... dark, quiet, desperate solitude. Still, Max felt kindly enough toward his unfortunate brother in cups to give him a small, weary salute.

"I feel you, brother," he said.

The man bared his teeth. "*¡Cierra el pico!*"

"Look, I get that you feel bad, but I'm trying to—"

The man raised up on his elbow and shot Max a look that could only be described as murderous. Max raised his saluting hand, palm out, in a gesture of peace.

"*¡Voy a matarte!*"

Max's eyes widened at the man's threat, and he was just about to scramble for his backpack and a weapon or perhaps *as* a weapon, when a deep voice rumbled behind him.

"You're not going to be killing anyone, buddy, and certainly not my stupid friend, here."

Max breathed a sigh of relief as he rolled over and looked up into Axel's broad face, which had forsaken its usual cheery expression in favor of one far more menacing. It worked. With bulging, frightened eyes the man turned away from them and pretended to snore.

"Ax! I didn't expect you so early."

His big friend raised an eyebrow. "Early? It's noon, you alcoholic. Time to be up and at 'em."

Max groaned. "Up and at who? Not Rosita, obviously. I figured you two would be making like rabbits all day."

Axel grinned, not all offended. "We already did that. Did I not say it was noon? Now, get up and let's go. It's lunchtime, and I want some authentic tacos."

. . .

OVER CARNITAS TACOS that came as close to melting in one's mouth as meat ever could, Max told his friend about Bembe and the surreal events of the previous night, conveniently leaving out any mention of Margarita. Axel listened with eyes that grew gradually larger as the story progressed, until Max was convinced they were going to pop out and land in his beverage.

"Are you ... serious?" Axel said, his deep voice wavering slightly. "You're not making this up, are you?"

Max shrugged. "I don't *think* so. I mean, not on purpose, anyway. I have wondered if it was all just a crazy dream. It certainly sounds absolutely nuts."

"Well," Axel said, inhaling his third taco, "I know how you can find out for sure."

Max held up a hand. "I know what you're thinking."

"And?"

"And the reason I haven't yet done so isn't only because my brain is just now starting to function properly."

Axel groaned. "You two had another fight, didn't you?"

"It wasn't a fight, exactly. Just a disagreement. Actually, it wasn't even that. A discussion, is all it was."

"A discussion that ended up with you proclaiming your independence in that annoying tone you get, whenever you think someone is trying to trample your rights?"

"No, I—wait, what annoying tone?"

Axel sighed. "Dude, you'd wear the Don't Tread On Me flag as a cloak, if I'd let you."

"Do you have one? Because that would be ... anyway, is that so wrong?"

"Not necessarily. Depends on what you're trying to accomplish. Which, in this case, is having a cordial relationship with your father."

"I hate it when you make good sense," Max grumbled. "Fortunately, it doesn't happen that often."

Axel growled. "Don't forget that I'm at least twice your size."

"So, what, you'd beat me up?"

"Well, no—but I might steal your tacos."

Max shuddered. "I think I'd rather get beaten. These things are to diieee foooor!" He ended the sentence in a high-pitched singsong.

"But your illusions of total independence may not be. Your dad's a smart and connected guy. Is your pride worth that loss?"

"It's not about pride, Ax, it's about principle."

"Principles," Axel said, making a gagging sound. "Yuck. Principles are just pride dressed up in the robes of piety."

Max couldn't help but laugh. "They are inconvenient things, aren't they? And ... whoa! Nice proverb. But back to the issue at hand—yes. The reason I have not already called my father to ask about Bembe's info is because our last conversation did not end in the best possible way."

Axel shook his head. "You two are so confusing. Both of you obviously love the other, but then you've got this never-ending conflict. I wish you could just put it to bed."

"As do I," Max agreed. "And I do see his point. He's in the lap of academia. He's expected to toe the line on things. Having a son who calls himself an archaeologist and goes on digs without the oversight and blessing of an institution is something of an embarrassment."

"It doesn't help that you're more successful than any of his peers," Axel interjected wryly.

"Exactly. And to be honest, I think that's a large part of it. Sure, some are sincerely concerned that I'll destroy invaluable finds with my 'uneducated' endeavors, but even most of *them* are just furious that I'm constantly showing them up. It makes them look bad, which makes it that much more difficult to apply for grants. My dad told me that a friend of his applied for a grant to do a dig in central Mexico, and the chairman of the grant asked him if he could, quote, 'provide the same results as that Maxwell Barnes guy,' end quote."

Axel cringed. "Ouch."

"Yeah. Ouch. So, my dad is caught between me and his stuffed shirt, status quo pals in the ivory tower."

"Look, I get it," Axel said. "But, still, you gotta call him and ask about Bembe. There's just no other way. And he will never say this, so I will. He's the one who taught you everything that makes you so good."

Max nodded and sighed. "I know, I know. He is, and I will. But after I finish these tacos. In the meantime, how about a little play-by-play of the night's doings with Rosita?"

Axel's grin spread so wide that Max thought his friend's face might split in half. "Sorry," the big man said. "A gentleman never kisses and tells."

Max grinned right back, completely okay with the fact that he was being an enormous hypocrite. "Two problems with that excuse: first, you ain't no gentleman; and second, I'm pretty sure you did more than kiss, you naughty playboy."

"As I said," Axel repeated, his face so complete a picture of smugness that Max desperately wanted to slap it silly, "no kissing and telling. Now, call your dad."

Max sighed but dug into his pocket for his cell. He poked his dad's number on the Favorites list and waited while it connected. It still boggled his mind that he could connect with his father, who was thousands of miles away, directly and in a matter of seconds. Living in the future had its drawbacks, but also very definite advantages. As recently as his dad's day, neighbors often shared a party line and could listen in on each other's conversations. These days, the only parties one had to worry about eavesdropping were bored government officials and algorithmically-driven mega retailers.

"Maxwell?"

Anderson Barnes always said that first thing, even though Max knew that his face and name showed up on his dad's screen. And he was also the only person who consistently called him Maxwell. His mother had always done so, saying, "If I wanted him called Max, I would have named him Max," while Anderson had always said "Maxy" or "Champ." But ever since his mother had passed away, Anderson had taken up the torch, so to speak, and carried on the maternal tradition. Max suspected that his dad did so because it reminded him of his wife, and perhaps it was also a way to respect her memory and to connect the three of them.

"Yeah, it's me," Max said, putting the call on speaker. "Is this a bad time?"

"No, not a bad time. Are you still in, where is it this time? El Salvador?"

"Guatemala, Dad. La Libertad."

"Oh, right, *that* La Libertad." Anderson chuckled lightly. "I just can't keep track of you. Old stomping grounds, right, Ax?" he asked, guessing Axel would not be far from Max.

Axel grinned and leaned toward the phone. "True that, Prof. Good times, huh?"

Max smiled thinly at the irony.

"Any luck out there?"

"Just some basic stuff for Crabtree," Max said.

"So this is a social call, then. Just couldn't wait to chat with the old man, eh?"

"Well, not exactly."

Anderson laughed. "I knew it, I knew it. What's up?"

"I had a pretty weird experience last night. And I'm hoping you can help clear it up."

"Okay, shoot."

As Max had talked, he'd noticed a man moving along slowly on the far side of the street. Normally, he would not have paid any attention—save for the never-ending vigilance that was bred of both experience and his paranoia which always lurked in the back of his mind—but this man was different. First, he was a striking man. And, while Max had eyes only for the ladies, he could admit when another male was good-looking. This man, with his swarthy skin and sleek black hair, could have graced the front of any number of celebrity magazines. Those features, along with his piercing black eyes, straight and thin nose, and sharply defined jaw, would have set the hearts of many women aflame. He was dressed smartly in pressed slacks, a cream-colored shirt, and a tan vest. But aside from his striking appearance, Max was keenly aware of the interest the man seemed to be taking in their table. A thought that at the same time pleased and worried him ran through his mind. *Rosita's dad, perhaps? Margarita's?*

"Maxwell?"

"What?" Max's attention was drawn back to the phone call by his father's sharp tone.

"The weird experience? You were going to tell me about it?"

"Oh, right. Sorry. Yeah."

Max told his father about his encounter, or possible dream, with Bembe, and waited with nervous anticipation as Professor Barnes remained silent for a long moment after Max had stopped talking.

"Bembe? Seriously? He's gotta be getting gray by now! He

was just about twenty when I knew him and that was, well, let's see ... forty, forty-five years ago? Long before you boys were born." Professor Barnes seemed to be attempting to make light of it, but to his son it sounded a little like he was forcing the issue.

Max now took his turn at the long, dramatic pause. As weird as this was already, a skater stuck in time was pushing things a little far.

"Must not be the same guy. His kid maybe? This guy's a skate punk wannabe, no more than nineteen or so himself."

"Skater? Hmm. So was the Bembe I knew. In fact, he told me he'd recently moved back home from Venice Beach. He said all the best skaters came from there."

"Well, I guess kids follow in their father's footsteps all the time ..." Max began, before hearing his own words and biting down on them.

When Anderson Barnes answered it was in a voice which contained hints of both sadness and aggravation.

"Some more closely than others."

Max took the phone off speaker as Axel nervously tried to pretend he hadn't heard every word spoken as well as the even louder unspoken things.

"Dad—"

"Maxwell, I'm sorry. I didn't mean to start down that road again. So let's stick to this whole Bembe thing. Whether this is the Bembe I knew, or Bembe Junior is probably less important than what he told you."

"About the crystal?"

"About everything. The ritual. The invaders. How detailed do you remember the telling being?"

Max paused again, but not for drama this time. He was

thinking back through the fog of drunkenness and whatever else was going on.

"Pretty stinking detailed, now that you mention."

"Kind of like he was remembering, as opposed to retelling. That level of detail?"

Another pause. "Exactly that level."

"And you're sure he said the crystal was still in Ahrum?"

"He ... said it *could* be. He wasn't certain."

There was now no doubt in Max's mind that his father knew as much about the city and the crystal as Max did, perhaps more. While his father was clearly interested in hearing what Max was saying, not much of it was coming as a surprise. Feeling the tension had passed, he put the phone on speaker again, setting it between himself and Ax. If his father *was* preparing to tell them anything useful, he'd want Axel to hear it too.

"He didn't happen to have the GPS numbers for the city did he?" Professor Barnes laughed nervously. Clearly he was hoping for just that, or something almost as good.

"No. But dad—"

"What, Maxwell?"

"He gave me something. A piece of map," Max said.

Silence.

"And it matches the piece of map that you have," Max continued

More silence.

"And he gave it to me," Max concluded with conscious redundancy.

The old saying about hearing a pin drop came nowhere near describing the abyss of absolute quiet that ensued. It went on so long that Max began to wonder if his father had succumbed to an aneurysm. He glanced over at Axel and saw a similar expression of curious concern on his friend's broad face.

At last, Professor Barnes cleared his throat.

"Ahem ... and you ... have this map in your possession? Right now?"

"Piece of map, yes. It's in my pack."

"And did Bembe explain anything about what it showed?"

Max shook his head, even though his father could not see him. "No, and for two reasons."

"Which were?"

"First of all, he didn't need to. This part of the map shows Ahrum right on it. It's even labelled."

"It's—"

"Labelled, Dad. It says 'Ahrum' right on the map."

More of that now-familiar silence.

Finally, "And what was the second reason?"

This time it was Max who cleared his throat. "Bembe, uh ... well, he vanished."

"Maxwell," The professor said, his voice adopting a new level of tension. "I am eager to speak about this more at length. But, look ... I don't know how much more I want to talk about this on an unsecured line."

"Aw, jeez, Dad. And here I am in the middle of Guatemala without an encrypted line in sight."

"Hilarious."

"Well, seriously. How are we supposed to talk securely? And why do we need to?"

"What did I teach you about paranoia?"

Axel and Max answered in unison:

"Paranoia is not always pathological. It's often nature's way of telling you ..." They both stopped in mid-sentence, because in the original teaching they were required to break into the song by the old rock band Spirit, which since becoming adults they only did when they'd been drinking for a while.

"I don't feel like singing right now either," Anderson said. "So instead I'll find a way to get in touch with you. But it might be a bit. Just keep your heads down and *be careful.*" He stressed these final words.

"Yeah. I've got to try to scare up something pretty for Crabtree anyway."

"There used to be a guy not far from the highway. By the Catholic Church, he had a small yard."

"Yurí," Max interrupted. "Yeah that dude's almost as old as the one or two genuine pieces he might have on hand, but I'd forgotten about him. Thanks."

Professor Barnes was the sort of person whose smile you could hear without seeing it. "Good to hear from you guys. I'll be in touch."

"Okay, Dad. Bye for now."

"Wait! Maxwell! I almost forgot. This is all really flakey still. Still forming up in my head. But ... just in case ... you should probably keep your eyes open for someone named Estrada."

"Estrada," Max repeated slowly. For some reason he looked back across the street, to the place from where the striking man had been observing Axel. He thought that the dude had been eyeballing Axel, but now...

The man was still there, but as Max repeated the name, he looked even more intently at the table before standing and rapidly walking away.

"Yeah. I'll be on the lookout."

"Alright. Good. Thank you, son. I'll talk to you soon."

The line was disconnected.

"There!" Axel beamed. "Was that so hard? A nice phone call. An *almost* nice phone call."

"Did you hear the way his voice changed?"

"Well, for gosh sakes, you said the single stupidest thing you could have said. Nothing like smacking him on the sunburn. Idiot."

"It was an accident."

"So were you, probably. No one holds *that* against you."

"Uh! Why don't you go back for another round with Rosita? You started out nice and now you're all Axel-y again."

"She needs time to be herself, man. That's why you're always alone and drunk. Because you don't know how to treat a woman."

"Hey, I got lucky too." The words were out of Max's mouth before he could stop them, and he watched Axel's eyebrows rise almost in slow motion, followed by an equally slow grin.

"That's the thing, Maxi-Pad," his big friend said. "With you it has to be luck. With me it's skill. It's inborn Latin lover stuff. You'll never understand."

"Huh. Looks like Rosita's father's back," Max said, indicating the direction he didn't want Axel to look yet with the cast of his eyes.

Axel and Max had been in enough "situations" to know the meanings of one another's non-verbal vocabulary. So the big man did not look, but he did adopt a pretty surprised expression.

"I don't think they let you 'back' from where Rosita's dad is."

"Where, jail?"

"Cemetery."

"Okay, look now, he's trying to be casual. I don't think it's his forte."

Axel stole a glance and had an immediate reaction to the man. It was almost as if looking at him was making him physically ill.

He was awkwardly watching them, trying to appear to be looking everywhere else but.

"Does he look like an Estrada to you?"

"He looks Spanish as it's possible to look, I will say that."

"As in from the Iberian Peninsula Spanish?"

"Yes. That kind. A citizen of the European continent."

"An invader."

"An invader."

"He's really good looking."

"I'm sure he'd be flattered to hear that. That was not a requirement for being a conquistador. Remember Cabeza de Vaca?"

"Not personally, no."

"Max! You know what I mean."

"Yes, I know about Cow's Head. They didn't call him that because he was ugly, Axel. It was legitimately his family's name. Don't try to trick me on conquistador lore."

"Well, I don't know who this guy is, other than he's Spanish, and he gives me a sour belly. But I am so close to one hundred percent sure that he is not a Conquistador that I will round up to that number with no fear."

"Whoever he is, he's gone again. Does Rosita have any brothers? He's very interested in you."

"How do you know he's not interested in you? You got 'lucky' too."

Max hated him for the air quotes he put around the word with an intensity only brothers can reach. As quickly as it came the vitriol evaporated, and he grinned.

"And I didn't have the sense to find myself an orphan," he teased.

"Rosita's mom is alive."

"Oh yeah?"

"Stop it. You're gross, dude."

"What? I said nothing."

"You don't even have to. I know what you were thinking."

"Still am."

Just then a hand landed gently on Max's shoulder, and he spun around to find himself looking directly into the dashing face of the man in question.

"Señor Barnes," he said, his accent refined, but decidedly European. "Allow me to introduce myself. I am Estrada."

5

Max stared at the man. Every warning bell in his head was clanging hard enough to recreate the alarms from the night of the Great Chicago Fire. The only thing missing from the noisy cacophony was the apologetic mooing of Mrs. O'Leary's cow.

"Estrada," he finally said. "I've heard of you, although not until a few moments ago. The bigger question, though, is how you've heard of me."

The man laughed, showing white, even teeth. "Ah, but you underestimate yourself. Many of us in the field have heard of you and, shall I say, follow your exploits."

"The field? So you're an archaeologist?"

Estrada was still smiling. "Not exactly, no. I am what one might call an enthusiast."

Max now smiled back at the man, but his own expression was more wry than warm. "I've been called that myself."

Estrada waved a hand. "By the envious professors who prefer theory to reality, and talk to action? Forget them, my friend. You—

and your rather enormous friend, there—are carrying on a long tradition. The antiquarians came first, paving the way, and the professionalists came after." Estrada laughed again. "Just like those types, isn't it? To come in and take over something, then tell you that you aren't good enough to be a part of it."

The man was definitely speaking Max's language, but the warning bells were still sounding. The man was too smooth, his words too perfect, his smile too wide and easy.

What kind of a world do I live in where it's suspicious for someone to be pleasant and friendly? Max wondered.

Aloud, he said, "That all sounds very familiar. And I'm flattered."

Estrada waved his hand again—in fact, he had never quite stopped waving it. "Not at all, not at all. But enough of these pleasantries. I did not interrupt your pleasant repast merely to annoy you with mundane prattlings."

"Yes," Max said, nodding. "I noticed you were taking quite an interest in us from across the street."

Estrada gave his head a contrite little nod. "I apologize if I appeared sinister or made you uncomfortable. I merely wanted to make sure you two were the ones I was looking for." He reached for the inside pocket of his vest, causing an involuntary moment of anxiety for the men. Then to their relief he withdrew a piece of glossy paper. He held it up so that both Max and Axel could see a picture of themselves staring back at them.

"Ah," Axel intoned. "The *Popular Archaeology* feature piece."

Estrada sniffed in amusement. "Yes. While I don't necessarily take much of its reporting as gospel, the article on you was detailed and informative."

Max cocked an eyebrow and, as he did so, he realized that his hangover headache was nearly gone. "And that's what got you interested in meeting us?"

"On the contrary, I've been interested in your career for some time. This article simply gave me a good idea of where to find you."

As Estrada spoke these lines, two things occurred to Max, almost simultaneously. The first was that he should be much more careful in the future about what he chose to reveal to reporters, especially the highly attractive, fawning female variety, who preyed upon his pride to get what they needed for their stories, then beat feet once the file was in her editor's inbox. He realized this flash of mental acuity was as unpredictable as useful. The second revelation was that Estrada seemed to be largely ignoring Axel. This may not have been particularly strange, given that Max was the front man of the duo and had his father's name recognition to give him added notoriety, but contrasted with Estrada's apparent interest in Ax from earlier when he'd been merely observing them ... well, Max thought, it just didn't make sense. He considered calling Estrada on it, but decided he'd first better find out what the man actually wanted before confronting him about something that may not make any difference at all.

Instead, he asked, "And why exactly did you want to find us?" Max made sure to include Axel in the question, both because his partner deserved inclusion and to see how Estrada reacted.

Estrada paused and looked down at his hands, which now rested on the table, as if he was expecting to find them clasping a drink of some kind. Max considered asking if he wanted to order one, but he was growing impatient and didn't want the delay. He also didn't want Estrada to feel too at ease at their table. Offering someone a drink is an invitation for an extended visit.

"Well," Estrada said, "It has to do with your father's research."

And then Max knew. The man was speaking of Ahrum. While Professor Barnes had been involved in many different archaeological projects, the one that defined him the most, certainly in the public's eye and definitely in his own, was his life-long interest in, and search for, the lost city of Ahrum.

"You mean Ahrum," Axel said, echoing Max's thoughts.

"Yes," Estrada said, his eyes flickering quickly to the big man before returning immediately to Max.

Max frowned, and the paranoia in his mind, which had been chattering away ever since seeing Estrada across the way, increased its volume. This one goes to eleven. "What is your interest in Ahrum? Merely professional?"

"Oh, hardly," Estrada said laughing. "I am not, after all, a professional in any field related to the ancient city. It is true that I have a strong fascination with the place, but not *merely* for archaeological reasons."

"What other reasons are there, at this point?" Max asked. "If Ahrum truly exists, it has to be, at best, mostly buried in the jungle by now or someone would have found it."

As Max had spoken, he'd noticed that Estrada's swarthy face had clouded over and his dark eyes had narrowed.

"There is no question about the city's existence," Estrada said, his voice low and even. "It was a powerful city in its day, and it still waits to be found."

Max shrugged. "Okay, I can see you feel strongly about this. But we—" and here he gestured again to Axel "—rely on facts, no matter what the detractors say. While there has been a lot of speculation about the city, no one has yet provided any solid—"

"It is real!"

Estrada's shout brought the entire area to a sudden halt, as if everyone was momentarily frozen in time. Slowly, over a period of seconds, people began going about their business again, but not without casting annoyed or curious glances at the trio's table.

"Keep your voice down," Max hissed.

"Ah!" Estrada said, his voice marginally quieter. "You are afraid people will hear! If it is a myth, why are you so concerned?"

"I didn't say it was a myth," Max replied, still keeping his voice soft and level, hoping the low tone would pressure Estrada to do the same. "I said that I haven't seen evidence—real evidence. But never mind—I'm willing to set that aside for a moment in order to get back to the point. What is your interest in Ahrum?"

It took a few moments for Estrada to compose himself, during which time Max began to reconsider his decision not to order Estrada a drink. The man was clearly high strung, a fact that surprised Max more than it should have, perhaps, given that hot Spaniard blood.

When Estrada had gathered the reins of his temper once more, he gave a forced smile. "I apologize for my outburst. You see, the subject of Ahrum's existence is a very personal one for me."

"How personal?" Max asked.

"Quite personal. As you know, my name is Estrada. What you do not know is that I am a descendant of the man who conquered Ahrum many, many years ago: Francisco Estrada de León."

Max felt rooted to his chair. He yearned to cast a look toward Axel, to see how his friend was digesting the news, but he didn't dare move.

The two men stared at each other, unspeaking, for a full minute. Then Max croaked,

"I think we all need a drink."

This brought a smile to Estrada's face.

"I thought you would never ask," he said, making himself more comfortable. He understood the implied meaning of the gesture.

They ordered drinks and once settled and left alone by the server, got back to business.

"Well," Max said, letting the single word sit there for a while. Then he repeated, "Well." He took a drink. "I suppose that explains your conviction regarding the city's existence."

"Indeed," Estrada said. "After all, the contrary would have great implications as to my, well, my ancestor's legacy."

Max heard Axel begin that low growl. It started low in his chest and slowly worked its way up his throat. This sort usually developed into a roar and culminated with a powerful fist punch in the general direction of whatever—or whoever—had instigated the growl in the first place.

"Anyway," Max said more loudly than the situation called for, hoping to nip *that* eventuality in the bud. But it was too late.

"Legacy?!" Axel roared, causing everyone's attention to once again swing to their table. "You mean the legacy of murder and genocide? Raping, pillaging, cruelty, and disease?"

Estrada barked out a laugh. "Cruelty! You speak of cruelty? Shall we then visit the practices of the Maya?"

"Oh my god, you guys." Max wanted to crawl under the table."

Axel half rose from his chair. He leaned forward and fixed Estrada with a glare so hot and fierce that Max wondered if their guest would burst into flame. Max reached over and tried to press his friend back down to a sitting position, but the effort was akin to pushing against a Ceiba tree.

"Ax, come on—"

"No! I will not sit here and listen to anyone play an apologist for the conquistador, certainly not one of their descendants!"

Axel rose fully and stood towering over the table. For one tense moment, Max felt sure he was about to witness a gruesome murder as his friend tore Estrada limb from limb. But instead, the big Maya simply turned and stalked away, his ham-sized fists clenched, arms held rigidly at his sides.

Max looked back to Estrada, whose face was an obnoxious mix of disdain and amusement. Max knew he should demonstrate solidarity with his friend and abandon the meeting—but the allure of what information Estrada might hold kept him rooted to the seat of the chair. He felt like a traitor, but he simply had to find out what the man knew.

"That was a shit thing to say," he said.

Even as he said it, he realized why Estrada had stared at Axel before joining and had ignored him after. The man had recognized him as Maya. And, apparently, some of that old conquistador blood still coursed through his veins. As Max stared at Estrada, he felt the battle lines drawing up in the back of his mind. Estrada was not on their side. Still, however, the man might hold valuable information, so Max swallowed back the taste of bile that lurked in the back of his throat.

"Let me be clear," he said. "Axel Morales is my best friend, one of the kindest, most decent men I know. In fact, I consider him my brother. Any disrespect shown toward him will constitute a personal affront to me. If you want any help from me, you will do well to remember that." Max said this without much idea regarding what help he could offer Estrada regarding Ahrum. He had two pieces of a map, neither of which he had any intention of sharing with the man, and a few mysterious carved arrows in the jungle, which may or may not have anything to do with the matter at hand. But he wanted to make sure that Estrada knew the ground rules.

The Spaniard appeared to get the message, and he nodded. "Of course, of course," he said, calmer now that Axel had left the table. "It has been centuries. Let us put the old feud to rest. After all," he added, smiling with what Max thought to be an odd light in his eyes, "none of us were there."

Max nodded cautiously, somewhat unnerved by the man's sudden switch in demeanor. "Agreed," he said. "At least for now. But getting back to the earlier topic, and why we are actually speaking, why exactly are you here, right now, talking to me about this?"

Estrada took his time answering, finishing his entire drink before launching into his narrative.

But it was worth the wait, Max decided, as he listened to Estrada lay out much the same tale as had Bembe the night before. The only real difference was that in this version, the Spaniards were the heroes of the story. But everything else was the same right down to the crazy story about the power of the Mayan gods being encapsulated in the crystal, waiting to be released, at which time current civilization would be destroyed.

Max sat there, his drink entirely forgotten, and listened to the rantings of a man he now viewed as a psycho megalomaniac. And that, he decided, was a *second* major difference between the two tellings. Bembe had recounted the story in a much more matter-of-fact way. Estrada's version was overshadowed by flashing eyes, the wicked twist of lips, and the cold eagerness for chaos and destruction. Had Bembe also felt that desire? He hadn't seemed to, but the young man may very well have simply been a more charming storyteller.

"Once the crystal is found," Estrada went on, his face flushed with excitement, "civilizations will crumble and power structures will collapse."

Max stared back at the man. His heart was pounding so hard he was certain everyone around them could hear it, and he fully expected it to burst from his chest and lie there on the table, contracting in its final attempts to keep pumping. In his mind, Max had a sudden vision of a human sacrifice atop a pyramid, during which that very thing would occur. A shaman bringing down the knife, then plunging his hand into the victim's chest and ripping the muscle from its resting place, holding it up so that it would be the last thing the wretched sacrifice would ever see: his own heart throbbing and glistening in the hot, equatorial sun.

"But ... why?" Max said at last, not even recognizing his own voice. "Why would that even be something you'd want?"

Estrada grinned horribly, and Max had to wonder how he'd ever thought the man handsome. His resemblance was now closer to what Max might have guessed the devil to look like.

"Out of chaos," Estrada said, his voice oily and slick, "a ruler always arises to fill the power vacuum. I intend to be that ruler. I have many connections and the groundwork is laid out. All that remains is to find the crystal. And that all begins with Ahrum, which is where you come in."

"I don't follow you."

Estrada grunted. "You are being intentionally dense. Isn't it obvious? I want you to find the crystal."

"But ... why me?"

"Again, it should be obvious. You are experienced, clever, young, independent and beholden to no one. You are also driven by money, if I may say so, and the desire to show your prowess in the field. Well, my friend—"

Max held up a hand. "We are not friends."

"Very well," Estrada nodded. "We needn't be. Regardless, I can make you the wealthiest and most renowned archaeologist of all time. Forget merely showing up those stiff-collared idiots in the universities. You could own them, Maxwell Barnes! Those old tenured fools who gave you such a hard time?" Here Estrada paused and drew one finger across his throat in a cutting motion.

Max was not so pure of heart that the idea was not theoretically appealing, at least as a pleasant daydream, but he also was not foolish enough to believe any of what Estrada was saying. What this man was proposing was sheer folly—not to mention horrifyingly evil.

"Estrada," Max said, speaking slowly. "You are a raving lunatic. And I wouldn't work for you if a gun was put to my head."

Even as the final word left his mouth, Max felt a hard, cylindrical object press to the side of his head. He'd felt that kind of object in the past, and he knew what it was. A gun barrel.

He chilled in the warm air and felt the hairs on his arms stand at attention. He looked at Estrada, who was still grinning.

"That is a shame," the Spaniard said, "because I came prepared for that exact eventuality. Mr. Barnes, I regret to inform you that you are now my prisoner."

6

Axel had walked almost the entire distance to Rosita's dress shop. He knew she'd be busy. She'd told him with great excitement the night before that she'd had a windfall in the form of an upcoming wedding and was going to start working on the bridesmaids' gowns today, after they'd reluctantly parted. He remembered the stern look Rosita's mother had given him as he'd left earlier, looking for Max. She had been sweeping the sidewalk in front of the shop and made clucking sounds to show her displeasure.

Ax had cast her a grin and said, "*Cuidado con el paseo, Mamá gallina.*" ("Mind the walk, mother hen.")

He'd thought it was funny. She'd swatted his butt with the broom, but her lips had twitched upward a little while doing it. No one could stay mad at Axel Morales for long. Often, like this morning, his charm did the trick. But more than one man had stopped being angry because Ax had stopped *him*. With extreme prejudice, as they say in the espionage movies. Still, even as big as he was, he knew better than to tick off a woman's mother, even if her only weapon was a broomstick. He knew what kind of women wielded broomsticks, and he knew his own limitations.

But now, as he came within a block of the place he thought about Max.

Before Estrada had come to their table, they were both relatively sure, especially after talking to the professor, that the man was, if not bad news, certainly not long-awaited good tidings.

After meeting the man face to face there had been no doubt. At least not in Axel's mind.

It was not really like him to make grand statements of his people's struggles. His birth father was of Hispanic ancestry, but it was no fault of his. And, as well as Axel could remember, he was a pretty great guy. Not only had he shown his only son nothing but love, he had been a tender and caring husband to his Maya mother.

But this man—Estrada—had claimed, even *bragged about*, being descended from the invaders. The Conquistadors. Axel spit as he thought the word, just as Max did when he thought about Crabtree. But, unlike his *hermanito*, he had no mixed feelings. The past being the past was something Axel could deal with—no living person could control what had happened before their own time on earth—but eagerly donning the cloak of past injustice was another thing altogether.

However, the fact that he had grown up as Professor Barnes' ward and Max's life-long companion was in part due to the actions of a new breed of conquistadors. And that, Axel realized now, was probably what had sickened him most at the man's approach. Axel did an amazingly good job of treating just about everyone with good natured respect, merely by default. He was of the mind that every human deserves the benefit of the doubt. But he had no problem retracting the good will if, as in this case, a person proved themself unworthy of it.

There was no quicker way to see what happens when Axel Morales withdraws his good will than to make him think of the village in which he'd been born.

But now, so close to Rosita that he could imagine he was smelling her perfume, he realized that a man who caused that violent of a reaction in him was not one Max should be alone with.

He turned on his heels and walked back to the small plaza where they'd eaten, getting angry at *himself* now, for leaving Max with Estrada, for letting the Spaniard's misguided devotion to some long-dead ancestor rankle him to the point that he had to walk away ... or kill the man.

Murder in a public plaza wasn't really Axel's style. So, he had walked away. He'd left quickly, but as he thought more about Max, he moved much more rapidly as he retraced his steps. He'd left Max by himself, but that didn't mean Estrada had been likewise alone.

Max was a lot smaller than Axel, but there was no one the big Maya would rather have on his side, and the two of them had fought their way out of some improbable spots, Barnes always more than holding his own. So he figured Max could probably handle Estrada.

But perhaps not Estrada and an accomplice.

By the time he reached their table he was in full gallop, but he skidded to a stop on cobblestones as he realized that both Max and Estrada ... were gone.

He wanted to tell himself his anxiety had been an aftereffect of his bout of high-octane righteous indignation, and that Max had obviously dealt with the Spaniard and moved on.

He wanted to tell himself that, but the chair in which Max had been sitting—now lying toppled over, the round metallic seat still rocking back and forth slightly—was telling another story altogether.

"He's taken Max," Axel growled.

He quickly assessed the situation. He knew that three streets led into the plaza. One he'd just traversed to return here. That left two other possibilities. Axel grinned a hard, horrifying grin. He knew the wider street would have brought them directly in front of the local police station and assumed Estrada would know that too.

He started walking with deadly purpose down the third *calle*. Any inkling Axel might have entertained about giving Estrada the default level of respect was now lost. As his alert eyes scanned every possible nook and shadow, he knew that when he found the conquistador's *descendiente*, that man would beg for the time when the mere loss of Axel's respect was the worst of his problems.

7

It didn't take Max long to work through what was happening. Estrada had been several steps ahead of him mentally, and Max now realized that fact, and the decision he himself had made to tell Estrada to drop dead, had made being here inevitable.

As to where "here" actually was ... that was a different matter.

He couldn't comment on its appearance, since as soon as they were far enough from the plaza that no one was paying them any attention, they'd placed a black hood over his head. It was still in place, zip-tied closed around his neck, a little too tightly for his taste. After that, he'd been stuffed into the trunk of a car, which had driven over some lousy roads for what he calculated was about thirty minutes, more than long enough to have left La Libertad far behind.

When the ride ended, he'd been taken from the trunk, roughly dragged and deposited wherever he was now.

His hands, also zip-tied, were bound behind his back. A third tie, around his ankles, had been improperly tightened, and Max had managed over the past hour or so to free himself from that. He didn't immediately stand however, as he had no idea if moving blind in his current situation was wise. He probably *wasn't* standing at the edge of a thousand-foot ravine, but one could never rule it out.

Sadly, this was not the first time Max had endured any of these things. Not his first black hood, not his first trunk ride. Certainly not his first zip ties. Even still, it was not the sort of experience to which one ever grew accustomed, and generally caused one to closely consider one's life choices, both past and future.

Later though. Not while the bag was still on one's head. First things first. And the first thing Max needed to do was get rid of the hood, and that meant freeing his hands. And *that* meant finding something with a sharp, or at the very least a rough, edge. But his preliminary groping had revealed nothing that would fit the bill. Everything seemed inconveniently smooth, giving off the annoying impression of newness.

As he carefully continued to feel about, he also began to shuffle his feet, still clad with shoes, as he hoped they might kick against something useful that his tethered hands could not reach.

He thought about the fact that they hadn't taken his shoes. "What a bunch of ams," he said aloud, remembering Bembe saying that about the punks that had beaten him.

Immediately after having mumbled the short sentence, Max heard a door open. The time juxtaposition made him sure someone had been posted outside to listen for anything untoward. A moment later, he felt himself grabbed roughly by the shoulders of his shirt and he was pulled into an upright seated position. He then heard the newcomer move behind him, accompanied by the sickening and unmistakable sound of a knife being pulled from a sheath.

Max was not a coward, but neither was he an idiot. Bound and blinded, he knew struggling would only invite the stinging slice of the blade. While he knew such an event was likely inevitable, he was not foolish enough to invite it by straining uselessly. And so, he did not battle or speak a word of protest. He merely waited, forcing down the almost overpowering urge to throw himself into a spasm of infantile flailing. He merely waited, tense and ready should a moment of real opportunity present itself.

But instead of the smooth slide of a sharp edge across his throat, opening his carotid artery and gently guiding him off this mortal plane, he caught the scent of the most alluring perfume he had ever encountered. A second later, he heard the most unintentionally sexy woman's voice to have ever whispered in his ear. Her accent was heavy, Hispanic in a variety he identified as European, similar to Estrada's.

"You do not fight me. That is wise. That is good."

A moment later, he felt the knife nick his palm, but resisted the "Ouch," as he also felt it slice through the zip tie, freeing his hands.

He still remained motionless, but an instant later there were two additional sensations which got him moving in earnest. The first was the sound of a clunk and the weight of something touching the side of his leg, and the second was the door once more being opened and then closed, followed only by the sound of his own breathing, hot and fetid inside the hood.

His hands, newly freed, quickly went to feel the object that had landed on the floor and touched his leg. Still not ready to believe good fortune would find him in this hiding place, he was surprised and overjoyed to feel a knife in his grasp, like the one that had just solved the second of his three immediate problems.

He used it now to remove the third and final issue; the

plastic tie around his throat. His hands were tingling, having fallen asleep after a few hours of being tightly secured, and he was yet a little wary about using the knife this close to the throat he'd only a moment before resigned to being slit, but without any self-harm he cut the zip tie and pulled the mask off to reveal …

A broom closet? Really?

Yes, there could be no other name to hang onto this space. He was very near the back wall and surrounded by cleaning supplies, dusters, mops, and yes, brooms.

"Better than a dumpster, I suppose," he thought, rising to his feet.

The untightened leg tie, having been long ago kicked free, meant that his legs did not tingle as his hands still were, and now that he could see there were no hazards other than the odd jug of mop solution and random flotsam, he walked toward the door.

After pressing his ear against it and hearing nothing, he tentatively tried the knob, fully expecting to find the door locked.

It turned without resistance, and he pulled. It gave way, opening in toward him ever so slightly. After a moment, he pulled it a little further, enough to peer through.

There was no one.

He slowly pulled the door open far enough to exit the closet and saw the storage area emptied directly into an outdoor space. He looked around and saw there was no one near, not even the woman who had unaccountably aided him.

It was already nighttime, and Maxwell Barnes stepped from the closet and into the darkness. He moved cautiously, the paranoid part of his mind yammering out all manner of horrible possibilities.

Vicious guard dogs, it insisted. *Vietnamese tiger traps, deep holes in the ground with the sharp sticks pointing vertically upward, just waiting to impale a falling body. Landmines! Snipers!*

Max knew most of these were highly unlikely—*except maybe the tiger traps*, Paranoia griped—but one thing was for sure: it was all far too easy. A broom closet with an outside door? Someone to come in and cut his bonds? In Max's experience, anything that seemed too easy usually ended up being very unpleasant. His mind again recalled his old spy friend, Henri Absil, who had recounted an old KGB trick, in which a party member would offer a suspected enemy agent an unbelievable windfall of information—the espionage world's version of a grand slam. It was always, of course, a trap, and the western agent would reveal themselves by showing up to the drop or exchange, only to be met by Soviet officials. The ruse was only ever played on the young and inexperienced, because seasoned spies like Absil knew and lived by the old adage: "anything that seems too good to be true, probably is."

Max was not old or particularly seasoned, at least by comparison to Absil, but he also lacked a younger generation's disrespect for the elders. On the contrary, Max considered older people to be fonts of wisdom. And so, while also attempting to keep his macabre imagination in check, he gave Paranoia a length of rope by which to hang itself.

With this in mind, Max moved along the edge of the building he'd just exited, reasoning that any traps or snares would likely be set farther out. Besides, he was getting a sense that the outlying area was large—difficult to tell for sure in the darkness-and keeping close to a wall made it easier to maintain his bearings. If there were guard dogs on the loose, which despite Paranoia's two cents Max considered the most likely of his current worries, he might need to retreat back to the closet, and he had no desire to get lost while doing so.

After a few minutes of painstakingly slow movement, he reached a corner and eased his head around it just enough to allow his line of sight to take in what lay in store. And there he saw the first glow of lights and, if he listened closely, the sound of voices. First there were only male voices, but then a peal of female laughter floated to him through the darkness. Was it the same woman who had cut him free?

At that moment, Max heard the crunch of a foot on dry ground. He whirled, only to be blinded by a flashlight shone directly into his eyes.

"Señor Barnes," a man's voice said, not unkindly. "I see you have found your way from the closet."

Max was a bit taken aback by the casual tone. He'd expected the stern bark of orders or even the report of a gun. He held his hand up to shield his eyes.

"My apologies," the man said, lowering the light. "I had to be certain it was you."

"Who else would it have been?" Max grumbled. He squinted, now just able to make out the man's features. Hispanic, wearing a guard's uniform ... smiling.

"Oh, you can never tell, señor," the guard said. "The compound is remote, but we still get people occasionally finding themselves where they should not be."

"Compound?"

"Sí," the guard said, nodding. "Señor Estrada's headquarters."

"Okaaay," Max replied, drawing the word out. "This may be a weird question and one tempting fate, but ... why are you being so nice? It was my belief that men who guard compounds hidden in the jungle are not known for their hospitality."

The guard clapped an open hand to his chest. "Oh, you wound me, señor! Surely, you do not believe that you are a prisoner here."

Max frowned. "Yes, that is exactly what I believe, not unreasonably, I would say. All of the other times I've been stuffed in a trunk, hooded and zip-tied, and then thrown in a closet have ended up being some sort of captivity. Are you suggesting this is the way Estrada welcomes all his guests?"

"Only those he likes," the guard said, a moment before bursting into laughter.

Damn it, Max thought. *I'm starting to like this guy.*

"Look," he said aloud, "just tell me what's going on. I usually like surprises, but this sequence of events is becoming downright inconvenient."

"I am not the man to tell you these things."

"Then who is?"

"Why, Señor Estrada, of course."

Max shook his head, as if clearing cobwebs from his neural pathways. "And you expect that I'm of a mind to go seek out the man who just had me kidnapped?"

The guard shrugged. "You may as well, señor."

"I don't follow you."

"Well, it is only that I do not see what choice you have."

"If I'm not a prisoner, why can't I just leave?"

The guard made a *tsking* sound and shook his head. "Oh, señor, you do not want to do that. It is dangerous outside of these walls, and you are miles from the nearest town. I would feel it my duty to see that you remain safely within the walls."

Max nodded slowly. "I'm beginning to understand. I'm free to move about the compound, but I can't leave the perimeter."

"I do not like the word *can't*," the guard said. "I prefer to say that we strongly encourage you not to do so."

"And if I leave you and walk to the other side of the compound?"

The guard shrugged again. "Then there will be another guard who will demonstrate the same concern for your well-being as have I."

"Well, you're all just a crew of regular Mother Theresas, aren't you?"

The guard bowed. "Ah! She was a great woman. We try our best, señor."

"I wish you'd stop being so charming. It's making it difficult to be incensed."

"Ah, then perhaps you could simply put off such pointless emotions and consider joining Señor Estrada for a glass of wine and some delicacies. Sí?"

Max heaved a sigh but knew that he was left with little choice. Finally, he looked up at the guard, grunted, and said, "*Sí.*"

8

Axel entered Rosita's dress shop and found his girl hard at work. The mass of fabric surrounding her looked like complete chaos to him, but Rosita labored with intense efficiency and focus, suggesting that she, at least, could make some sense of it all. Axel always marveled at her skill and was completely baffled by the minute stitching, much of which she did by hand. His own enormous paws had more chance of pounding nails barehanded than accomplishing that sort of detailed, intricate work.

Rosita looked up as he entered, her expression first annoyed at the interruption but changing quickly to concern as she saw the look on Axel's broad face.

"What is it?" she asked, struggling to free herself from the swaths of material surrounding her. "What has happened?" She came to him, putting her arms as far around his bulk as she could and looking up at him. "Something is wrong, *mi rey*; tell Rosita."

"It's Max."

"Your friend?"

Axel nodded. "*Sí.* I left him in a plaza with a man named Estrada."

The two lovers conversed in Spanish, as they almost always did when alone, the romantic Latinate language adding an extra layer of intimacy to their interactions.

"You left angry," Rosita said, demonstrating that she knew her man very well indeed. "You left him angry, and when you returned?"

"He was gone."

"You were angry with Max?"

"No," Axel shook his head. "With Estrada. He spoke proudly of the conquistadors."

Rosita squeezed her arms tighter and buried her face in Axel's powerful chest. "But you are not really so angry about events so long ago. Are you, *mi rey*?" Her tone suggested that she knew the answer to her question without it even being answered.

Axel shook his head again. "No."

Then the memories poured into his mind, and he felt his shoulders shake just once in a massive, heaving sob.

Rosita reached up and gently wiped a single escaped tear with a delicate index finger. "And now you are worried about your friend?"

"Yes," Axel said, his deep voice like gravel rasping on iron. "He is in trouble. It is my fault, and I have to find him. Don't wait up for me tonight, I think."

MAX APPROACHED the lights and laughter, following the guard. At first, he thought it odd that the guard would lead the way and not prod him along at gunpoint, until he remembered that this was a captivity unlike any other he'd ever experienced. And, while he had no desire to be precious about it, he had to admit that he far preferred this to the variety to which he'd grown accustomed. Rat-infested hovels, chains, and beatings had nothing on what he now experienced: good humor, a relaxed atmosphere, and even an odd and developing sense of camaraderie.

These positive aspects were only bolstered as the duo drew closer to the activity, where soon Max could make out several figures. Three men and one woman sat around a fire pit, each holding a glass in hand. A couple of the men had cigars, and Max could smell the enticing scent of tobacco and wood smoke.

All at once, the scene turned absolutely idyllic. The night air was warm but less humid than normal. The jungle fauna sent up a distant buzz of nocturnal activity. The smells of the fire and, Max now detected, some sort of cooked meat awakened something primal inside of him.

Do not let down your guard, Paranoia hissed.

Max's stomach growled, and he realized it had been a very long time since he'd eaten his previous meal. He already decided that he had little choice but to see this whole thing through, so he might as well fill his stomach while he was at it. Besides that, Max had to admit to a deep well of curiosity. There had to be a reason why he was not yet dead, why he'd been set free under such suspicious circumstances, and why he was being treated like some exiled prince. But learning the answers to these questions wasn't only a matter of bland curiosity; Max also suspected that such knowledge might also prove to be useful.

At last, their approach was noticed by those around the fire. One man, whom Max recognized as Estrada, smiled widely and held up his glass.

"Ah! Excellent! I see you've escaped your bonds. Come and join us, my friend."

Before, Max had quickly corrected the man when he'd used the term "friend," but now he thought it might be wise to let the inaccuracy pass. It might be necessary, Max realized, to play an unsavory role in order to achieve a full understanding of what was at stake in this scenario.

Estrada stood as Max walked up, and then he gestured to one of two empty chairs next to his. Max nodded, went to the nearest empty chair, and sat down. Someone, Max assumed a member of the wait staff, handed him a glass of dark liquid, which upon smelling turned out to be a rich red wine. Max swirled the drink and then smelled it again, this time with more appreciation than suspicion. He looked up to see Estrada watching, a not entirely unnerving smile on his handsome face.

"Teso La Monja," he said. "It is from Toro. And, I might add, pairs nicely with the evening's meal."

At the word "meal," Max's stomach commenced an urgent series of demands, loud enough to be heard by everyone around the fire. All but one laughed good-naturedly, and Max allowed himself a sheepish smile.

"Does that answer the question?" he asked.

"It does indeed," Estrada said. He snapped his fingers, and the same server as before appeared with a white plate adorned with a garnish of green and an artful trail of sauce. But the real star was the medallion of meat in the center.

"Wagyu beef filet," Estrada said, still smiling.

Max's mouth was watering so much that he surreptitiously wiped at the corners to make sure he wasn't drooling.

"Please, eat," Estrada said. "We've already dined."

Max accepted the offered utensils and cut into the prime meat. The moment it touched his tongue, he was transported into a heaven of gustatory perception. Olive oil, butter, a light seasoning of salt and pepper—perfectly seared on both sides and rare in the center. He chewed slowly and thoughtfully, mesmerized by the flavor, and then swallowed it down with a chase of the wine. The red added a complexity to the taste that caused Max to instantly mock everything he'd ever eaten in the past. The hints of oak and vanilla, along with the robust dryness of the wine, mingled with the beef's profile and sang a song of angels all the way down, and then lingered on his tongue like passion's afterglow.

He realized he'd had his eyes closed during the entire experience, and when he opened them again, he found everyone watching him with expressions both amused and understanding —the dish had apparently had a similar effect on all of them.

"Take your time," Estrada said. "Enjoy and savor it. A far cry from the tacos in La Libertad, is it not?"

Max grinned. "A far cry indeed." His humor dampened a bit as he realized that the fact that Estrada mentioned the tacos meant that he'd been watching them a bit longer than Max had originally thought. And it also reminded him that this was no luxury resort, although it was beginning to feel that way.

Are you really going to be bought off by a steak? mocked Paranoia. *Keep your guard up.*

Max finished the steak with no less enjoyment but more efficiency. He wanted to lick the plate, but refrained, settling for a refilled glass of wine instead. He passed the dishes off to the mute server, and then sat back in his chair and looked at Estrada.

"First of all, thank you for the best cut of meat I've ever had, if you don't count those spicy beef sticks I used to get at the corner pharmacy when I was a kid." Estrada smiled indulgently, but Max shook his head. "You think I'm kidding, but to a nine-year-old kid, those things were the pinnacle of fine dining. Tonight, this was the pinnacle of my adult years."

Estrada's smile became slightly less condescending, and he nodded in acceptance of the odd compliment, although it was clear he did not entirely share Max's sense of humor.

"Second," Max continued, choosing to ignore the bombed joke, "I think it may be time to fill another hunger—that of my own curiosity regarding the point of all this." He swept his arm wide, indicating the entire compound. "Why am I here?"

Estrada took his time answering, filling the long silence with a savoring sip of wine. At last, he said, "Put simply, Mr. Barnes, it is because I have a great deal of faith in your intelligence and sense of inevitability."

"I don't follow."

"I think you do. You will recall my offer in the plaza, after your large friend stormed off to wallow in self-pity."

Max felt his hackles rise but forced himself to keep things together.

"At that time, you refused me," Estrada said. "And that refusal forced my hand. After having revealed my plans to you, even at a superficial level, I couldn't simply allow you to trot off and relay this information to anyone you pleased."

"Then why not simply kill me?" The moment the words left his mouth, Max cringed. It was probably not advisable to voluntarily bring up the topic.

"Because, as stated, I have a great deal of faith in your intelligence and sense of inevitability. I was convinced that having time to consider all your options, you would come to the same conclusion as I have—that is the intelligence part. Everything will happen just as I said earlier today, and you can either be a part of it, or you can sink with the rest—that's the inevitability part."

"And if I continue to refuse to help you?"

"Then you will have to be killed, of course," Estrada said.

Max wasn't sure if the chill running up his spine was a product of what the man had said or the extreme casualness with which he'd said it.

"Wow," he said. "That's a pretty convincing argument."

"There's that intelligence again," Estrada smiled, his perfect teeth seeming even whiter against lips stained redder with the wine. "And I will tell you that my decision to give you a second opportunity was not a unanimous one."

Max felt he could guess who had cast a dissenting vote: the man who had refused to laugh at his hilarious stomach rumble. The same man who had continued to watch him balefully throughout the meal.

"But before we get too much further into this, allow me to introduce everyone." Estrada looked across the fire. "The man wearing yellow is Sánchez."

The man, who was indeed wearing a shirt that looked suspiciously like the yellow jersey worn by the Tour de France frontrunner, laughed jovially, lifting his drink in a toast to Max.

"This dour-faced gentleman is Colón, one of my oldest associates."

Max had been expecting the phrase "oldest friends," and thought he saw the man chafe in the firelight at the use of the alternative. Although his eyes never left him, he did nothing to acknowledge Max, so Max responded with a curt nod.

"Over there," Estrada said, motioning to an empty chair sitting across the fire, "is where another of our party should be sitting." As he spoke these words, his expression saddened and his eyes glinted. "Unfortunately, that member, Raul, met an untimely end recently."

"Oh?" Max wasn't sure what to say, but had the distinct impression that Estrada expected a response. "A sudden illness."

Estrada shook his head. "From all appearances, he got into the wine a bit too heavily, and then fell out of a window, breaking his neck."

"I'm sorry," Max said awkwardly.

Estrada roused himself with a shake of his head and his previous expansive mood returned. "And his sparkling beauty is Isabel María Garcia." He reached over to pat the woman's bare knee. She laughingly pushed the man's advance away with one hand while touching the hilt of a knife on her belt with the other.

"Easy there, Estrada, or I'll be removing *your* sparkling beauties."

"Ah yes. She always lets me know where I stand, but she also knows how to follow instructions."

The woman flashed him a smile that seemed more than a little ingenuine to Max. A breeze passed across the fire, and it carried not only the comforting aroma of the burning wood, but a trace of a familiar scent – a hint of perfume ...

Max, whose own drink had again just been refilled by the seemingly omniscient service staff that continually appeared at precisely the correct moment, now lifted it to the four people across from him. "Greetings to you all. Here's to me remaining not killed."

"Hear hear!" Estrada exclaimed, raising his glass in response, immediately followed by Sánchez and Isabel. Estrada leaned forward toward Max. "Now perhaps we can talk about you moving *beyond* mere satisfaction with the continuation of your life."

"That's a pretty lofty goal in my book."

"No, no, no, Mr. Barnes. A lofty goal is, say, world domination. Staying alive—protozoa do that."

"'World domination.' Not words you hear a lot in the twenty-first century, Señor Estrada. And, if I can be so bold as to point out, things seldom go well for the men ..." in what Max hoped was a gesture whose irony would be appreciated he lifted his drink again, this time to Isabel. "... *and* women who have bandied it around."

"Women are too smart to sign up for that garbage job," she laughed. Max thought that her accent made the word "garbage" just about the most beautiful thing he'd ever heard.

"Besides, Max—may I call you Max?" Estrada paused to ask.

"Everybody does except my dad." Max looked closely at Estrada's eyes as he mentioned his father and was positive he saw them narrow slightly.

"Max. Those men, and yes, women, they defined, and therefore pursued the concept of dominating the fate of the world incorrectly. They saw it as a question of military might, of strategic alliance and intrigue. They envisioned their reach spanning the world, spreading out from their homeland, gaining one painful inch at a time.

"But we, Max, we know differently."

"We?"

"Men of vision, men of clarity. Men who would rule the world *... in an instant!*"

"I get that you all have been sitting here a little longer than me and have probably tossed back a few more of these than I have." Once again, he lifted the glass, and if anyone had been observant enough, they would have noticed that he was doing much more lifting than drinking. "But that sounds like some drunk-ass talk right there."

"No, no, nuh." Estrada burped out the final, strangled "no." "Alright, perhaps a bit." The Spaniard held his thumb and forefinger a fraction of an inch apart. "But what, Max, if there were a way?"

"A way? With all due respect, what are you talking about?"

"The Crystal, Max! It's not just a myth. Not a legend. Not a story to frighten naughty children."

Max took a sip of the drink now, listening intently to the man. Listening for a hint that he was lying, or even more insanely, that he *believed* what he was saying. "Even assuming it was real," he said at last, "we don't know where it is, and if we somehow found it—"

"Think of it, Max! Think of everything you've done, said, even hinted at in your illustrious, if somewhat loose-cannon career. You would have the right to look at any stuffed suit academic and tell him to shut his pompous mouth."

Max raised an eyebrow.

"I wouldn't hate *that.*"

"Exactly. And I ..." Estrada's voice was suddenly almost quaking, and he stopped himself, regaining a measure of composure. "I would gain some vindication as well."

"Vindication," Max echoed.

"Vindication, for us both. Side by side."

Now Max was sure of a few things. One was that the man most definitely believed the story of the Crystal, and the power that would come to the man or woman who possessed it. He was also certain that, while Estrada might want Max by his side, it was only because it would mean he could get the mysterious man what he desired. Should Max decide to go off and spit in the eyes of a mile-long line of professors and—it chilled him to think—doctoral candidates, those bloodthirsty research assistants who looked further down their noses at Max than even the department chairs ... well, Max knew that Estrada could not have cared less. But that was the gambit. He was dangling the carrot of equality.

And *that*, Max thought, was something he could play along with. Because all of this was, indeed, play. He had one immediate goal, and that was to get out of this compound in one piece. So, a bluff well-played appeared to be his best option.

"Well, then, if an assist from ol' Max Barnes, rebel archaeologist, is what you need, and I can tell all those wannabes where to go ... I'm in! Let's show the creeps."

Much to Max's surprise, this at last drew a hint of a smile from Colón, and Estrada clapped his hands in ecstasy. Max smiled across the smoky fire, but when he looked at Isabel, he saw no smile upon her face. The heat of the flames seemed to wither in the frost that issued from her eyes.

Barnes realized he was in danger of losing a potential ally. He had no doubt that it had been Isabel who'd freed his hands earlier, and he wanted for her to know that he was aware. Taking advantage of the moment's levity he mouthed the words, "Thank you."

He was rewarded with a softening of the furrows that had formed on her lovely brow, and she gave him an almost imperceptible nod.

"Well then!" Estrada said finally, "I think perhaps we should all get some sleep. It has been a long and stressful day, and tomorrow promises to be filled with excitement! Sánchez, will you show Mr. Barnes to his quarters?"

Before the man in the yellow shirt could answer, Isabel stood.

"He is near me. I will walk him. Sánchez has been enjoying his cups a bit too much. He will walk into the fire!"

"Very well," said Estrada, clearly not thrilled that she had volunteered for the task, but too happy at Max's apparent acquiescence to be concerned enough to object.

They walked away and, after a few paces, Max ventured a look over his shoulder. Colón and Estrada had already quit the scene, but Sánchez was still seated, slumped a little sideways, fast asleep.

9

Axel's mood hadn't improved after leaving Rosita—it never did—and now he'd been walking the streets for two fruitless hours. He was thirsty, sweaty, and completely prepared to manually behead the first person who asked him what time it was.

This was his dangerous mood when he spotted the little Maya dressed like a skate punk. Even in the midday heat, he was wearing long, baggy cargo pants, a Vans tee and, on his feet, the shoes that his shirt advertised. He was leaning against a wall, his skateboard propped on its edge beside him.

Axel's first instinct was to close the distance between them and grab him by his little chicken neck, but something held him back.

When Max had been describing his experience with Bembe, and indeed when he'd described the young man himself, Axel had felt himself on the edge of belief, but no closer. To be fair, the story strained credulity more than a little, but now Axel saw that at least the physical description was spot on, except that the knit hat with its dangling chin ties was absent. At some point, even a stupid skater would have to make that concession to the swelter.

So you've decided not to bring the hammer of Thor, Axel thought to himself. *What else ya got?*

He decided to hang back and observe him for a minute ... but only for a minute. Max was still his primary concern. This Bembe character would stay on his radar exactly long enough to find out if he was going to be of any use at all.

Bembe hadn't moved. He continued to lean back in a little oasis of shade, his eyes closed. His left leg was bent into a figure-four with his low topped shoe resting flat against the wall. Axel wasn't completely sure the kid wasn't asleep standing up.

The big man moved slowly, making use of a particularly busy burst of foot traffic to blend in—to the degree that he could, standing head and shoulders above the majority of the crowd. When he arrived by the skater in his quiet reverie, he looked down.

Bembe opened one eye and focused it on him.

"Stand right there, brah," he said, emitting a sigh of pleasure. "You just increased the shade by about double. Dang, you got big, Axel Morales."

"Hold up. You don't get to use my name. We haven't met."

Bembe opened the other eye and assumed his full stature. It somehow made him look even smaller.

"Oh no? Don't think so?" Bembe gave him a full scan then shook his head. "Some gratitude."

At the speaking of those two words, the cognitive equivalent of a pipe bomb went off in Axel's memory. And just like one of those cylinders of destruction, shrapnel flew in every direction on the mental rose compass.

He remembered the day he ran from his village, his family

gone, killed before his eyes. He ran off alone, except for one Maya that he didn't really remember seeing around before that day. But his memories from then were little more than snatches – flickers of moving light projected against the back of his skull.

Which added to the unsettling nature of *this*. Because Axel could see it clearly. The Maya urging him forward was smallish in stature, but Axel could see he was a teenager. Somehow his diminutive size helped Axel trust him as he led them both deep into the jungle, never hesitating as he took turn after turn, clearly knowing even the densest parts like the back of his hand.

This boy? This skate punk? How could that be? And yet Axel felt certain.

And the rest of the expanding shrapnel of memories was no less sharp. He saw the professor finding him a few minutes later, after the young man had told him to wait in the roots of the mango tree. And after that ... once or twice when Axel was still a boy he recalled seeing this young man again, from a distance and speaking earnestly to the prof.

What the ... ?

Axel had a decent memory in general and could certainly tell many things in detail from his past. But he'd never remembered anything like this ... in this way ... with this degree of clarity.

It was fascinating in the way a scary story told by the firelight is. Equal parts enlightening and unsettling. Axel shook his head.

"What?" Bembe said. "You getting dizzy, brah? Grab some wall. I don't want you falling on me. I already got my butt kicked last night, I ain't looking to have to mend anymore bones."

Axel put one hand on the wall, indeed feeling his legs' integrity grow a little suspect.

"I don't know what you're talking about," he lied at last. "And I don't care. Right now I need to find Max Barnes. He says he talked to you last night. Is that true?"

"We enjoyed a cold beverage together, yes."

"How *many* cold beverages? Because the story he told me would require a few, I think."

"Well, I only had one. Max too, while we were chatting. I can't say what he did after. He looked pretty thirsty."

"He ... er, wha—" Axel did not like feeling this flustered, especially by a vaguely familiar tiny dude whom he could easily snap in half. "Listen. Max. He's missing, and I need to know ..."

"He's not missing, brah. He's just not here."

"What?"

"No one's ever missing. They're always somewhere."

Axel stared at him for a few seconds. Whoever this guy was, he was doing things to Axel's head that were not enjoyable, and the time he had allotted for being patient with him had expired.

"Okay, two things," he said to Bembe. "First, you're making my head hurt, and I don't like it. Second, instead of dropping these useless philosophical cow patties, how about you tell me if you have any idea which 'somewhere' Max is occupying currently. Alternatively, I could just tear your arms off now, then continue looking on my own. Entirely up to you."

Now it was Bembe's turn to do the long stare. But not too long, because he sensed Axel wasn't kidding.

"Estrada has him."

"I knew that already."

"At his compound. In the jungle."

"Jungle compound. Sounds sinister," Axel said, again not quite ready to fully step into belief.

"Dude, you have no idea."

"Okay, then. Off to the jungle I go."

"You'll never find it."

"Duh. I was being sarcastic."

"Duh. I *invented* sarcastic," Bembe said with a grin so infectious that Axel momentarily forgot he was supposed to be scaring information out of him.

"Sooo ... ?" he asked the diminutive Maya, letting the question trail off expectantly.

Bembe seemed to be trying to make up his mind, then let out a sigh of resignation. "Come on. It's not that far if you know the way."

MAX STRETCHED out on the low bed in the room where he'd been escorted, and quickly left behind by Isabel, after leaving the snoring Sánchez, the more jovial of the two men who'd been dining with Estrada. While the escort had been smiling and in seemingly good spirits, Max thought he detected an undercurrent of danger lurking beneath the placid surface of goodwill. The other man, Colón, made no secret of his feelings toward the American newcomer, and somehow Max found that easier to deal with. He disliked artifice and fakery, especially in humans. Not only was it weak and pathetic, but it was dangerous in situations where an accurate judgment of character could be the difference between life or death. Max suspected that when not sleeping drunkenly Sánchez may be the kind of man who would slice an enemy from stem to stern and smile during the entire operation. Maybe even comment on the pleasant weather.

He looked around the room. Dim lighting, provided by a single bulb in an open ceiling fixture, cast the small accommodations in shadows, but there wasn't much to see in any case—a chair and desk, both basic and old, and then the bed on which Max now rested. The room did have its own bathroom, sans shower, and was as tiny as it was clean. In fact, the room itself was practically spotless. Max shrugged inwardly. He'd stayed in much worse conditions, although he had to admit that when Estrada decided to change his status from prisoner to co-conspirator, he'd hoped that such a promotion would afford lodgings worthy of the opulence that the main compound could clearly afford. Still, this was much preferable to being bound in a closet, and he wasn't about to go complaining to the management.

Max scooted back and up until he was in a sitting position, with his back resting against the stucco wall. He was in a precarious spot, and he knew it. Walking the proverbial tightrope between maintaining Estrada's belief in him as an ally and defeating the very plan he was supposed to be aiding—well, that would be a trick indeed. And that was if, Max reminded himself, Estrada bought Max's capitulation act in the first place. It all seemed far too easy, and Estrada was too intelligent to not at least have some doubts about it. More than likely, this would be more of a delaying tactic than anything, a way to stay alive while he, first, figured out exactly how Estrada was planning to carry out his domination quest and, second, how to get the hell out of here with that knowledge.

So deep in thought was Max, that he visibly started when a small tap sounded on the door to his room. He pushed away from the wall and sat up straight, his heart thrumming into overdrive.

They've talked about it and decided you're not worth keeping around. They're here to drag you off into the jungle and shoot you in the head, Paranoia squawked.

If they were here to kill you, they wouldn't be tapping politely on the door, Reason rebutted. *They'd burst in to take you by surprise.* While there was a lock on the door, it was almost laughably flimsy and wouldn't keep out a determined toddler.

Max felt the conflicting viewpoints carried equal weight and, so, he rose from the bed to answer the door, but did so with as much caution as his current status as quasi-prisoner afforded. He approached the door slowly and quietly, crossing the floor on bare feet. He took up a position on the side of the frame opposite the door hinges in case whoever was waiting decided to burst through without further warning.

"Who is it?" he asked, keeping his voice as low as possible while still assuring that whoever waiting on the other side of the door had a reasonable chance of hearing.

Max considered this a reasonable question, but no voice responded. Instead, the tapping sounded again.

"I'm not opening this door until you identify yourself," Max said, putting his mouth to the crack between the door and the side jamb. His stage whisper would have been worthy of even the most venerable theaters around the world. A weighty pause ensued, and then the tapping returned. Max clenched his jaw in irritation.

He was just about to return to his bed and ignore this rude caller ... when a familiar fragrance hit his nostrils.

"Isabel?" he breathed.

"Sí. Let me in."

Max unlocked the door and stepped back, giving the woman space to enter. She did so and shut the door quickly but quietly behind her, resetting the puny lock. Then she turned to him with blazing eyes. When she spoke, it was in a harsh, furious whisper.

"You left me standing there in the hallway with my ass hanging out. I could have been seen."

Max involuntarily cast a glance around at her backside. "Your ass doesn't appear to be—"

"It is just an expression, you stupid dumb," she hissed.

Max tried not to grin, but he simply could not help himself. He'd never enjoyed being insulted so much in his entire life, and immediately began plotting more ways to anger Isabel, to again be referred to as a "stupid dumb." Her wonderful accent—and her scorching beauty—made the inexact name-calling sound like music.

"And stop your *estupid* grinning," Isabel continued. "This is serious!"

"Of course, of course." Max nodded. "It must be very serious to bring you to my bedroom door at, what, one o' clock in the morning?"

"It is, how do you say, serious as a heart assault."

"Attack. A heart attack," Max corrected, although he was beginning to feel an assault on his own heart, mounting unwittingly by Isabel herself. While the woman did not seem to be particularly fond of him, Max was quickly becoming a big fan of hers.

Proving the former point, Isabel scowled at him. "We stand here in mortal danger, and you choose to make tedious corrections."

"Sorry." Max narrowed his eyes. "What makes you think we're in mortal danger? When we broke up the festivities earlier, Estrada seemed pretty happy with my decision to help him."

Isabel let out a muffled snort of derision. "He was no more convinced than am I. He might want to believe it, because you can be useful to him, but trust me when I say that he has his doubts. At the first sign of betrayal, you will be killed. He may even choose to get rid of you earlier than that, if he thinks he can dispense with you."

"And why are you in danger? He seems pretty fond of you." *And I can totally see why,* Max struggled to keep from adding.

"Because he has his doubts about me as well," Isabel said. "I have managed to remain somewhat neutral, but he is growing suspicious. The closer he gets to his goal, the more ruthless he becomes with those who are not completely on his side." Isabel cut off speaking suddenly, and stiffened, straining her ear toward the door.

"What is it?" Max whispered.

She waved frantically at him to be quiet.

Finally, after several long minutes, she relaxed slightly. "I thought I heard something in the hallway."

Max stepped softly to the door and, unlocking and opening it, peered out into the hall. It was empty in both directions, with not a sound to be heard except for the distant noise of the jungle at night. He looked back at Isabel and shook his head, then silently closed and relocked the door.

"Forgive me," she said, "but I am, how to say, a package of nerves."

"A bundle of nerves?"

If he'd been close enough, Max was certain she would have struck him. Which he would also have enjoyed. *You have a problem, dude,* he chided himself. *She obviously hates you. Accept it.*

"So why don't you tell me why you're here," Max said.

"I became acquainted with Estrada several years ago. I was younger then, and much more foolish. I found him handsome, charming, and clever."

Max nodded. "He is all of those things."

"And I fell for him," she continued, ignoring Max's input. "Before long, and without even noticing it, I was assimilated into his lifestyle. Gradually, I began to realize that he was not the sweet and charming man I thought that I knew; that he was, in fact, vindictive and cruel."

Max frowned. "I don't get the sense that he's an angel, but ... cruel?"

"Ah, you are falling into his trap of charms as well, I see. Do not be fooled. Estrada hides his evil with an exterior of light, but inside he has the blackest soul I have ever known." Isabel looked at him and, while Max had tried to retain a neutral expression, skepticism must have clouded his face. "I see you have doubts," she said. "Then let me give you an example. Some time ago, we were traveling to a remote village in Campeche. A young boy, an orphan, crept into our tent late at night to steal some food. Estrada saw him running away into the night with a bar of chocolate and a bag of rice, and he raised his pistol and shot the boy in the back."

Max's eyes widened, and a sickness began forming in his stomach. "And ... he *knew* it was a child?"

The corners of Isabel's mouth tightened. "He said that he had been staring into the fire and so his night vision was not good enough to tell. But, even if that were true, I saw him go to the body and retrieve the food without a backward glance and scarcely a shred of emotion. That was when I truly began to understand what kind of man he was. And what a terrible mistake I had made."

"And you couldn't leave?"

"Not at that time, no. We were deep in the jungle, and I did not then have the experience or skills necessary to survive on my own. And I have to admit that I was afraid. Estrada, as I said, is a cruel man. I have seen what he has done with previous prisoners, and I have never felt truly secure in my position here."

"What has he done with these other prisoners?" Max asked.

"I'm assuming by your expression that things did not end well for them."

"No." Isabel shook her head. "Their deaths alone would have been enough, but it was how they died that made it so much worse."

"Well, now I *have* to know," Max said.

Isabel grimaced. "Estrada has a formula that makes people unconscious. And when they wake up, they are paralyzed. He then has them taken into the jungle where they are slowly eaten, alive and conscious, by jaguars or jungle insects."

"How charming," Max said. "Where does he get this ... formula?"

"It is made here, at the compound, from an ancient recipe. I do not know exactly what the ingredients are, but they come from the surrounding jungle."

"Okay, you've convinced me," Max said. "Estrada's a cruel bastard."

"Yes," Isabel said. "And I now know that I would not have been allowed to leave, even if I had possessed the skills that I have now —I am little more than a prisoner here."

Max wondered briefly what "skills" Isabel was referring to, but his thought was interrupted as she continued speaking.

"If I so much as approach the walls, the guards turn me back. And I never go into towns unescorted." Isabel sighed. "And besides, even if I escaped, where would I go?"

"You have no family?"

"I have aunts and uncles in Spain who might assist me. But what if they did? What would I do? I cannot take what I know and simply go about my life as though nothing were happening, and my story is not one that would be believed or taken seriously by the authorities, or by *anyone* who might make a difference. Until you arrived, I had resigned myself to biding my time until a moment came at which I could make a difference, if even in some small way."

"And that's why you had a strong reaction when it seemed I might be taking Estrada's side over dinner," Max stated.

Isabel nodded. "Yes. I had helped you get free and, for a moment, I thought you were turning against me."

"And now?"

"I do not believe you are on Estrada's side." Isabel's deep brown eyes searched Max's face for any sign of treachery. "Are you? On his side?"

Max paused. *She's setting you up!* Paranoia shrilled. *She is here at Estrada's behest, trying to get you to betray yourself to him!*

And then, he slowly shook his head. "No," he sighed. "I am not. I could never be." He waited, almost expecting the door to fly open and hear Estrada shout, "Aha!"

But nothing of the sort happened.

Instead, Isabel's entire body seemed to slump with relief, as if she'd been standing at attention this entire time.

"I did not think so," she said. "But I have lived a lie among liars for so long, that I no longer completely trust myself."

Max nodded in understanding.

"And now," Isabel said, "the question remains of what are we going to do?"

Max paused, thinking. "Well," he said at last, "there isn't much we can do tonight. And whatever we end up doing will require rest. It's late. Let's sleep and find a time to confer tomorrow. In the meantime, I'll be thinking of a way out of here. And you as well—you know the compound much better than I do. Perhaps make a mental list of the weakest security points."

"I will do that," she said, turning to the door. "And now, I should get back to my room."

"Could be dangerous in the hallways," Max said. "You could also stay here. You know, to avoid detection."

Isabel scowled at him. "That was, how to say, a pleasant try, *cochino*. But I can assure you that being found in your room is just as likely to get us killed as would being found roaming the halls. And that is assuming I would even want to stay here with you, which I definitely do not. Good *night*, Señor Barnes."

Max could only grin as Isabel unlocked and opened the door, looked both ways, and then disappeared into the hall.

"Good night, Isabel," he murmured. "You might not like me now, but I've got a few tricks up my sleeve." He walked back to the bed, lay down and stretched. Yes ... once he pulled out the old Barnes charm, that poor woman wouldn't know what hit her.

10

The next morning, Max was lured from his room early by the wafting smell of coffee. He had awakened abruptly and, pleasantly surprised at still being alive, he had lain in bed for a few minutes, simply staring up at the ceiling. He'd at least half-expected Estrada to send someone to his room in the wee hours to insert some pointy object "under the fifth rib," as the Bible would say. Instead, Max found himself very much alive, very much un-stabbed.

His next thought had been of Isabel, and her lovely-smelling perfume. And then his thoughts had strayed to other lovely aspects of her. He might have gone down a lustful rabbit hole at this point, except for the fact that the scent of coffee—that blessed nectar of civilization—began tickling the edges of his olfactory senses.

Opening his door, he peered out, demonstrating an abundance of caution and handing Paranoia a minor victory. (He could almost hear its smug grin.) After all, as it had earlier suggested, there might be someone waiting with a sharp blade to finish him off upon exit.

But there was no one.

Following his nose, Max made his way down the hallway until he heard the low sounds of voices and the muted clink of cutlery. He came around a corner to find Estrada and his two henchmen, Colón and Sánchez.

Estrada looked up when Max came into view.

"Ah! The slumbering babe awakes. Come, Max. Join us for a light repast." The Spaniard gestured toward an empty chair at the table, one of two—and the second empty place brought Isabel immediately to mind. Where was she?

Max walked around the table to the indicated spot and took a seat. He looked around for the coffee carafe, but at once a waiter was there and setting down a steaming *café con leche.* This was followed immediately by a small plate containing a mouthwatering *tostada con tomate, aceite, y jamón*. Max took a sip of the coffee and then grabbed the tostada. He took a generous bite and had to close his eyes in pleasure at the combined flavor of warm bread, olive oil, and Iberian ham.

Once he'd regained control of his senses, he swallowed the mouthful of food, sipped at the coffee, and looked at Estrada. The man was watching him carefully, not gauging his reaction to the food as any conscientious host would do, but looking for signs of ... well, Max wasn't sure quite what.

Max made a show of looking around the table.

"And where is the lovely Isabel this morning?"

Estrada displayed a small, tight smile. "She is indisposed for the time being. You know how women can be—they can't bear to be seen not looking their best. She is, no doubt, engaged in the many mysterious rituals of the feminine routine."

"Huh," Max said. "I didn't take her to be particularly vain." This wasn't exactly true; Max did see a streak of vanity in Isabel, but it was not about her appearance. If anything, it was pride at being self-sufficient. He remembered her making a point to say how much more skilled she was now than when she'd first landed in Estrada's clutches, and Max suspected that Isabel had been engaged in a great deal of maturation and self-discovery during her time here. And it had no doubt been a journey she'd had to take alone. Max felt a twinge as he began to realize how isolating and lonely an experience it must have been, and his respect for the hauntingly beautiful woman deepened yet further.

"It is not mere vanity," Estrada was saying. "The señorita understands what is expected for a woman of her position."

"Speaking of that," Max said through a mouthful of tostada, then raising one finger to indicate that he needed a moment. He chewed, swallowed, then continued. "Exactly what *is* her position here at the compound?"

Estrada paused. "How do you mean?"

"Well ... what does she do here?"

"Do?"

"Yes, do. I can't imagine a woman like Isabel is content just sitting around, coquettishly fanning herself."

Estrada's face darkened and his lips tightened. "Our dear señorita is well cared for. You needn't worry about her. In fact," and here Estrada leaned forward in his seat, peering at Max with an intense stare that seemed to burn into the younger man's skin, "you would do much better to worry about yourself."

At these words, and Estrada's hardening manner, Max felt a cold tickle run up his spine to his neck, where it froze the short hairs in an upright position.

"Estrada," Max said slowly. "If you have something to say to me, I'd ask that you simply go ahead and do so. It is much too early to play word games. I don't even tackle *The New York Times* crossword until after lunch."

Estrada gave a short, sharp nod. "Very well, then. I will get right to the point. Your room, my dear Mr. Barnes, was bugged last night. My lieutenants and I heard every word you and Isabel said to one another."

Max's heart leapt up to his throat and his stomach hit the floor. He forced himself to remain still… and discovered that the effort was much easier than he'd expected.

"I see," he said. "So you heard our passionate lovemaking, then? She called out your name, by the way. Very awkward."

Estrada emitted a small laugh. "Joking in the face of danger. Such an American thing, and I do admire it. But comedy cannot help you now, Mr. Barnes. Both of you have betrayed me in the most callous way. I abhor traitors; they commit a cardinal sin and must be punished for it."

"Awww," Max said. "Am I being sent to my room?"

Estrada smiled and sat silent for a long moment, which Max found somehow creepier than when the man was speaking. Finally, he said,

"How are you feeling, Mr. Barnes?"

"A little embarrassed that I didn't search for listening devices, but otherwise—"

"You aren't feeling a bit sluggish? Stiff? Lethargic, perhaps?"

Max frowned. Come to think of it, he was feeling a bit heavy and listless. Sensing he could use more coffee, he tried to reach for it, but discovered that his arm felt as if it weighed a hundred pounds. It moved, but just barely, and seemed to be growing heavier by the second. He raised a stricken face toward Estrada, his neck fairly creaking with the effort.

"You've ... drugged me."

His tongue was growing thick and useless, and he felt his entire body begin to lean sideways as he lost his balance on the chair.

Then he was falling ... falling ... falling toward the floor. And as he fell, the floor morphed into a swirling black vortex that seemed to be reaching upward toward him, sucking him in.

Falling ... falling ... falling.

And then there was nothing.

As they had been walking quickly through jungle paths that Bembe seemed able to find and traverse with zero difficulty, Axel was alternately groaning and shaking his head. Bembe had been telling him surfer jokes the whole way.

"Okay, okay. Listen to this one, brah. What do surfing and oil have in common?"

As he had every time, Axel shrugged his shoulders.

"Dude! It's so easy! They're both measured by the barrel!"

Head shake.

"Oh! Wait till you hear this one! How does Mick keep cool before a heat? Fanning!" The young Maya was overcome by his own joke and laughed so hard he stumbled briefly.

"Listen, man," Axel said at last. "I don't get ninety percent of those jokes, and the ten percent I get just aren't funny."

"What are you talking about? This stuff is gold! You tell one of these jokes on Venice Beach – everybody cracks up. Everybody loves you." As Bembe finished speaking he let a branch snap back and the edge of it whipped across Axel's neck, scratching it.

"In case you haven't noticed, we're not in California."

"I know, I know, dude. I'm just trying to pass the time, but now we're getting close, so you should probably hold it down."

"Me? You're laughing so hard at your own lame jokes, I'm surprised they haven't sent out a welcoming party."

"We won't be welcome."

"I thought you said you invented sarcasm?"

"Still, I probably don't use it to the degree that treasure hunters do," he said, his voice oozing in the very mode of expression they were discussing. "Now, hush."

Bembe pulled back a branch and pointed. They were about thirty yards from a well-lit compound, surrounded by a tall chain link fence, capped off with some nasty looking razor wire along the top edge. Oddly the gate was open, but Axel could see there were at least three men with AKs guarding it.

"How nice, they've opened the door for us," Bembe said.

"Not an invitation I fancy accepting," Axel said. "No way am I waltzing up to that gate."

"Why not, brah? You're big but you'll fit."

"Fit? It's not a question of fitting. You could drive a truck through it. The issue is those dudes with the automatic rifles. They can put a lot of holes in a guy, fast."

"Oh, don't sweat those guys."

"Little man, I am reaching the limit of my patience with you." Axel growled menacingly. "What are you going to do, hit them with your skateboard?"

"I could, but what I mean is, I think they're coming to us. Check it, dude."

Axel sighed, but took a moment to, indeed, "check it." And what he saw made his stomach twist. His fists clenched, and the hot blood of anger began creeping up his neck. Two more guards had appeared through the open gate, dragging something—some*one*—behind them.

And that someone was Max.

Axel started to charge forward, but Bembe grabbed him with a strength that was surprising from such a small frame.

"Wait!" he hissed.

"But it's Max," Axel growled back.

"Brah, I have my own two peepers. But as you said, 'holes in guys,' remember?"

Axel did remember, and it was only the obvious folly of charging in that kept him in place. Everything in him screamed for him to go full Rambo on these bastards, but he bit down hard on the inside of his cheek until he tasted the metallic tang of blood, allowing the pain to center him once more.

Both men watched as Max was dragged unceremoniously across the clearing that separated the compound walls from the jungle. Then they disappeared into the treeline, still dragging the limp form behind them.

"Where are they taking him?" Axel growled, more to himself than Bembe.

"Probably leaving him for the jags," Bembe whispered. "Or bugs. Any number of bad things in the jungle that just love an incapacited meat sack."

Axel had the sudden urge to put the little Maya in an extremely tight headlock. "That 'meat sack' just happens to be my best friend. We're not leaving him to the bugs."

"Course not," Bembe said distractedly. "Just answering your question."

Axel huffed quietly. "One thing you might want to figure out sooner rather than later, is that I don't have a great sense of humor when it comes to the health and well-being of my friends."

"Or at all," Bembe muttered under his breath.

Axel shot him a hard look and ground out, "What was that?"

"Just sayin', ya didn't exactly go into paroxysms of mirth over my surfer jokes either. Might wanna see a doctor about that lack of levity, brah. It's bad for the digestion."

"Look, you little stain," Axel snarled. "I laugh when things are funny. In case you've lost sight of the objective, let me remind you that we're on an SAR, not at the local Dr. Yuk's comedy club."

"I—" Bembe started to respond but fortunately for him, given Axel's increasingly rage-filled expression, he was interrupted by the sight of the guards reappearing through the treeline, this time sans their human cargo.

"Looks like you were right," Axel huffed. "They're leaving him out there to die. Let's get the hell over there and find Max before something else does."

11

Max's eyes blinked open slowly, reluctantly. For a moment, he thought he'd gone blind, but then realized that his surroundings were merely darkened, and that he could just make out the dim, hazy glow of light to his left. He tried turning his head, but his muscles refused to respond, as if he were encased entirely in cement.

He groaned and, at the sound, felt rather than heard movement behind him. And then a face peered down—it was Bembe.

"Dude, you are in really bad shape. You must have taken in a real heavy dose."

As Bembe spoke, Max realized that he felt as bad as he apparently looked. His immobile body seemed to be on fire with fever, his damp and burning skin made worse by the close, heavy air of the jungle. He tried to speak but discovered he couldn't form words.

"Let me guess," Bembe continued. "They offered something fancy and delicious, and you stuffed yourself like a pig."

Another face appeared, and Max experienced a welcome surge of relief as Axel's broad mug hovered over him.

"You moron," the big man said affectionately. "You've gotten into a lot of stupid messes over the years, but this one takes the cake."

Bembe's face brightened. "Cake? We have cake?"

"No," Axel said. "But I'll make you one myself, if what you told me earlier is true."

"Would I lie to you?" Bembe said, scooting out of Max's line of sight.

Axel looked back to Max. "Our weird little buddy claims to not only know what ails you, but also how to cure it."

"It's a fifty-fifty chance!" Bembe called out, sounding much more cheerful about those odds than Max thought he should be.

"Anyway," Axel went on, rolling his eyes, "he thinks you've been poisoned by some sort of paralyzing agent. I don't know how he knows this stuff and, honestly, I don't much care as long as it works." He lowered his deep voice to a raspy, emotional whisper. "I'm not going to lie to you, buddy. You're in damn bad shape. I'm not sure you'd survive a trip out of this jungle and to a hospital. And they probably wouldn't be able to treat you anyway. I'm not entirely comfortable trusting Bembe with this, but I also don't see we have much choice."

Max struggled to respond, to tell Axel that Bembe's story entirely matched what Isabel had told him about Estrada's cruel method of disposing of the unwanted, but his voice and throat were frozen and useless.

Bembe reappeared, holding a small, crudely carved wooden bowl. Whatever was inside the bowl was steaming and, Max noticed next, smelled like an absolute abomination.

"Okay, brah," Bembe said, his tone utterly matter of fact.

"Here's the skinny. You're, like, about to croak from that poison Estrada gave you. I have an antidote for it, but it's not been, you know, exhaustively tested."

Axel cast him a glance. "Yeah, you already said fifty-fifty. How many times have you used this antidote?"

"Well ... two, actually."

"Two?" Axel stood up from where he'd been leaning over Max. "That's a horrible sample size!"

"Hey, I didn't exactly have major government funding, okay?" For the first time since meeting Axel, Bembe displayed a bit of temper. "The dude can take it or not. But without it, his chances drop from fifty percent to right around nil, so you do the math."

Axel sighed. "Fine. We'll leave it to him. Max, the choice is yours. Blink twice for yes, once for no."

Max didn't even have to think about it. He set his eyelids fluttering as fast as he could.

"Okay, then," Axel said. "That settles it. Give him the antidote."

Both men knelt down and, as Axel held up Max's limp upper body, Bembe held the shallow bowl to the patient's lips and let the steaming, vile liquid trickle into Max's mouth.

As the concoction entered his body, Max felt his entire being revolt. A strange, internal blackness that seemed to start at his feet, rushed upward toward his core, where it churned and boiled before flooding up into his head. His eyes went dark, and in stark contrast to the falling sensation that he'd experienced in Estrada's presence, now he felt as if he were shooting skyward, leaving his body behind.

Rising ... rising ... rising.

This is it, he thought, as the curtains of his consciousness fell closed. *I'm in the fifty percent who don't make it.* And then, in a moment of relief, an additional thought appeared: *At least I'm going up as I die. Maybe I wasn't such a bad person after all.*

In what was becoming a familiar routine, Max found himself easing back into consciousness. He lay for a moment, not even trying to move, assuming his body was still trapped in paralysis. But then there was a noise to his left, and his head involuntarily jerked at the sound.

It took a second for him to realize what had just happened—he'd moved! He tried to wiggle his fingers, and they responded immediately, as did his toes. One by one, he tested the various mobile parts of his body, and they all responded appropriately. He still felt heavy and sluggish, but the paralysis seemed to be a thing of the past.

Max took advantage of his amazing new abilities to finally take in his surroundings. He was lying on the floor of a cave, with an opening that was partially concealed by hanging vines. The light that filtered through cast a dim, greenish hue over the interior of the cave, creating a sort of greenhouse appearance. And it felt like a greenhouse—hot and sticky and close. But it was nothing like it had felt when he'd been in the ravages of the intense fever from earlier.

The sound he'd heard grew closer, and he looked toward it, even rolling halfway onto his side. He saw Bembe coming toward him with another bowlful of steaming concoction, with Axel looming up behind him like a cast shadow.

"Brah, you're awake!" Bembe said. "Looks like my antidote just increased its effectiveness by a whopping ... well, whatever percentage that would be."

"The hell with percentages," Max rasped, relieved to hear his own voice. "I'm just glad it worked on me."

"Yah, well, you still got some crud in you. But this second dose of the antidote should knock that right out."

Bembe knelt and held the bowl to Max's lips. Max felt silly being essentially spoon-fed but understood that his newly regained motor skills were still on shaky ground.

"Will this ... knock me ... out again?" Max asked between sips of the horrible brew.

Bembe shook his head. "Nah. It should actually get rid of any leftover effects in a few minutes. Just a heads up, though, your next trip to the little boy's room could be interesting."

"What?"

"Never mind," Bembe said, grinning. "You'll find out."

Max was going to press him on the issue, but at that moment they all paused as the sounds of rustling came from the mouth of the cave.

In a moment, Axel was pressing himself against the rock to the side of the entrance, as always impressing Max with how quickly and quietly the big man could move.

The rustling noise stopped, and everything was quiet, save for the continuous sounds of the jungle. After a minute or two, Axel shifted his position and eased sideways until he was able to peer around the edge of the cave's opening.

There was a sudden flurry of movement and in the space of a blink, Axel had a knife blade pressed to his throat. Someone stood before Axel, knife extended upward with the tip digging into the big man's carotid artery. The newcomer was somewhat silhouetted by the light of the entrance, but Max could tell it was a lithe figure dressed in jungle gear. And in the next flashing moment, he knew who it was.

"Isabel! Stop!"

Everyone froze at Max's outburst, which he'd delivered in a voice much more powerful than he'd have expected, given his recent flirtation with the Reaper.

Then the figure spoke: "Max? Are you—?"

"I'm okay. These two are friends of mine."

Slowly, ever so slowly, Isabel removed the knife from that most tender point on Axel's neck. The big man grimaced and rubbed at the spot, as if to make sure his life's blood wasn't gushing onto the cave floor. He looked over at Max.

"You know this wildcat?"

Max nodded. "She was in the compound with me."

"She is with Estrada?" Axel's forearm muscles flexed, as if they wanted to leap out and strangle the woman.

"Not exactly," Max hastened to say. "More of a prisoner than anything else. She's with us."

Axel relaxed minutely and reached up toward his neck again. "She has an interesting way of introducing herself," he grumbled.

"No time for the tender reunion," Isabel said, her musical voice holding just a hint of humor.

Axel's rigid body relaxed just a bit, and he allowed himself a small smile, despite the recent unpleasant proximity of the lovely dark-eyed woman's blade. He pointed toward the knife.

"Who'd you get that from, anyway? Crocodile Dundee?"

"I do not know your friend Dundee," she said, making her own concession to diplomacy by sliding the knife back into a sheath strapped to her strong thigh. She looked back at Max. "And you—Max. I saw you," she said, her voice a mix of confusion and relief. "They were dragging you into the jungle. Estrada's poison—"

"Has an antidote," Max interrupted. "Bembe concocted some sort of brew that purges it from the body."

Isabel frowned. "Who is Bembe?"

The Maya skater stepped forward and grinned. "I'm Bembe. You're just gonna *love* me."

Isabel snorted, and Max found even that adorable, coming from her. "Every time someone has said that to me, it has turned out to be the lie. And I see no reason to more believe you."

Max would not have put money on ever seeing Bembe speechless, but Isabel's glib smackdown to the little guy's hubris did exactly that. Before the Maya could recover, Isabel continued.

"And now we must run. I was spotted leaving the compound and they must be getting close now."

"Oh, wonderful," Axel groaned. "You led them right to us. Who needs enemies when you've got allies like—"

Isabel's big eyes flashed. "I had no way of knowing Max had already been rescued by a ragtag team of one *ratón pequeño...*

Axel pointed to Bembe and laughed. "She called you a little mouse!"

"And one *gorila de gran tamaño!*" she spat out.

"Oversized gorilla! Ha! I prefer being a little mouse. Easier to hide than a big-butt monkey." Bembe was laughing altogether too loud for their current circumstance.

"Gorillas aren't monkeys, they're apes," Axel countered. "And I bet they *eat* mice. And even if they don't, they can kick the little mouse's a..."

"...*And* they would likely have to found you eventually anyway also. The jungle surrounding the compound is monitored closely all the time. I'm surprised you two idiots got as close as you did."

Axel turned to Max. "Can you stand?"

Max sat all the way up and waited for the inevitable dizziness or nausea, but it never came. In fact, he felt pretty darn great. Just the hint of a headache lingered behind his eyes, but that was all that remained of the illness that had so recently rendered him entirely impotent.

"Yeah," he said, surprise in his voice. "In fact—" and here he rolled to a crouching position and then straightened all the way up, "—I feel well enough to get the hell out of here."

Isabel gave Max a grin so wide that it made him feel like a knight who'd just galloped back to the castle with a dragon's head under his arm.

"Okay," she said, her pronunciation making Max decide that he'd be just fine if "okay" was the only word she ever said. "Then we should go—now. We have only minutes at the most."

12

The four had finally reached the cleared land outside of La Libertad. Max's stamina had held up remarkably well, but he was now flagging badly. Even so, they pushed ahead until they were in the outskirts proper. With Bembe leading the way, they passed through alleyways and private yards as easily as he'd traversed the jungle.

After a few moments, Max realized they were heading to Bembe's lean-to and when they reached it the Maya ducked inside.

"Okay, peeps," he said. "We can chill here for a while. They can't find us now. Plus, I wanna grab my board."

"What's that?" Max asked, pointing to the one he'd carried through the entire getaway.

"I want my *competition* deck, okay? Big things ahead."

"He'll find us," Isabel said, mostly to herself, but Bembe scoffed.

"Nobody can follow the trail. Certainly not Estrada's goon squad," he laughed. "We can hang until we move on."

"Uh-uh," Axel said, shaking his head. "Don't be talking like La Libertad is just a layover. That's my final destination. Now that I got this numbskull out of trouble, I have a girl to go see."

Isabel shook her head. "Estrada is not a fool. Where do you think he'll go looking first? He'll be in the city within the hour."

Axel groaned. "But ... Rosita!"

Bembe looked over his shoulder at Axel with a sly grin.

"The dressmaker? Your girl is the dressmaker?"

"Yeah ..." Axel replied, a little suspiciously.

"Doh!" Bembe said, his Homer Simpson spot on. "Well, you'd better bring her with when we do move. She won't be safe once Estrada starts asking questions."

"Then we should go now and get her," Isabel said, her voice increasingly urgent.

"Then what?" Axel asked, almost shouting. "If we don't stay in the city, where are we going?"

Isabel leveled a steady gaze at the big man. "You are familiar enough with area. If not in the city, then where are we?"

"In the jungle," Axel said, disgustedly. "We just came out of the jungle. After Max and I just came out a couple days ago. I don't want to be in the jungle for a while. I prefer coming out of it!"

"So, you want to be the dead then?" Isabel said pointedly. "Both you and your girl?"

Axel growled. "She's not going to be happy."

"I don't know," Max said. "Maybe she's ready for a little time off. A little get away."

"Getaway is a right term," Isabel said.

This time Max's tired lungs hurt too much to correct Isabel's grammar, even though he sorely wanted to.

. . .

When they reached the dress shop, Axel walked around to the back of the building. Light could be seen through the pink sheer curtain in a second-floor window and Axel looked at the ground. Spotting a few small pebbles, he scooped a handful and after three near misses managed to hit the window, making a light tapping sound. When there was no response, he threw another four off the mark before a fifth again contacted the glass.

"Now I see why he grab so many," Isabel whispered to Max.

"Don't pick him for your softball team," he replied.

A few seconds later the curtains parted, and the window was pushed open.

"*¿Axel, que pasá?*" she whispered harshly.

"No time to explain, baby. We need to go."

"So, go!" the pretty dressmaker said in English, her face making no attempt to hide her displeasure. "I have a wedding dress to finish in the ... what's that?"

Rosita pointed to the sky behind where Axel and his companions where standing. They all looked up.

"It's a drone," Axel groaned. The flying device was moving in a straight line and its remote operator didn't appear to have noticed them. It continued on and was soon out of sight. "That right there," Axel said pointing in the direction it had flown, "is why you have to come with me. Right now. I'll explain everything, just please come with me."

Rosita's face softened. "Are you certain?"

"Lady, if you stay here you're not gonna finish the dress anyway," Bembe said, drawing his finger across his own throat and making his "dying human noise" to indicate her pending demise. Axel looked down at him and gave him a gentle cuff.

"Shut up, fool," he said as Bembe was deposited on his backside. Axel's gentle cuffs were nothing for anyone to sneeze at, especially someone as small as the Maya.

"He's right, though, baby. It's not safe. You have to come, *right now.*"

The woman hesitated.

"Let me leave *mama* a note. I'll be right down."

A moment later she emerged from the shop's back exit. She'd left the note and thrown on something a little better suited for travel than the nightgown she'd been wearing as she leaned out of her bedroom window.

"Ok, everyone follow Bembe," said the Maya, brushing off the final traces of his recent introduction to the ground. He walked to a small wooden fence at the back of the shop's small yard and pulled at the bottom of the widest slat. It pivoted out as if hinged at the top.

"I have lived here all of my life and have never seen this alley," Rosita said as she slid through the opening. When they had all passed through Bembe followed and let the slat settle back into place.

"I know all the alleys," Bembe said in an only slightly dismissive tone, moving forward at a moderate pace, the skateboard he'd taken from his lean-to tucked under his arm.

He led them along a twisted route that eventually brought them out of the city, heading in the direction from which Axel and Max had arrived when they returned to town the day before yesterday. Three times as they made their way through the city, they heard the whine of the drone's rotors as it continued to pass overhead. Each time, it continued on its path.

Now they were again more in the open than they were comfortable being as they headed back toward the jungle, this time on the opposite end of the city from which they'd arrived in

La Lib, escaping the compound. They approached the end of the cleared outskirts and were about a hundred yards from the jungle's obscuring shroud. Then they heard the whine in the sky behind them.

As they turned, they saw the drone moving out from the city in the same direction they'd gone, though at a slightly different vector.

"Get into the trees!" Bembe shouted as he broke into a full run.

The others, to a person, had longer legs than him, and they began to pass him as they dashed for the protection of the foliage. Max was a step or two behind the others and heard Bembe speak.

"I've had more than enough of this noisy toy."

Max looked over his shoulder in time to see Bembe point his skateboard in the direction of the drone. He spoke again, although Max could not understand the words. It sounded a little like the Maya he'd heard spoken in Guatemala much of his life, yet completely different at the same time.

Whatever the language, a moment later the drone's steady hum became suddenly choppy as though the rotors were stopping then restarting. Then it grew silent altogether, and a heartbeat after that it fell to the ground.

Bembe turned to follow the others and saw Max standing still, his mouth opened in shock.

"Crazy coincidence it just quitting like that, huh?" he said, running past the stationary man.

Max frowned after him. "Yeah ... crazy."

Instead of running to join the others, he jogged to where the drone had fallen. It lay upside down, on its rotors, two LED lights flashed alternatingly red and green on the craft's underside. Max knelt and saw a camera attached between the lights. He reached out to disconnect it, but suddenly his shoulder was nearly crushed by a vise-like grip that yanked him back several feet.

"Don't touch it!"

Axel stood there, his face set in an expression of combined fright and anger.

"Hey, watch it!" Max grunted. "You almost broke every bone on the right side of my body!"

Without speaking, Axel pointed at the drone. Max followed the point and saw, for the first time, a thin red wire protruding from the back of the craft. He gulped.

"Is that what I think it is?"

Axel nodded. Then he stepped forward, picked up the drone, avoiding the wire, and lobbed it as far as he could. What Axel lacked in accuracy, he made up for in power. The drone sailed so far into the jungle that Max lost sight of it. But that didn't stop him from seeing the blinding flash when the entire thing exploded as it hit a distant tree.

"Why, those insufferable jerks," he muttered.

Axel coughed out a laugh. "If you're talking about Estrada, I'm pretty sure they warrant stronger language than that."

"Oh, definitely," Max said. "I'm just so awe-struck by their insanity. That thing could have crashed and exploded anywhere in town: a restaurant, playground, medical clinic..."

Axel grunted. "Yeah, they don't care. In fact, causing a little collateral damage in the way of innocent civilians would probably make their day. Like finding a shiny centavo on the ground."

By now, Bembe and Isabel had returned, albeit slowly and cautiously, and gathered around.

"Are we being shot at?" Isabel asked her hand on the knife hilt, and Max thought he detected a small note of hopefulness in her wonderful voice.

"Just a little boobytrapped drone going off in fine style," Max said. "Nothing you don't see every day in the field of archaeology."

Isabel's smile widened and her eyes twinkled. "Ahhh, so you *are* Indiana Jones."

"Okay, fine," Max said, scuffing the ground in the perfect simulation of an "aw shucks" moment. "You got me. Maybe my life actually *is* that dangerous and exciting." He paused and considered. "A little dangerous and kinda exciting."

Axel groaned. "Break it up, you. We have actual problems here, and you know exactly what the situation is calling for. We need to get to the airport and hop on the bush plane."

Max nodded enthusiastically. "That would certainly make things a lot easier."

"And to do that, we need the jeep," Axel continued.

"Makes sense. Tizimín is a bit far to commute by shoe leather express."

Axel smiled. "Ha! The prof."

"Yeah. Dad's favorite euphemism. 'You boys don't need a ride! Take the ..."

"... shoe leather express," the men said in unison.

"So, back to La Lib, then?" Bembe asked. "Jeez, I'm just a kid! You guys are going to do me in before my time!"

"Then what is next?" Isabell asked, her anger and frustration bubbling to the surface once more. "A jeep, a plane? Then what? We all go up a nice flight? Take in sights?"

"*On* a nice flight," Max corrected. "Otherwise, you're just walking up stairs."

A second punch, with even worse intentions, told Max this might not be the time for an English grammar lesson.

"But to answer your question—yes. We go up in the plane."

Isabel shook her head. "I do not think the plane will help us spot Ahrum. You would not think the jungle could so totally reclaim a city as great as Ahrum was said to have been, but I know the jungle. Unless you know what to look for, I am sure it would be very difficult to spot on the ground *or* in the air. You have to know the signs ..."

"She's right, but that's where I can help," Bembe said smugly. "If you can get me a bird's eye view of the vicinity, I can probably narrow it down."

"Narrow it down?" Max said. "Using what?"

Bembe smiled and tapped the side of his head. "Knowledge, brah. First-hand information." He pronounced "information" as one might if they were performing a very bad French accent: "informaysheeown."

Max rolled his eyes. "Okay, Inspector Clouseau."

"Which raises the question," Axel said, "can we get close enough for Bembe to use this, er, knowledge?"

Max nodded, taking his turn to appear smug. "And this is where *I* can help."

"Oh really?" Axel scoffed. "You've never been of help to anyone before. What exactly are you bringing to the table this time?"

Max's self-satisfied expression never faltered. "Bembe has his knowledge and I have ..." he indulged himself in a lengthy dramatic pause "... technology."

Axel looked at him for a moment. "I'm getting the unpleasant idea that you've been hiding something from me. What do you know that I don't, Barnes?"

"Just a little thing that Crabtree bought for us awhile back that I've never had the excuse to use."

"Bought for *us*? And you're just now telling me about it?"

Max waved a hand, as if that were sufficient to dismiss Axel's indignation. "I know how you are with new tech. Always wanting to use it right away and then breaking something. It was expensive when Crabtree bought it, and I didn't want your meaty, bumbling hands making a mess of things."

Axel growled. "Fine. I guess I have to wait to give you the wedgie-from-hell that you so richly deserve. Right now, let's get the heck out of the jungle and to the airport."

"The perfect plan. Let's—" he broke off suddenly and held up one hand. "Do you hear that?"

"What," Axel said, "the sound of the entire world shouting in unison about how annoying you are? Yes, I think—"

"Shut your trap; I'm not joking. Listen!"

Axel did as he asked, cocking his head and even going so far as to cup his ear. "Uh ... either I'm going deaf, or—wait ... oh no."

"Oh yes," Max replied. "Another drone." Max ground his teeth together. "Great. I was hoping to cut back through La Lib and grab a ride to the airport, but as long as they've got a fleet of these flying bombs hovering all over the place—"

"Maybe I could, ya know, take care of those?" Bembe suggested quietly to Max. "You know. More... coincidences?"

Max raised an eyebrow. "I have many questions about that, but now is not the time to ask them. And to answer *your* question—thanks, but even if you were to 'take care' of this one, we have to assume there will be a third and even a fourth. And, regardless, even if we keep knocking them out of the sky, it will still give away our position. We'll just have to stay under cover of the jungle until dark. After that, we can try to stealth our way into town."

Bembe scoffed. "Modern technology. Such a downer. Okay, follow Bembe. Again."

13

Darkness fell much faster than Max expected. That was partially due to the thick jungle cover they'd used to conceal themselves from the drone, and partially because he'd been so exhausted that he'd fallen asleep while waiting for the sun to set completely before attempting to enter the city. The others, no doubt understanding his condition—after all, being paralyzed by a poison and then being brought back from the death's front porch by an antidote does tend to weary a man—let him sleep, waking him just minutes before the sun dropped below the horizon.

Axel, of course, had a responsibility as Max's best friend to not let him off the hook so easily.

"Seriously, Max," he said. "This right here is why I'm always bugging you to run and workout with me. You've got the energy of an eighty-year-old."

"What I wouldn't give!" said Bembe absently.

"Huh?" Max asked the small Maya.

"Oh, uh … what I wouldn't give for an ice-cold beer," quickly amending the off-hand statement.

"Yeah. I'm down with that notion."

"No time for beer," growled Axel.

"I didn't say I was going to have one," Max retorted angrily. "Just that I want one. That's what 'I'm down' means you illiterate Central American."

"Shut it up," Isabel said. The hurried escape had left her breathless and her skin still shined with perspiration in a way that Max found irresistible, and immediately took his mind off both beer and his pain-in-the-neck best friend. As is the case with friends close enough to be brothers, however, the rancor between Axel and Barnes dissipated as quickly as it had come up. "Now," Isabel continued, "how about we do less of the bickering and more of the figuring out what we do next."

Now Max turned to Axel, their bristling entirely forgotten, and mouthed the word, "Hot."

Isabel saw and gave him a not-so-playful punch to the arm.

"Ow! You tell us to behave, and then you go and slug a guy? Again? Are you sure you're not working for Estrada?"

"Yes, Maxwell Barnes. I'm sure. You too should be by now. If I was to kill you for Estrada, you'd already be dead. Remember? In your bedroom last night? I was thinking about it then, until you assured me you were trying only to fool Estrada."

"Which, by the way brah, you didn't," Bembe said, grinning.

"You don't need to rub it in. Now come on, let's get to that Jeep."

AS THEY EMERGED from the jungle, Max and Isabel were in the lead. Almost immediately, Max saw they were not far from the boarding house and, despite his weariness, began to run. He heard Isabel's footsteps quicken beside him and assumed the others were following suit.

The boarding house loomed at the end of the street and Max was just about to redouble his efforts, when he heard Isabel stumble. She cried out and stopped running, which caused Max to involuntarily curse as he forced himself to stop. He turned and grudgingly made his way back to her. She was sitting awkwardly on the street, her pretty face turned in a grimace.

Max knelt beside her. "What happened? Are you all right?"

"I think I twisted ankle. Am sorry, Max."

"It's okay. I'm more worried about you. Can you stand up?"

She held out her hand and Max took it, helping her to stand. She was in the process of testing the ankle's strength when the others caught up to them.

"Whew!" Axel said. "Forget what I said. For an eighty-year-old, you can actually shake a leg. I guess you just needed to feel motivated." He glanced at Isabel. "What's up with her?"

"Twisted ankle," Max said. He did his best to make his tone neutral, but Axel knew him too well and gave him a tiny, commiserating eyeroll. Then he paused and squinted down the street. "Uh ... and that may have saved your bacon, man."

Max cocked a brow. "What do you mean?"

Axel pointed toward the boarding house. Max looked. At first, he saw nothing but the massive dark rectangle of the building, but then he saw the smaller outline of the Jeep ... and the now-distinct glow of a cigar cherry.

"Someone's waiting by the Jeep," he muttered. "Now who do you suppose that might be?"

"I could guess," Axel said. "But whoever it is, I feel running headlong into their waiting arms would not be an amazing way to end the day."

Max nodded. "I'm guessing you are correct. Let's get in the shadows at the side of the street and ease our way forward, shall we? I want to get a look at this guy."

They all followed his instructions and moved into deeper darkness, with Isabel bringing up the rear and grumpily muttering something about, "Oh, no, don't worry about me. I will be fine as a hair frog."

Not far from the boarding house, Max ducked into an alleyway, and the others followed. From that vantage point, he observed the figure standing by the Jeep. There was, as far as he could tell, only one man. But this man was very large and very armed, cradling what appeared to be a Brügger & Thomet MP9 machine pistol in one of his massive arms. He was dressed in sort of para-military fatigues and was smoking a cigar that had to be at least a 70 ring gauge.

"Ridiculous," Max muttered. "Anything over 64 is just overcompensation for something else entirely."

"What are you talking about?" Isabel asked, having crept up beside him. She still sounded grumpy, but Max didn't notice, being so amazed by the fact that someone could still smell good after spending so much time in the jungle.

"Nothing," he said. "Not important."

She gave a curt nod, taking his word for it. "We should just rush the Jeep and drive away like hell bats?"

"Not a chance," Max said, shaking his head. "That machine pistol would cut us all down. Besides, there are some things in my room that might come in handy. Once I get those, we can grab the jeep and get out of Dodge."

"'Out of Dodge?' You like to correct *me*, but is your Spanish so bad that you don't know La Libertad means Liberty?"

"It's just an expression," Max said. "It means to get away fast, probably because someone's looking for you. Comes from the old American West. Dodge City."

"Ah! *Sí!* Matt Dillon. *Pyew pyew*!" She made little six-shooters with her hands and mimed a fast draw.

Behind them, Axel made a muted barfing noise. "Have I ever mentioned how tedious I find you both? Let's just get the Jeep and split."

Max turned his attention back to the guard, then he glanced back at Axel. "He looks pretty tough. You think you can take him?"

Axel looked as if he might incur internal injuries from the explosive laugh he was suppressing. "Can I take him. You're hilarious. Of course, I can take him. It's just a matter of getting to him before he turns that pea shooter on me."

A slow smile spread of Isabel's face. "You need a, how to say, distraction?"

Max nodded. "Yeah, that would be perfect. You think you can do that?"

The smile froze, as if Isabel had suddenly taken offense. "Of course, I can do that. I mean, look to me—"

She made a sweeping gesture with her hands, indicating her entire body.

"I think you mean, 'look *at* me,' but I get your point," Max said. "However, on second thought, maybe we should send Rosita over instead. That guard might know you, given your association with Estrada."

Isabel grudgingly nodded. "You are right. No matter. Rosita can wield power of her own." And with that, she have the other woman a conspiratorial wink.

Rosita smiled in return, and then stepped out of the alleyway and into the open. She glanced back at the others. "The guard is a man; I can do that."

The three men watched her walk toward the guard, and there was a special spark in Axel's eyes.

"You know," he said, almost to himself. "I've often said that the most attractive quality a woman can have is confidence. Turns out, I could not have been more correct."

Max snorted. "I don't think I've ever heard you say that, pal. You've mentioned plenty of attractive female qualities, but confidence has never been one of them."

Axel scowled at him. "Shut up while I go bag myself a guard." He slipped away into the darkness, surprising Max for the millionth time by how quietly and stealthily the big man could move.

Turning his attention back to Rosita, he felt his pulse quicken at the fact that she was moving into extreme danger. The guard might very well view her as a threat and cut her down, knowing that no authority in La Lib would move to stop him. But what made the move more impressive was that Rosita was not "one of them" in the same way Isabel was. She was not trained or hardened by a life of danger, action, and intrigue. And yet, when called upon, she had--quite literally—stepped forward.

She was now close enough to speak to the man, who had straightened to attention and held out his hand for her to stop.

"*¡Alto!*" the guard said, his tone sharp enough that Max could hear even from a distance.

He also heard Rosita's voice, but her words were too soft to be understood, his sketchy Spanish notwithstanding. Whatever she was saying, however, appeared to be having its desired effect. The guard's upraised, outstretched hand slowly dropped. He took the cigar from his mouth and smiled broadly. Rosita cocked her hip to one side, placing a hand there, as if giving the guard some alluring backtalk. The man let out a laugh—but that was the last sound he ever made.

Axel came from the shadows like a hound on the moor, one brawny forearm going around the guard's throat. The man struggled and clawed at the choking limb, but within seconds, he was sagging helplessly. Axel slowly lowered the limp form to the ground, then raised two fingers to his mouth and whistled sharply.

Max and Bembe ran forward, Isabel following. The little Maya cut a wide berth around the fallen guard, while Max approached and gazed down with at least cursory concern.

"Is he—?"

Axel shook his head. "Nah, he's not dead. Just off in la-la land for a while. Still, we should get moving ASAP."

Max bent and scooped up the B&T, hefting it a bit. He grinned and caressed the barrel.

"Feels good."

Axel raised an eyebrow. "Should we all give you and your new gun a private moment?"

"Hey, not all of us carry a personal arsenal in our biceps," Max grunted. "Besides, I have a feeling this lovely piece of mechanical engineering is going to come in handy."

"I don't think we have time to caress any guns, dudes, euphemistically or otherwise," Bembe said. "Let's hop in this hunk of metal and peel a nanner outta here."

"Peel a nanner?" Max said. "You one hundred percent just made that up."

"Nope, it's a thing," Bembe insisted. "But I don't have time to explain it, and it's super disturbing anyway." He jumped into the backseat of the Jeep. "Can we just *go*, pleeease?"

Axel spared a few seconds liberating the keys from the fallen guard's person. "I'm driving."

"Lost your love of hotwiring vehicles?" Max asked in a low voice.

Axel grinned. "Not at all. Still one of my favorite things. But why ruin the electrical wiring when I don't have to?"

Max regarded his friend with a look of amused thoughtfulness. "Maybe having a steady female friend is doing you good. You didn't used to be so responsible. I remember a day when ripping things apart was something you did just for fun, necessary or otherwise."

"And I remember a day when you weren't so annoying," Axel growled. "Oh, wait—no, I don't. Okay, everyone, let's go."

"Hold on," Max said. "I want to grab my things from inside."

Axel growled. "What the hell could be so important?"

"You'll thank me later," Max said, and then disappeared into the building.

After what seemed like at least two eternities, he reappeared and hopped calmly into the Jeep, without so much as an explanation or apology, and dropped his backpack on the floorboard at his feet.

Axel dropped into the driver's seat. "Are you ready now? You got your teddy bear and lollipops?"

"Sure do! Some bubble gum too!" Max grinned, not taking bait.

The others piled into the Jeep,

He cranked the key and the engine sputtered to life. He called over his shoulder, "Hold on to your butt cracks, people, because it's going to be a bumpy ride."

14

Axel had not simply been speaking metaphorically. It was, quite literally and painfully, a bumpy ride. To say that the road to the airport was in "bad repair," was to commit the understatement of the millennium, and possibly even a crime against language... *any* language. Even the potholes had potholes, and some could have almost swallowed the Jeep whole, had Axel not been so adept at grinding the steering wheel back and forth, weaving them through the treacherous maze like a sapper leading his company through no man's land. The wheel appeared comically small in his meaty hands, and he gripped it as if it was the only thing keeping him this side of the eternal vale—which it might have been.

The saving grace was that the distance was only five or six kilometers—a bit of a jaunt on foot, but certainly manageable by Jeep, even with the horrendous road conditions—and Max was beginning to experience a resurgence of good humor. Thinking back, it was clear to him that he, and by extension everyone else, was in much better standing now than they had been just a few hours prior. Estrada and his minions were, of course, still a definite threat, and they still faced the uncertainty, danger, and daunting challenge of locating Ahrum. Those two things, accompanied by the nagging periphery concerns regarding Bembe and Isabel—neither of whom Max *fully* trusted yet—still occupied the lion's share of his mind. Still, he could feel the tide shift just a little bit in their favor. Maybe not enough to give them the advantage, but at least to the point where they had a fighting chance.

He grinned against the night air on his face as they bumped and joggled along in the open Jeep and was just about to break out into a rousing, whistled tune ... when he thought he heard something that made his blood run cold. He gave Axel a solid thump on the shoulder.

"Turn off the headlights," he said.

Axel cast him a scowl and released one hand from its steering wheel death grip long enough to rub the place on his shoulder that Max had just assaulted. "First of all, ouch. Second, if I turn off the headlights, we're going into the ditch for sure. Off course, this road is so bad that I'm sure we'd even notice—"

"Turn off the lights! And pull over and stop."

Axel growled but knew his friend well enough to hear the little something in Max's voice that meant he was deadly serious. He flipped off the headlights and then brought the Jeep to a crawl, then a stop.

"Kill the engine."

Axel did so. "What the—" he started, but Max held a finger to his lips. And then Axel understood.

A distinct *whump-whump-whump* sound cut through the night air.

"Is ... that what I think it is?" Axel said.

Max nodded. "If you think it's a helicopter, and almost

certainly a scary one, then yes—that is exactly what you think it is."

"And you think it's after us?"

"I think we are in no position to assume anything other than exactly that. It would appear that Estrada has upgraded his flying machines, which means we absolutely need to get to ours. How much farther to the airport?"

Axel pointed. "It's just across that field."

Following the point, Max saw the sickly yellow glow of an HPS light that was most likely hanging from an airport service building. He then listened again to the helicopter.

"Okay—they're not right on us yet. Can you make it without the headlights? They'll certainly see us when we reach the airport, but it would be ideal not to advertise our position before then."

Axel tightened his already vise-like grip on the wheel, to the point where Max worried the thing might actually snap off and nodded grimly.

"Nothing but an ASM is going to stop us."

Max grimaced. "Don't even talk like that."

Isabel had leaned forward to hear the conversation better and now she spoke up. "What is this ASM you talk about?"

"Nothing," Max said. "It's just Ax talking crazy again."

"It goes boom," Bembe piped up. "Along with everything else in close proximity."

Max turned around in his seat, feeling very much like a harried parent on a long car ride. "Enough, okay! There will be nothing going boom—"

His words were cut off by the underwear-soiling sight of something fast and fiery flying past the Jeep. A moment later, something did actually go boom, just yards ahead and to their left. The shockwave rocked their vehicle, and somebody screamed. Max glanced over at Axel.

"Did you just scream?"

"Maybe," the big man growled. "I'm actually not sure. Now shut up—I have to drive."

And drive he did. Wrenching the wheel to the right, Axel drove the Jeep off the road and into a large dirt field. Max braced himself but was surprised and pleased to discover that the field was actually far smoother than the road had been. Apparently, it served as some sort of extended area for parking aircraft and was routinely graded.

"There!" he pointed ahead at an airplane, a Quest Kodiak 100, sitting on the runway. "That's ours!"

Axel gaped. "They had the plane prepped for us?"

Max grinned. "I told you that you'd thank me later."

"You sly dog. You called somebody, didn't you?"

"Maybe," Max said smugly. "We do know at least one person in high places, after all, and it would be foolish not to take advantage of him. Especially since he owns the plane. And this baby is fully STOL. Takes off in seconds. Just get us there and we have a chance." He turned to face the backseat again. "As soon as this thing stops, it's out and into the plane. We don't have any time to lose."

Just then, the chasing helicopter roared overhead and banked sharply. It was so low that the Jeep shuddered violently in the rotor wash.

"You think they've got any more missiles in that thing?" Max shouted.

"Who knows," Axel ground out in reply, his eyes not wavering from his rapidly approaching destination. "I don't think they actually want to kill if they don't have to. I think they're trying to stop us."

And, as Max watched, it appeared that he spoke the truth. The helicopter had banked again and was now beginning to descend even more, almost blocking their path to the plane. The side door to the helicopter opened and a man in black tactical gear appeared. He held an immense firearm and brandished it menacingly.

"Yeah, he wants us to stop, all right," Max said. "And I am going to suggest that we do the opposite."

Axel hazarded a tight grin. "Hey, we've been bad boys and girls so far. I see no reason to turn over a new leaf quite yet."

And with that, he stomped even harder on the accelerator, jerked the wheel, and spun around the hovering chopper. Max heard the armed man shout something unintelligible and then the chatter of automatic weaponry caused him to involuntarily duck his head.

"Stop us, maybe. Considering there's nothing like a bullet in the head to at least slow a brah down," Bembe shouted. He looked over his shoulder and saw that the chopper had yawed sideways, and that the gunman would soon have a better angle.

"I tell you what. If a thing was meant to fly, it ought to have feathers IMHO." He said each letter separately and with great emphasis. Max turned to look at the little Maya, and as he had when the drone had followed them to the edge of the jungle, he now waved his skateboard, holding it by the rear truck and making circles with the rounded front end of the spiffy deck. As had been the case at the tree's terminus, he muttered something in his odd-speak. Max was now thinking of it as "broken-Maya."

Bembe, crammed into the back of the jeep between the two girls continued to mumble and twirl… with absolutely no effect at all. Again a show of bullets flew over their heads, though considerably closer this time.

Max remembered the previous "coincidence," as Bembe had called it.

"This is a lot bigger than that kid's toy you appeared to bring down when we were heading for cover. I don't think the skateboard is up to it."

"Shouldn't matter," Bembe said, looking quickly at his deck. "Oh, duh!" Max watched as he turned it around and grabbed the front truck and started spinning the tail-end. He turned and looked sheepishly at Max.

"Backwards!" he giggled, as though enjoying himself.

This time when he started muttering the chopper began to sound much like the drone had. The engine began to sputter, and the whirly-bird's rotor began to work only intermittently. The tail rotor stopped first, robbing the pilot of its stabilizing effect, causing the entire machine to begin to spin as the main rotor continued to turn, taking the tail boom with it. After only a few seconds the air was again pushed in every direction, radiating uniformly out from the blast caused when the chopper made ground contact far harder than its landing skids were rated for. They folded outward like Bambi's legs on the frozen pond and the fuel tank ruptured in a blinding flash. They again felt a buffeting shockwave.

Just then Axel pulled the Jeep back onto the road, which turned out to be the wrong choice, as the flat field had been vastly easier for the vehicle to traverse. The big man immediately hit the biggest pothole they'd encountered thus far.

"More like a *cave*," Axel muttered.

The resulting bump caused Bembe, who was admiring his handiwork, to lose his tenuous balance. He tumbled rearward and if both Isabel and Rosita hadn't grabbed his ankles he'd have been a goner. But a second later the little man called out.

"Wait! Stop! I dropped my deck!"

Axel slowed the Jeep to a stop, then put it in reverse causing the transaxle to whine commensurate with the pressure he put on the gas pedal. Bembe shouted again.

"Brah, don't run over it!"

Axel slammed on the brakes, and this time Bembe flew toward the front of the vehicle, between the front seats. He turned to look at Axel after groaning for a moment.

"You don't have to rush for a minute or two anyway. Those guys aren't going to be an issue anymore." He regained an upright orientation and complaining about a new set of aches and pains, he hopped out of the Jeep.

"This might be, though."

Bembe lifted the skateboard from the ground ... in two unevenly-sized portions. It had snapped in half close to the front wheel assembly. Max was confused as Bembe looked at the two parts, especially the back end, then tossed the smaller front piece aside.

"Aw ... dude," he said, showing off a pout that would have put a toddler to shame. "

"Bad news?" Axel said, raising an eyebrow.

Bembe scowled. "You know many things that are improved by being snapped brutally in half?"

"Crab legs?"

"Shut up."

Axel sighed. "Look, I'm sorry your boom-toy got broken. But we still need to get on that plane. That chopper might have friends. And now that you're essentially useless to us—"

"You go ahead," Bembe said, and for a moment Max thought he might start weeping. "I'll just walk."

"Suit yourself," Axel said, yanking the Jeep into gear and passing Bembe about halfway to the open gate, giving him a nice cloud of dust through which to walk.

"Brah! Not cool!" he shouted as the vehicle bounced past him.

Max glanced back and saw the little guy trudging through the dust cloud, shoulders slumped, one piece of skateboard in each hand.

Once through the gate, Axel quickly proceeded to their plane. Bembe followed at a lagging distance, but when the others started piling into the plane, he picked up his pace and ran after them.

Isabel waited in the doorway of the two-toned plane, yellow on top, white underneath, and held out her hand which Bembe grabbed just as Max and Axel, who had taken up the two front seats of the plane, eschewing a proper preflight check, got the plane rolling.

"Max, brah!" he said as he scrambled aboard, with Isabel virtually pulling him through the hatch. He felt what he said got his message across, so he added nothing, laying on the floor as Rosita reached over him and pulled the door shut, securing it.

It was at that exact moment that a vehicle, a Jeep eerily similar to the one they themselves had utilized, careened onto the airstrip ahead of the rolling Kodiak. It came to a sliding halt and a man jumped out, waving his arms in the air.

"Holy crap!" Max said. "Is that ... ?"

"Estrada?" Axel said. "It certainly is."

"Not a good idea, buddy!" Max shouted, as though the man could actually hear him.

"Rosey, hand me that pea-shooter," Axel said, turning to face the variously arrayed passengers. He pointed to the machine pistol they'd recovered from the man guarding the jeep, who should just now be waking up with a very bad headache and the burden of explaining how he not only lost a Jeep but his weapon as well.

In Rosita's life before meeting Axel, the most dangerous thing she ever handled was the antique sewing machine in her mother's shop. She picked the gun up like it was a very dirty baby diaper. "Here. Have it!"

"Thank you, *mi querida.*"

Even with Estrada's recent actions, Axel had no burning desire to fill him with bullets. People often thought Axel, with his brawn and hard, blunt looks, was as tough on the inside as he was on the outside. Truth be told, there was more than a little teddy bear inside that thick hide. The problem here was that the plane, controlled by Max—who had decidedly less teddy bear—was accelerating directly toward the man and showing no signs of slowing. The propeller was 100% going to end his day early. Unpleasantly early. Axel pointed over Estrada's head, slightly to the left of him, and squeezed off a short burst. As he hoped, the man dove to the right, out of the way of the plane.

Max cast him a look. "Feel better about yourself?"

"I just didn't want to damage the props," Axel grumbled. "Besides, don't give me grief for not wanting to slice a guy with a propeller."

Max shrugged.

"Pretty cold, Max."

Max was in no mood.

"Listen," he said, "if it was a question of avoiding him, slowing enough to let those other folks catch up ... and then we have to ... while you might enjoy attending that party, have at it."

"You sound like a blithering lunatic right now," Axel said, as he began paying more attention to the navigation than the people they were rapidly leaving behind. "Are you sure you're capable of flying this aircraft?"

By way of answer, Max pulled back on the yoke, bringing the small craft into as sharp a pitched climb as he dared.

"This 747 will def make our lives easier," Bembe said. "It ain't a short hike."

"It's hardly a 747, Bembe," Axel said.

"Because here's the deal," the little Maya went on ignoring the big man's correction. "Either we get to Ahrum, get the crystal that's there, as well as the others, which is a whole other gnarly can of worms, and reunite them to complete the ritual ... or Estrada will. Come hell or high water, he won't stop if *we* don't stop him."

"We'll be in Tiz before you know it," Max said. "We'll pick up the equipment, and then you'll earn your keep, Bemberino."

"Oh, my good Itzamna, no matter what happens from here on out, no matter how bad things get or how good things go, puh-lease don't ever call me that again."

"Party pooper," Max said, as he leveled off the plane and headed to the Mexican border.

15

Max had touched down at the private airstrip to the southeast of the Mexican city of Tizimín, and not at the city's Cupul International Airport, where they worried about things like passports and visas and all those inconveniences.

The airstrip was currently unoccupied except for a barebones crew and an airplane mechanic who seemed to have been expecting them.

As Max and Axel walked over to talk to the man, Isabel pulled her cell phone from her pocket and made a quick call. Then she stood with Rosita while the men huddled together. She couldn't help but laugh.

"They look like little boys, planning to do mischief," she said to Isabel in Spanish.

"They *are* little boys," Isabel said, smiling nonetheless.

The men, well out of earshot, obviously did not hear her quiet comment, and probably would have laughed had they. At the moment they were engaged in earnest conversation with the keyholder, a young man in greasy overalls with the name "Manuel" sewed onto his chest. He wore a Cruz Azul F.C. hat turned backwards, his long, dirty hair thus kept out of his eyes. Although Cruz Azul played in Mexico City, it was not unheard of for places without a nearby team to root for them. They finished in the number one spot in the Liga MX. His work boots were oil stained and dusty.

"So," Axel was asking, "You think you'll need the help of one of us to install the lidar on the plane?"

"Sí. Is not difficult, but requires two people," the young man said in great earnest. "Señor Barnes, Señor Crabtree request you await him at Bar Bomba."

"Sure! How do I get there?"

Manuel held up a set of keys and pointed to a much nicer Jeep than the plane-crash-simulator model that they'd used to get out of La Libertad.

"Is already programmed into GPS," he said, with a smile that was at a 50% deficit in terms of front teeth.

Max turned to Axel. "Do you want to stay and help? You can do all the heavy lifting."

"Might as well," the big man said, "so I know it's done right! Rosey can stay in case I get sad."

Max snatched the key from the mechanic's outstretched hand. "Works for me," he said. "Why don't you keep Bembe here with you, on account of he annoys me, and you might need help. Oh, wait, I forgot," he said, pretending to just remember a key point. "His skateboard is broken."

Bembe shot him a look that could have chilled Vesuvius during its most infamous eruption.

"It'll ride again, brah. Don't you worry."

The women walked over, while Bembe sat in the dirt next to the taxiway, inspecting his broken skateboard from several angles.

"Dang, this was a good deck, too," he said, mostly to himself. He seemed to be picking at something on the underside.

"Isabel, do you want to ride into town with me?" Max asked her.

The beautiful dark-haired woman seemed to consider this for a moment. Finally, she nodded. "Sí. We go," she said, giving Max his comeuppance by stealing the keys from him. "I will drive. Have had enough of men rear of the wheel."

"Yeah, generally in America we say, 'at the wheel.'"

Isabel stared at Barnes for a minute, then cracked a smile. She was beginning to understand that Max was just teasing her.

"Well, Max Barnes, this is not America. Correct again my English today and I stick your head beneath wheels and run it over."

"'Run over it,'" Max said automatically as he walked to the passenger's door.

Isabel started the vehicle and looked over at him.

"Go. Go stick your head under wheel so can I run over it,'" she said, mocking him with yet another butchered sentence.

He smiled and opted for the front seat. Max had kept the MP9 and now he slid it beneath the seat as Isabel navigated toward Bar Bomba. He felt that 571 miles from Estrada and his lackies was distance enough to only need it close, not held at the ready.

THE RIDE WAS MUCH MORE peaceful than most of the recent travels, and Max found himself surprised—and dismayed—by how quickly death-defying journeys had become the norm. As a result, however, the ride also seemed absurdly short, although that may have been due in large part also to the fact that his traveling companion was the beautiful and charming Isabel. Max had to admit that, while he had some reservations about her trustworthiness, he was beginning to harbor feelings toward her that went a bit beyond the fact that she was insanely attractive. He was not "in love" or even infatuated, but there was a magnetism between them that he had to believe was not entirely unnoticed by her. How was it possible that he could feel it so plainly, but she did not? And, if she did, then what were they to do with this mutual attraction? Max had certainly been with his share of women. He'd never been a major playboy, and frankly found that whole lifestyle to be stupid and meaningless but was also a red-blooded male with a strong appreciation for the opposite sex. Additionally, he'd never had to work very hard to find interested women. He knew they generally found him attractive, merely judging from the heads that turned whenever he walked into a nightclub—which was, admittedly, a fairly rare occurrence—and a couple of purchased drinks and a turn on the dance floor usually got him where he wanted to be. But he'd never been interested in abusing this gift; he found it to be a stupid game for stupid guys. Still, this thing he was feeling for Isabel—just the initial, tickling tendrils of connectedness—was something else entirely. He'd only experienced it one other time in his life—and that had turned out very badly. And so it was, that whenever he felt that twinge around Isabel, he experienced both a rush of excitement and a crush of dread.

Max snapped back from his thoughts to find Isabel pulling the car to a stop alongside a street curb.

"We're here?" he asked, almost in a daze.

"If here is Bar Bomba, then *sí*," Isabel said, smiling at him with only a hint of question. "You are all right?"

"Huh? Oh! Yeah—sorry. I guess I'm not used to not being shot at while in a moving vehicle."

Isabel frowned in confusion, then shook her head as if feeling sad about her traveling companion's lack of mental acuity.

"The restaurant is across the road." She pointed.

Max followed her point and saw a light blue building with dark blue trim. There was a large Corona sign attached to one side, and the entrance was a swinging half door, like those ubiquitous in western movies.

"Perfect!" Max said, swinging out of the vehicle. "I just realized I could drink approximately twelve Coronas!"

"Twelve?"

As they started walking across the street, side-by-side, Max grinned at her. "Little known fact," he said. "'Corona' actually means 'twelve' in ancient Mayan. And if you drink less than that in a single sitting, a conquistador comes back to life."

Isabel shook her head and tried to scowl at him, but Max could tell she was fighting back a laugh. "Isabel thinks you are lying to her."

And Max thinks it's super-hot when you refer to yourself in third person, Max thought. His step hitched as he tried to figure out if he'd said that aloud, but Isabel had not reacted so he assumed he must have kept verbally quiet, even if he'd shouted it in his own head. He was pretty sure she would have slapped him otherwise.

And Max thinks that might not be all that bad—stop it! Max mentally slapped himself in an effort to move out of this dangerous territory. It did not work.

Fortunately for his state of mind, they had reached the sidewalk in front of Bomba and were now pushing through the bar doors. The dim light forced Max to focus more on where he was walking and less on the sketchy fantasies his mind seemed intent on projecting onto the silver screen of his imagination.

They found a booth—that shuddered ominously as they put their weight on it—and ordered Coronas and tamales. The food arrived quickly—almost too quickly for Max's comfort, as if they'd been sitting on the steam table for a while—and they tucked in. Immediately upon seeing the food on the table, Max realized he'd never been so hungry in his life. Yes, there was that time he and Axel had gotten lost in the Amazon and spent a few days living on grubs, but as he savored the delicious, gloriously greasy tamale, he did not believe he'd ever been this close to starvation.

"It is good?"

Max opened one eye, as he'd apparently closed them both in ecstasy. "Huh?"

"You have the look of a man who is very much enjoying something," Isabel elaborated.

Max almost choked but managed to control himself enough to smile and say, "Er ... yeah, these are delicious." He chugged the rest of his first beer and waved for another. He gestured toward her plate. "You haven't touched yours, yet. Do you know something about this place that I don't?"

Isabel shook her head. "It is only that I like to watch a man eat who is hungry." She smiled, a bit coyly, Max thought.

"Well, that's me," he said lamely. "I'm a man. Who is ... hungry."

"I know you are a man," Isabel said. "Maybe you can tell me a thing."

"Tell you ... ?"

"I have always wonder," she went on, ignoring his confusion, "why it is that some women in America like a man who has no hair."

"You mean bald?"

Isabel shook her head. "No, I mean on the ... " She made a circular motion around her bosom with one hand.

Max almost choked again. "The, er, chest?"

"*Sí!* The chest. I am think that if a man does not have hair on the chest, then he is not a man."

Max shrugged, trying to will his face not to blush. This was ridiculous. He was not easily embarrassed, but now he felt like a schoolboy who'd been caught looking at a Victoria's Secret catalogue behind a propped up math book.

Isabel pointed at Max's chest. "And I can see that you have not made to shave your chest."

Max chuckled nervously in a most unmanly fashion. He tried to stick a tamale in his mouth, missed, and smashed it into his chin. "Well, that's me," he chortled like a crazy person. "Manly to the boner ... er ... ha! Bone ... er ... hey, more beers you can bring, thank you? I mean, please? Can you bring more beers?" His face flaming redder than matador's cape, Max forced his miserable eyes toward Isabel's face ... and discovered that she was laughing. Without malice or cruelty, but still laughing at his expense.

He scowled. "You've been toying with me this whole time, haven't you?"

Isabel had to take a moment to compose herself, her dark eyes sparkling with merriment. "Oh, Max. You are so easy to know."

"What?" Max found himself feeling suddenly offended. "I'm no such thing. I'm a man of mystery."

Isabel shook her head. "Isabel read you like a book. I have known you have a little crush on me."

"I have no such thing. Sure, I find you attractive, as would any man in his right mind, but—"

"It is not to be ashamed, Max. I am used to it. And it is a harmless thing."

For some reason, Isabel's words caused a sudden plummeting in Max's mood. Why her designation of his "crush" as "harmless" should have affected him so much, he didn't know. But he didn't like it at all. Not that he wanted her to feel threatened by his feelings toward her, whatever the heck they were, but calling them harmless seemed ... dismissive? Max sighed inwardly. This situation was one that would require much more contemplation, away from the teasing, discombobulating influence of Isabel.

"But no more of this," Isabel said, shaking her head as if to rid it of frivolous things. "I need to talk to you about something serious."

Max froze in mid-chew. "I hate it when people say that. It usually means I owe them money and missed a payment."

Isabel opened her mouth to answer, but then she too froze, her lovely red lips forming a small "o" shape. Her eyes stared off into a corner, but were not vacant—rather, her gaze was sharp and focused, and a small wrinkle appeared between her brows.

Max swallowed his bite of tamale. "What is it? Isabel?"

No answer.

Max turned on the bench, half expecting to see some horrible monster sneaking up behind him. Instead, as he followed Isabel's stare, he saw a small television sitting on a low table in a corner, playing what appeared to be the aftermath of some action movie battle scene.

"Isabel," he tried again. "What's wrong?"

She pointed at the television. "Don't you see?" Her voice was low and slightly ragged.

"The TV? Well, yeah, and I agree the picture is terrible, but I don't think that warrants—"

"Enough of the jokes, Max! Look!"

And he did.

Displayed on the screen was an inferno, but it was not an action movie, as he'd initially assumed.

It was a newscast.

As he watched, a news anchor appeared and began speaking, the Spanish too fast and clipped for him to catch more than a few words. But he did understand as the anchor recited the name of the private airstrip where he'd left Axel, Bembe, and Rosita—an airstrip that was now engulfed in raging flames.

16

Max tried to look away from the horrific image on the flickering television screen, but he sat immobile ... unblinking. In his mind, he kept picturing Axel in the hangar at the airfield—a hangar that was now just a huge pile of twisted, scorched metal. And there was Bembe and Rosita, of course, but they were footnotes in his sea of mounting grief. Axel was like a brother to him—WAS his brother, and Max could already sense a creeping notion that he should have been there, should have somehow foreseen the tragedy that now played coldly on the television. He'd seen similar images countless times from around the world, and they were always unfortunate ... but now he knew some of the victims, and that made all the difference.

Gradually, he became aware of a voice calling his name from a long distance away. The voice grew nearer and nearer, until suddenly it was shouting directly into his face.

"Max!"

It was Isabel, face drawn and eyes wide.

"What?"

"Come back, Max!"

He gestured weakly toward the television. "But … they … Ax—"

"I know, I know—" Isabel's voice was soft but underpinned with cords of steel. "But we have another thing to worry about *right now!*"

Max took a long breath, digging deep within himself, searching for the strength to not completely lose it. With great deliberateness, he placed his hands palm down on the table, as if to steady it—knowing he was really trying to steady himself. His mind whirled, and he was taken aback by not only the event itself but also his reaction to it. Max was no stranger to high stakes play, danger, and adversity. There had even been times when he'd been uncertain of Axel's survival—and Axel about his. But this was something different. It *felt* different, shrouded in an air of finality. Max hoped to God he was wrong, but he couldn't ignore the leaden lump of dread in his gut.

"Okay," he said, more to himself than the woman across the table. "Okay—I'm listening."

Instead of speaking, Isabel merely pointed out the nearby window. Max leaned forward to see from her vantage point, and then he immediately understood her urgency. There, crossing the street, were two men in black fatigues who were making no effort at all to conceal the automatic weapons they carried from straps over their shoulders. Two more men waited in a Jeep parked just behind the vehicle that Max and Isabel had taken from the now-defunct private airstrip.

Max groaned. "I'm guessing those aren't representatives from Publishers Clearing House, bearing good tidings of newfound wealth?"

"You speak nonsense, as usual," Isabel said, "but whatever they bring, is not the good tidings."

"Hey, maybe that's what they named their bullets," Max replied, surprising himself by joking in his current state of mind.

Isabel ignored this latest shred of lunacy and was already up from the booth, grabbing at Max's hand.

"Come, we go."

Almost dragging him along, Isabel headed directly for a set of stairs leading to a second floor. Up they went, making way too much noise and ignoring the shouts of the bartender.

"He's going to rat us out, isn't he?" Max said, indicating the irate proprietor.

Isabel nodded. "*Sí.* And I would like to send his, how you say, jewels up into his body, but there is no time."

Max shuddered, feeling quite convinced that "sending his jewels up into his body" was the most horrifying line he'd ever heard.

They were now in a hallway that appeared to run the length of the building, with several doors along the right side. Isabel began rattling doorknobs, finding them all locked until the next to last door, which opened upon command. They both tumbled inside but had no time to take a breath before the air was filled with shrieks and angry yelling. Max gaped at the sight that now accosted him. A man and woman lay entangled on a bed, having obviously been engaging in a very intimate moment.

"*¿Qué estás haciendo?*" the man shouted. "*¡Sal de aquí!*"

The woman simply kept shrieking.

"Sorry!" Max said, with complete and utter sincerity, although he felt even sorrier for himself. This was not a sight he needed in his brain. He tried to shield his eyes while backing into the hallway, but then heard the clatter of footsteps coming up the stairs toward them. "Sorry again!" he yelped, charging back into the room and, with Isabel right behind him, covered his head with his arms and crashed through the window, dropping to the street below.

Max attempted a tuck and roll maneuver, but as he'd cleared the window Isabel grabbed his ankle, causing him to land, which he did a second later... on his back, and driving the air from his lungs. Any oxygen that might have hidden and attempted to linger were driven out a half-instant later when Isabel landed face down on top of him.

She'd clearly been less shaken by the fall. Granted, she had a softer place to land, but as she continued to lie there he grew... less soft.

"Max! Is in your pants another tamale, or you are just happy to see me?" she teased.

Max was still unable to speak for a moment, but then something deep within his autonomic nervous system shouted loudly, "Breathe, idiot!" He did, in a deep gulping gasp that sounded like he imagined how the first breath of the resurrected would sound. With that first lungful he felt strong enough to choke out one word:

"Jokes?"

"You are right," she said, rolling off of him. She quickly gained her feet and held a hand down to Max, who was currently enjoying a second fresh gulp. With some effort he got up as well. "Come, we must reclaim jeep."

"I don't kno..." Max began, but Isabel had already moved around the corner of the building, her back against the wall as she passed stealthily. "Never mind," he added, rather impotently. He followed her lead and soon they were edging around the back of the building. Max glanced at Isabel's face and saw that her gaze was laser-focused on the two other Blackshirts waiting in the Jeep. Only seconds remained before the two men who had chased them up the stairs would be reappearing on the street, since odds were they wouldn't take the same exit as their quarry. But Isabel was not waiting for that to happen.

Before Max even had time to make the street crossing, Isabel had dashed along two other vehicles and had leapt into the back of the roofless Jeep, stabbing one man at the base of his skull, just below the occipital, which Max was pretty sure wouldn't kill him... not immediately. But it would render the use of everything below neck level useless, including his lungs. Max winced as he remembered just a tiny bit of that feeling of airless panic. He continued to wince when, an instant later, she drove the hunting knife through the top of the driver's skull, as he'd already begun to turn in reaction to his passenger's expression of shock and horror. She tugged hard to pull it out. It resisted, thanks to the serrations along the blade's spine.

Max had snapped out of his trance-like stupor and dashed past *that* bloody scene and toward the driver's door of their own Jeep. As he passed her he said, "Leave it Isabel! I'll buy you a new one."

"*Mierde!*" she exclaimed.

Max thought that everything he'd just seen her do up to that point was pretty shocking, but it turned out that it had only been a charming prelude to what he saw her do now: as he pulled on the door handle, he turned to see her standing on the dead man's shoulders, pulling on the hilt for all she was worth. After a brief struggle she was rewarded as the blade dislodged so suddenly she fell backward into the rear seat.

At the same moment, the two other men ran shouting from the

bar but to Max's joy they turned in the direction of the window through which he'd made his spectacular exit.

"Isabel, *please!*" he called.

Looking like a meerkat peeking cautiously out of its burrow, Isabel's head popped up. Seeing her beautiful face, smiling now despite the macabre scene in the front of the jeep, Max felt a chill run down his spine.

I'm glad she's on my side, he thought. Then as he saw her vault out of the rear of the jeep and run to the passenger door of the vehicle Max had already started and put into gear, he appended the thought.

Please, let her really be on my side.

She jumped into the vehicle slamming the door closed at the same instant that Max tromped on the gas pedal, just as the other *camisas negras*, having found nothing on the far side of the building, sprinted around the corner. As Max tore down C.51, he heard furious shouting behind them. With his sketchy Spanish, he couldn't quite decide if they were yelling, "We will catch you, skin you alive, and use your hide for bedsheets" or "Please return to us as we have many lovely pastries to share." Given his recent experiences with these hoodlums, he assumed the former and pressed the accelerator as far as it would go. He glanced over at Isabel, to see Isabel clutching her bloody knife in her equally bloody hand. She waved it in front of his eyes.

"Is a present from *mi madre*," she said calmly, reasonably. "I couldn't leave behind."

He swatted at her hand as she was seriously impeding his vision.

She moved her hand but smiled at him. "Max is grumpy pants when he fall down!" she laughed, reminding him of his awkward landing from the second story. "All judges show you *la terjeta cero!* Poor, poor Max. No gold medal."

Max had by now recovered sufficiently to be offended.

"Wha... they... they did *not* all show me the zero card. What about degree of difficulty?"

"*Sí*," she answered, "and you really... how they say? Ah, 'stuck landing!'"

When Max laughed it was spontaneous and genuine. He felt himself being pulled closer to that place, that reservoir of emotion in which he did not like to dip even his pinky toe. But before he could even fully realize what was happening he'd said, "Oh, I L—-"

She looked at him quizzically.

"—OVE me some Corona." The save was lame, but it was a save all the same.

"Well, you only drank two or three. So somewhere *el conquistador* has risen."

For the second time in only minutes, Max felt his spine tingle. The things he'd seen and heard in the past few days made his barroom joke a little too believable for his comfort.

17

While Max executed a series of turns designed to make it harder for them to be tracked by the Blackshirts, as he now thought of the men in their midnight fatigues, or *camisas negras* if he was thinking in Spanish, Isabel, who was essentially covered in blood spatters, sheathed her knife and took out her phone.

"Who you calling? Oh, don't tell me you booked a backup date in case I turned out to be a dud!"

"Ha! That would make this a date in first place! No. I call my boss."

In what was rapidly starting to feel very old to Max, he felt another brief shot of ice-cold electricity zip down his spine, thinking she meant Estrada. But a moment later she said, in English, "Let me speak to Emcee."

Just then Isabel's side of the Jeep's windshield splintered, the milky cracks radiating out from a central hole that had obviously been caused by a bullet. A split second later, Max heard the pop of a weapon from behind them. He glanced in the rearview mirror and saw the second Jeep coming down the road toward them, gaining ground at a distressing rate.

"Hey, uh, Isabel?"

She waved at him to be quiet. "Am on phone!" she hissed.

"Okay, but a bullet just—"

"Hello, Emcee," she said, interrupting him and speaking into the phone. "It would appear that Sr. Estrada was able to track us to Tizimín. We had to leave Bar Bomba ... prematurely."

The word rolled off her tongue in a way that threatened to reawaken Max's enchilada.

"Sí ... okay." There was a pinging noise as her phone received a notification. She pulled the device away from her ear and looked at the screen. "The text came. Sí ... gracias ... bye-bye."

The "bye-bye," made the threat a reality. For all his teasing about her English, her voice was beginning to sound like music in whichever language she spoke.

She was again looking at her phone, punching some GPS coordinates into the vehicle's navigation system.

"What's that?" Max asked.

"Coordinates."

"I don't need coordinates. I remember how to get back to the airstrip, and as soon as I lose these maniacs behind who are, as I've been trying to tell you, *shooting at us*, I'm going straight there."

"No."

Max felt his mind whirl. "Excuse me?"

"I said no. We are not returning to the airstrip. At least, not that one."

"What the... what are you talking about?" Anger was bubbling up inside Max's core. The worst kind of anger. It was the kind infused with grief. He felt his hands begin to shake, and he gripped the wheel tighter to prevent Isabel from noticing. He paused for a moment, during which several more bullets whizzed overhead. He took a right turn at an insanely high rate of speed, coming close to rolling the vehicle, but he didn't even blink. "Listen," he began, his voice so quiet that Isabel was forced to lean closer to hear him. "If you think for one minute that I'm going to leave Ax alone at that airstrip, then you have another—"

Max saw movement from the corner of his eye, and he hazarded a glance at his passenger. A passenger who was even now staring at him with steely eyes and pointing a deadly-looking handgun directly at him.

"Max. We are not returning to that airstrip. Anything that happened there has already happened. I am sorry. You cannot help friend by needlessly dooming us."

He saw red. For a brief moment, he legitimately saw red.

Fortunately for their safety, his vision cleared quickly, and his rage receded into a burning lump in his belly.

"Look—you may be right. In fact, you are almost certainly right. But what if I *can* do something? What if someone is hurt and needs help? What if Ax is hiding in the brush somewhere, expecting me to return to help—as he would certainly do for me? How can I just drive away?"

"Because I have a gun pointed at your head, and I am telling you to."

"The hell you—"

"I have things to tell you," Isabel interrupted. "But first we must follow the coordinates, and it would be better if we were not followed there."

"On that we agree," Max said, screeching around another tight corner. "Unfortunately, it looks like we're leaving the town and it's going to turn into more of a drag race."

Isabel shook her head. "No main road. You must follow the coordinates." A moment later, she screamed, "Here, turn here!"

Almost without checking to see where he was going, Max wrenched the wheel and turned right, causing Isabel to fall directly into him. There was a moment when he could have grabbed the gun and perhaps turned the tables ... but he didn't. And he wasn't sure *why* he didn't. Perhaps, in that brief window of opportunity, he didn't have sufficient confidence that he could wrest the gun from her before she put a bullet into his skull. Or perhaps he considered her point about the futility of returning to a good enough reason not to even risk getting a bullet put into his skull. Or perhaps—just perhaps—skull or no skull, he trusted her more than he was willing to admit, even to himself.

Whatever the reason was, he kept his hands on the wheel and his eyes on the road, which was now a dirt track leading away from town and toward the tree line.

Obnoxiously, the pursuing Jeep had somehow managed to remain on their tail and, if anything, was drawing even closer.

"You are terrible driver!" Isabel yelled at Max over the increased travel noise as they bumped along the dirt road. "How are these monkeys still with us?"

"Can't you shoot them?" Max shouted back. "Or are you saving all those bullets for me, in case I refuse to do your bidding?" There was more than a little bitterness in his voice, but he didn't care. In fact, he hoped she understood how furious he still was. If she didn't know now, she certainly would as soon as they were no longer in immediate mortal danger.

"I do not want to shoot toward town," Isabel said. "Innocent people there in the line of fire."

It was a responsible point of view, and one that suggested at least a certain level of firearms training. People did not instinctively look beyond their target when considering a shot, but that skill was certainly covered in any respectable training course. Even if a shooter hit their target, a projectile with that great an energy load has a high possibility of retaining enough of that energy to pass directly through it, perhaps coming to rest in an unintentional target. To say nothing of the bullets that missed and continued on, unimpeded by anything but natural atmospheric resistance.

Still, Max thought, their own hides were on the line right now, with no level of random chance involved. They were the primary target. And he was certain it was no longer a matter of merely slowing them down. The rounds being fired in their direction were coming far too close for the marksmen to be overly concerned about *not* hitting them.

Finally, the dirt road curved to the left, and took them behind a copse of trees, giving them momentary concealment, but not before another bullet hit their Jeep with a sickening, metallic, *kuh-clunk.*

Thank God they haven't hit the damn tires yet, Max thought.

The road curved again, back the other way, leading them through the last open area until they hit thicker tree coverage. Max tried to steal a quick glance in the rearview, but it promptly shattered and dislodged from its mount, dangling back and forth by a wire, clattering annoyingly against the spiderwebbed windshield. Clearly, the pursuing Jeep was closer than ever.

"While I admire your altruism," he shouted over to Isabel, "we're mere seconds away from finding out if that even matters in the afterlife. So how about returning fire?"

Isabel nodded and, while Max kept the Jeep as steady as he could (which was not steady at all), she released a series of shots backward.

"Any luck?"

"No—missed! You are terrible driver!"

"What?! This road is like—"

"You shut up now."

Another shot pattern rang out. A choked scream.

"That sounded better," Max said. "I mean, it sounded horrible, but also effective."

"Got one," Isabel replied simply. She shot once more, and then the slide of the pistol locked back. "Oh poopy!" she screeched. "I am out."

"Poopy?" Max laughed. "Watch your language, lady, I have virgin ears."

"Your ears are no virgin—they have bad words in every port."

Max nodded appreciatively. "Nice malaprop. But once you're done wordsmithing, how about reaching under your seat and grabbing that machine pistol we took off the guard in La Lib? In fact, I probably should have just had you use that from the beginning, but I assumed you were a better shot."

"You shut up now."

Isabel reached under her seat and pulled out the MP9. Max was just about to mansplain how to ready the weapon to fire, when Isabel racked the slide with the aplomb of an Army Ranger.

"Okay, then," he grinned, feeling put in his place in the most gratifying way possible. "I'll shut up now."

His satisfaction waned, however, when Isabel screeched again, this time using a much stronger version of her previous "swear."

"What now?" he asked.

"It is jammed. Piece of garbage."

"Can you clear the jam?"

"That is what I am trying, but cartridge is lodged bad."

"Okay—that B&T is a 9mm. What's your handgun?"

"A .45."

"Damn!"

They were now in full jungle cover, and the sunlight filtering through the trees gave everything an eerie greenish hue. The air was filled with the twin roars of competing V6 engines. Insect and bird sounds supplied a background ambience and provided a bizarre contrast of natural tranquility and extreme, man-made danger.

Max glanced over his shoulder and saw that the pursuing Jeep was very close indeed, and the driver was even now leaning out the side with a pistol. At this much closer range, he wasn't likely to miss. Even evasive maneuvers were limited, as they were now racing down a narrowing path with heavy brush on either side.

Max tensed, waiting for the sudden impact of a bullet, to be immediately followed by darkness.

And then, three things happened in such quick succession as to be almost simultaneous.

First, they broke out of cover into an open field, the sun bursting hot and heavy down upon them. Second, Max twisted the wheel sharply to the left in a last-ditch effort to avoid lead poisoning. And third, the sound of a single shot boomed through the humid air.

18

Again, Max tensed ... but the blow to the head or sudden darkness did not come. He looked at Isabel, half-expecting to see her slumped over in the seat—but she remained upright and looked as confused as he felt.

Then a fourth thing happened. The sound of the roaring engine behind them was interrupted by a loud crash, in dissonant harmony with screeching, tearing metal, all followed by the lone, nonstop blaring of a car horn.

Looking back, Max saw that the Jeep behind them had left the path and ended its impressive road rally career at the base of a massive tree. The vehicle now sat motionless, crumpled and useless, its driver slumped over the wheel and missing a good portion of his head. The part that remained had landed on the horn.

Slamming on the brakes, Max stopped the Jeep and jumped out. He took cover behind the Jeep, expecting Isabel to follow. Instead, she got out of the vehicle and stretched languidly in the sun, as if at a peaceful rest area break during a long road trip.

"Hey!" Max hissed. "In case you hadn't noticed, we're under attack right now. Get behind some cover!"

Isabel smiled lazily. "Calm yourself, Max. Weren't you paying attention to the GPS? We are at our destination."

"Uh, yeah, and so is someone else. Someone with a very powerful rifle. Did you see the condition of that guy's head? Hear the shot? That was no 9mm. We're outclassed, lady."

"Sí, but we are outclassed by a friend. He is on our side."

Max slowly, cautiously, stood up from where he'd been crouched behind the Jeep's back wheel well. "Who? Who is on our side?"

"Me, you young whippersnapper!"

Max's head snapped toward the voice, and he saw an elderly man walking toward them carrying a massive rifle with a suitably massive scope attached. The man sported a bushy white beard and was dressed in ratty jungle fatigues. Max had at first planned to laugh in the face of anyone using the word "whippersnapper," but upon taking him in he felt it was an appropriate choice.

To Max's shock, Isabel ran toward the man, her arms open wide.

"Uncle Philo!"

The two weirdos embraced, and Max shook his head, trying to clear the cobwebs.

"Izzy!" the old man roared.

After a long, warm hug, the two separated and stood side-by-side, watching Max approach. His face must have been a study in bewilderment because both burst out laughing.

"Not funny," Max huffed. "You can't blame me for being slow on the uptake. I've just gone through the entire spectrum of human emotions in about sixty seconds. I'm scared. I'm relieved. I'm exhausted!" He paused. "I'm also a little hungry."

Finally, Isabel took pity on him and stepped forward. She reached out and put a warm hand on his arm. "Max—you remember that I said at Bar Bomba that I need to talk to you about something serious."

He nodded. "Yeah. Just before my entire world changed."

"Sí," Isabel nodded sympathetically. "And we will get to that—but still I need to talk."

Max heaved a deep breath. He was in no mood for a long, explanatory discourse, but he also knew that he was in dire need of information. He felt adrift, with no idea what was going on or in which direction to turn. And perhaps whatever Isabel needed to say would help bring his world back into perspective. Because from his viewpoint, things were spinning wildly out of control.

"Okay," he said. "Shoot. I mean, wait—bad choice of words, considering what we've just been through." He turned to the old man and said, "Oh! I should tell you—that was a hell of a shot. Thanks for that."

Philo dipped his head and grinned, showing a mouth sparsely populated by teeth.

"It was my pleasure! Been a while since I've been able to knock a feller's head off his shoulder with good ol' Belinda."

"Er ... huh?"

"Belinda!" The old man patted his rifle. "Had her back in 'Nam and we've never parted since."

Without thinking, Max nodded at the rifle, as if acknowledging its presence. "Nice to meet you, Belinda."

The old man's grin broadened to a disconcerting level.

As if sensing that things were on the verge of plunging irreversibly into crazytown, Isabel gave a little cough.

"I will speak now," she said, and both men's attention returned to her. "I have not been completely honest with you, Max."

"That much I gathered."

Isabel scowled. "You shut up now."

"Okay."

"At the compound, that night in your room, I led you to believe that I became part of Estrada's group through an initial attraction to him, and that I only later learned of his cruelty and wicked plans."

Max felt his heart lighten just a fraction. "So, you never found him attractive?"

"That is not point! What I mean to say is that romantic interests were never part of my decision to join him at his compound."

"Then ... no?" Max was still interested in pursuing this thread of conversation, but Isabel moved on.

"I was there for a different reason altogether, and merely using the romantic angle as an excuse to get close to him."

"Ah," Max said. "You're an agent."

Isabel nodded.

"For which organization?"

"That is not important now," she said, waving a hand. "The point is that Estrada was not my employer."

"He sure made it sound like he was."

She shrugged. "What can I say? He is bad man. Bad men are often deluded. And they often lie."

"Okay, fine. If Estrada wasn't your employer, what was he?"

"He was my, how do they say? My mark. *Sí*. He was my target."

"You were there to kill him?"

"Eventually," she said. "But first my actual employer wanted me to work into his inner circle. There is a thing my employer wants very badly."

"Does this thing have anything to do with why you pointed a

gun at me and forced me to follow these godawful GPS coordinates?"

"Mostly business. Not personal. And, *sí* it has everything to do with it."

"And Philo?"

"He was only here to do a pre-flight check on the airplane. He works for the same man as do I."

"The … airplane."

Isabel smiled, nodded, and pointed.

Max turned.

And there, a dozen yards away, sat an airplane that looked like it might have been flown by the angel Gabriel when he visited the virgin and shouted, "Mary, you're gonna have some 'splaining to do!"

Max felt his stomach turn. "Um … you're not actually thinking we're going to leave terra firma in that thing … are you?"

"Of course," Isabel said. "Why else would we bring you here? We needed a plane, and now we have one."

"But … if we go up in that, we'll probably die."

"Now, son—" Philo ambled forward, still cradling Belinda. "That there aeromobile is a genyoowine 1918 Sopwith Camel biplane, manufactured and used in the First World War. Poor ol' thing was obsolete by 1920, but not before Billy Barker used it to shoot down over thirty Kraut planes."

"Billy … who?"

"Knew him well!"

Isabel sighed. "Uncle Philo, you are—how do they say—old as dirt. But never you met the Billy Barker."

Philo grinned. "Any woman who knows about Billy Barker is a woman worth knowin' herself."

"Only because you mention him every time I see you."

Max took another look at the plane. It was painted a color somewhere between rust and cow patty. He shook his head. "This thing should be in a museum, not flying through 21st century skies."

Uncle Philo gasped, as if Max had insulted his mother. "Son, flying this machine is a damn honor. And Belinda and I would be very insulted if you chose to turn down such an opportunity."

Max was having a little trouble keeping up the stream of names Uncle Philo was assigning everything, but he remembered Belinda was the rifle, and he remembered what a good shot she'd made to take out the driver of the Jeep.

"Well, by all means, let's keep Belinda happy ... and quiet!" Max said, as he walked to the plane for an even closer look. When he did, he noticed there had been a few modifications made to it.

Two were immediately obvious. First, the biplane had two seats, meaning this model had been built for training purposes. Max had never flown this configuration, or the single-seat version for that matter. He had logged a few hours in a different double-winged craft, but it had been the far more manageable de Havilland Tiger Moth, manufactured with the previous shortcomings worked out. In other words, he knew a little about flying *a* biplane, just not *this* biplane.

And he felt fairly comfortable in assuming next to no one had flown one with the second modification, which was a clear glass cockpit cover that had been facilitated by the Camel's cutout section on the top wing. Although this had been implemented to provide better upwards visibility for the pilot, it now served a dual function, as it also allowed for the opening and closing of the cockpit dome.

The plane was also equipped with twin .303 Vickers machine

guns. These would be synchronized to fire forwards through the propeller disc. Allegedly synchronized. Max had never fired a gun with this configuration and secretly believed the technology was impossible. In any event, he was hoping that the flight wouldn't afford the opportunity to find out. Whether it worked properly or not wouldn't come into play if they avoided any encounters. Max examined the guns closely nonetheless and noticed that they appeared to be in better repair than ... the rest.

It wasn't fair to be overly critical of the Sopwith Camel's design. All of the things about it that concerned Max the most were standard design of every aircraft from the period, with a wooden fuselage, plywood panels around the cockpit, with fabric covering the fuselage, wings and tail. In his mind Max heard a British voice narrating a documentary about the history of flight saying, "Almost at once it was clear that plywood was not very effective as armor ..."

While he assumed the imaginary reader was correct, he once again hoped it wouldn't matter. He peeked at the landing gear and was uncertain how they would hold up upon actually landing. Actually *attempting* a landing. In fact, he was uncertain how they were holding the plane up now.

He also saw that four Cooper bombs had been fitted to the underside of the ancient plane. He turned to Philo.

"Seriously?" Max asked pointing to the bombs, designed and, most likely *built* over a hundred years before.

"Ya never know who yer gonna wanna say 'Howdy!' to."

"Howdy. Yeah," Max replied, already moving on to his next thought, which was that the rust to cow-patty color scheme was actually accumulated patina on the canvas covering the body of the plane. So, while it wasn't rust, there was still a chance the fabric could just disintegrate. "Howdy," he said again.

The fuel tanks had been enlarged. Well, replaced with larger ones would be more accurate. It wasn't like one could climb into the tank and say, "First, we'll take out this wall, then we'll replace the northern exposure with glass for a lovely view of the valley."

The engine, a Bentley BR1, he almost hated to admit, looked sound and well-maintained, which was good, of course. But he was still in a whole bundle of trouble if the healthy engine was abandoned by the remainder of the sickly thing.

Finally, Max stood up straight and walked back to Isabel and Philo. He was shaking his head.

"I mean, I know my history. I know these things were able to do some pretty amazing things back in the day, but that was in 1918 air. With inflation ..."

Isabel scoffed. "Max, don' be estupid. There is no 'air inflation.' You know maybe your history, but your science—how do they say it? Ah, sucks. Your science sucks."

Philo laughed and pointed to a small shack. When they'd first arrived, Max had taken this for the place they stored the lawnmower, but the old man said, "Come in and get some chow before you go. I made chili."

Isabel's sparkling brown eyes lit up still further.

"Oh, Max," she said, "you have lived not at all until you try *Tío* Philo's chili."

"And ya might not live *after* you've tried it!" Philo chortled, as he pulled open the wooden door.

Max, who'd fallen in line behind him, stepped aside to allow Isabel to enter before him. She smiled at his gallantry, and he was happy that she didn't realize he was really going last to make sure the tiny building didn't collapse upon entry. It did not, but he was still uneasy as he followed, wondering if *he* would be the straw ...

When he looked around the dimly lit, windowless interior, he was amazed at how cozy the place looked. It did not appear expansively larger from the inside, like some insane world-connecting wardrobe. It was tiny. There was a twin bed of dubious cleanliness, and a small wooden table with a pair of chairs made from the same red oak as the board. A small wood stove, on which sat a large pot, was the only other fixture. Philo went to a small crate and drew out two bowls. When he removed the lid from the bubbling cauldron, Max immediately forgot about his physical surroundings, however, as the most enticing aroma he'd ever encountered filled his nostrils. *Well,* he thought looking at Isabel as she rubbed her hands gleefully together, *second most.* The memory of *her* scent may eclipse this. But not by much.

Philo set a steaming bowl in front of each of them. Isabel closed her eyes for a second and crossed herself an instant later.

"Amen," Max said, smiling at her. She was already eating however, seemingly immune to his sinner's flirting wrapped in a parson's pulpit robe. She'd downed several spoonfuls by the time Max reached for his own utensil. He was just about to open his mouth and see if it tasted as good as it smelled.

"Hold on there, ya frisky colt," Philo said. Max looked at him and saw that he was being handed a good-sized chunk of freshly baked bread. "Keep this in yer other hand so you can use it to put the fire out."

Max's forehead grew furrowed as he considered this.

"You didn't give *her* any bread."

"Son, she's Spanish. Her mama's milk was spicier than this."

"Whatever," Max said. Philo began to withdraw, so Max quickly added, "... but sure! I mean, it smells amazing."

Isabel laughed. "It smells better than the burning flesh of your mouth will, as the chili begins to cook you from the inside."

Max, now holding the bread in his left hand as he held the spoon aloft but halted half-way to his mouth. "Wha ... what?"

Her eyes crinkled devilishly. "I'm... how do they say? Screwing with you. Eat. Your change of life will come."

"She means it'll change yer life," Philo explained, stage whispering to Max.

"I'm beginning to decipher."

"Good. Probably a required skill in your line of work."

Max laughed and finally brought the spoon home. The flavors of the chili were multi-layered and vying for superiority, while at the same time complementing one another completely. It was the most amazing thing he'd ever tasted. Until a tick later, when all of those flavors seemed to expand outward at explosive speeds, causing him to choke and quickly take a huge bite out of the bread.

He was eventually able to take two, then three spoonfuls before resorting again to the leavened fire extinguisher. He had to admit to himself that he dared act no braver. And also that it *was* an act.

Philo sat on the bed. "So there's some things yer gonna need to know. Have you ever flown a Camel before?"

Max, whose battle with the chili seemed to be making him a bit hysterical, let out a snort. "I tried, but the humps kept blocking my view."

Philo stared at him with disapproval. "Son, that fine aerocraft ain't nothin' to joke about."

"Sorry." He shook his head. "No, I haven't had the pleasure."

Philo turned to Isabel.

"I thought ya said this one could pilot."

"He flew us here."

"Yeah, to an airstrip that blew up. Was it his fault?"

Max swallowed hard at being reminded of the disaster that certainly looked like it was not at all survivable. Isabel's eyes, capable of being so delightful, flashed at the old man in a way that clearly wasn't. He changed the subject.

"No matter. I'm sure it'll be fine. But here's the bulletin, Maxie: the fuel tanks have been enlarged. Now, this is just the opposite of what they originally did with these F1 trainers, where they shrunk 'em to allow for controlling the plane from either seat."

"So don't you lose the trainer controls then?"

"Sure, but what the hell? You don't lose much. Izzy's the girl you want on your side, but she ain't no pilot. Shouldn't really make a difference. Like Billy Barker used to tell me ..."

"*Cristo, Tío* Philo. You were born when? Around '36? No, '37?"

"On the nosey, nineteen and thirty-seven."

"Hokay. Major William *Jorge* Barker die in 1930! Seven *años! Haz las matematicas!*"

Max had just taken a spoonful of chili, but now he snorted in reaction to Isabel's admonishment of the old man. Translating he said, "'Do the math!' Ha! Burn!"

Unfortunately, his sinuses had begun to do just that, and the snort sent the active ingredients to places they were not meant to travel. Not even the bread could help him now. He had to ride it out. Philo and Isabel waited patiently while his death-throes gradually diminished.

"Wow," he said at last, tears streaming down his face.

"Okie-dokey, you can talk again. Means you can prob'ly hear too. So, these bigger tanks make it even more fun than normal. It handles like crap, especially with a greenhorn at the stick. Always has. It's got the dag-blamed engine, the pilot, the Vickers and the fuel all crammed into the front seven feet of the beast. Lots o' rookies crashed on takeoff. It's the worst time for the Camel. Then in level flight it's gonna try to go butt down on ya' so be ready fer it."

Max nodded his head, at the same time noticing that the chili no longer seemed quite so hazardous to his well-being. Perhaps the accidental nose indoctrination had deadened the requisite nerve endings, or perhaps the death chili's power waned when compared to crashing to the ground from a great height, trapped inside a plywood box.

"So, basically you're telling me that you've managed to make a plane that is notorious for handling like crap ... and you made it worse?"

"Pretty much, yep!" the old man said, once more flashing his disturbing demi-smile.

"Sounds perfect!" Max said. His enthusiasm, meant to be sarcastic, was unexpectedly genuine. He couldn't help but notice that his mood was considerably better than it should have been. It occurred to him that he should *not* feel this way but was disinclined to worry about it right now. He passed on a refill of the deep bowl, begging off on account of time, not out of disrespect for the cook.

"And we should really make some miles," he added, turning to Isabel.

"Kilometers," she teasingly corrected.

"You pick on me a lot," Max observed with a grin.

"Wait till you start flying with her behind you. She'll start flicking your ears and giving you noogies."

"Is that why pilots used to use those leather flying helmets?"

"No, that was just to try to keep most of his head intact when he got shot down. Increased the chances for having an open-casket funeral. Mighta helped that Jeep driver, though I kinda doubt it."

"Cheery!" Max said, not nearly as disturbed as he should have been. "And can I just add that I cannot tell you the last time I felt this good. In general. Like my life is suddenly okay, even though I may have just lost my best friend. Ha, ha. Crazy, right?"

"That's the chili talking, Max. Secret ingredient and all that."

A light bulb burned to life in Barnes' head. "You drugged me?" he asked, still grinning.

"All plant-based. Mood uppen-ators. Shouldn't impair yer ability to fly, but it's gonna make all those ear flicks easier to deal with."

They were outside again, walking toward the biplane. Without a backward look, Isabel climbed first on the lower wing and then into the rear compartment. Max followed her example, occupying the forward pilot's seat. As he looked into the space, he saw a leather helmet just as he'd joked about earlier. It even had flaps to cover his ears. Maybe they'd been designed to preserve the faces of the Aces, but if what Philo had said was true, it might provide him with a modicum of protection from the ear flicks, and a bit of a cushion against the noogies.

He looked at the cockpit controls. There weren't many. But there was another obvious upgrade: a modern radio for comms. He began to put the headphones on when he realized it meant removing the protective layer of head itself. Finally, he pulled off the helmet and seated the headphones over his ears, figuring he would still be protected in this regard. But he was defenseless against noogies, and he wasn't going to have an open coffin if the plane went down.

Philo had walked to the propeller and put his hands on it, looking at Max expectantly. He toggled a switch and called out, "Contact!"

With a downward pull, the rotary engine caught and coughed

to life. Max made some adjustments, and soon had it idling smoothly. Philo had stepped out the way and pointed them straight down the runway, then offered a thumbs up, which Max returned. At the same moment, he felt Isabel give him a light noogie. There was no pain, though. It was almost a caress.

"I could not resist," he heard her say in his headgear. He gunned the engine, and they began to roll down the dirt runway. It was not at all smooth, and the two of them were jostled as Max attempted to gain takeoff velocity. At a point far too close to the end of the runway—and the line of trees at the point where the jungle had stopped being cleared—he got the nose of the plane off the ground, yanking back on the stick as hard as he dared without causing it to stall.

In the end, they did clip a tree or two, but the plane seemed to bear out his suspicion that it was in better condition than the naked eye would permit one to believe.

"Okay," Max said through the comms. "Where the heck am I going?"

"You have noticed I am no longer pointing my gun at you," Isabel said through the headset.

"You ran out of ammo," Max retorted.

Isabel murmured a laugh. "But still you are following my instructions."

"I sort of got used to it." Max chuckled in return, and then grew serious. He swallowed back a rising lump in his throat. "And whatever has happened at the airstrip—with Ax—has already happened. And too much time has passed by now. Which I'm still angry with you about, by the way."

"Understood," Isabel said quietly. "And I would be too. But I have my own loyalties."

"Also understood." Max cleared his throat. "But perhaps we

can use this rig to fly to the airstrip once we've done whatever it is you're after."

"It is a deal."

"So … I guess you should tell me where the heck I'm going."

"You need only to follow the flight plan."

"What flight plan?"

"This flight plan."

Something appeared in Max's peripheral vision, and he spared a sideways glance. It was a folded paper that Isabel shook annoyingly.

"You want to unfold that for me?" Max said. "I'm a little busy making sure we don't dive into the ground."

"Such a whiny little baby."

"Look, I'm not Billy Barfer, okay?"

"Barker."

"Whatever. I'm new at this First World War stuff. And, I gotta say, I'm not a fan."

Max was pretty sure he heard Isabel huff into the comms, but the paper disappeared, and he heard the thick paper being unfolded in a very determined manner. Then it appeared again, this time in its expanded state. He took a quick look, then said, "Does this big red circle on the map mean that we're doing what I think we're doing?"

"That all depends on what you think we are doing."

"To look for Ahrum?"

There was a pause, and then Isabel said, "To look for Ahrum."

Another pause, this one considerably longer.

"There's a lot of jungle out there," Max said finally. "If you'll recall, we were hoping that Bembe's memory could get us within reasonable distance, and then we'd pinpoint the location of the ruins with the lidar. We have neither Bembe nor lidar."

"The circle on the map is based on historical records."

"Those are pretty vague. And notoriously inaccurate."

"But it is something."

"Barely."

"We will go."

19

The sun was well past its zenith by the time the two WWI flying aces double-winged their way into the general vicinity of Ahrum—or where historical records, in the form of Spanish journals, claimed it to be. These records, although certainly better than nothing, were frustratingly vague, a fact made all the more daunting by the sheer size of the area in question. More than one intrepid explorer had come away empty handed after searching for the city. A roughly equivalent number had never returned. Period. In addition, the location was some of the deepest jungle that Max had ever seen. He looked down from their lofty vantage point and allowed himself a little shiver. He was, of course, no stranger to surviving in these types of hostile environments, but even he would not relish having to do so now, unequipped and unprepared. He sent a mental message to the whirring engine: *You can do it. Keep chugging, pal.*

It's probably going to conk out, Paranoia chirped. *Right about ... now!*

But this time paranoia was wrong, and the engine continued to live its best life, propelling them through the sky at a speed not impressive by modern standards, but that certainly *felt* fast when moving at such a rate in a flying coffin.

As these morbid thoughts and metaphors were ricocheting around Max's head, he glanced to the other side, toward the east, and saw a dark smudge against the green canopy cover of the jungle below. The smudge was moving and, as he looked closer, revealed itself to be a helicopter very similar to the one that had chased their Jeep to the La Lib airstrip.

"Bad news," he said into his comm mic.

Isabel responded immediately. "What is bad news?"

"Oh, it's when you hear something you don't like and—"

"No, you idiot. What *is* bad news."

"Oh! You're asking—I see." He pointed out the canopy. "It's that thing. Down there."

"The black smudge?"

"Look closer."

"The black smudge that is a helicopter?"

"Yes."

"That is bad news."

"Told you so."

There was a beat of silence, then Isabel said, sounding far too chipper about the whole thing, "Well, that is not so bad. You will shoot it down with machine gun, yes?"

"My—"

And then Max remembered that the Camel was, in fact, armed. Was it ridiculous to go up against a modern chopper, armed with God knew what kind of technology and firepower? Yes, of course it was. Was he going to do it anyway?

Maybe.

"How do we know for sure those are Estrada's men down there? What if it's just a group of tourists?"

"I do not think tourists ride in helicopters armed with rocket launchers," Isabel said.

"How do you know it has—?"

Something appeared over his right shoulder, and he reached over and grabbed it with his left hand. It was a small pair of binoculars.

"Standard issue," Isabel said.

"I'll take your word for it." Max adjusted the glasses and peered down at the chopper. The binoculars were horrible, but they did magnify his target enough to confirm Isabel's words. "Yeah, you're right," he said. "That's definitely carrying Estrada's men."

"You will shoot it down with the machine gun, yes?"

"I'm going to try, yes."

"There is no try, there is only—"

"Oh, hush."

Max was no expert with WWI aerial combat tactics, but he did know that using the sun as a way to blind your enemy was a long-respected tradition. With that in mind, he turned the nose of the Camel so that the sun, which was lower now than even when they first arrived in the vicinity, was directly behind him. He already had a good altitude advantage over the helicopter, and he was hoping that the craft below was not equipped with any sort of military grade radar to go along with its rocket launcher. Otherwise, they had likely already been spotted.

"Hold on to your stomach," he said into the comms. "We won't get a second chance, so I'm going in hard and fast." A beat, then he added. "I really would like to make a joke about that."

"For later," Isabel said. "Right now, is bang bang time."

"And I would really like to make a joke about that as well."

"Go kill!"

"As you wish."

Slowly, steadily, Max turned the airplane's nose downward, and their dive began. He lined up his target and felt a surge of adrenaline sharpen his focus and send his heart into an overtime rhythm.

This must be just a taste of what those WWI pilots felt when they were closing in, he thought.

It was horrifying in many ways. The violence, the death, the carnage—and yet it still awakened the ancient warrior inside of Max's chest. As the dive intensified and the airspeed increased, the engine began to scream and the wind tore past the canopy, creating a shrieking sound that steadily increased in both pitch and volume. There was a section of Max's brain that knew he should be keeping an eye on the instruments, making sure they weren't going too fast, putting too much strain on the old aircraft, would be able to actually pull out of this insane downward charge …

The helicopter came closer and closer. Max wasn't sure what the range on the Camel's machine guns were, and he didn't want to fire until he was sure they were close enough. He knew, at the first volley, the pilot of the chopper would go into evasive maneuvers, and Max had no desire to engage in a dogfight.

"Shoot!" Isabel screamed into the comms. "Shoot them! We're going to crash!"

"Just a little closer!" Max could feel his lips pulled back over his gritted teeth, knew he must look grotesque and insane, but he couldn't help it. The strain, the adrenaline, the pressure from the dive, the shrieking engine (and woman), the flapping canvas.

"Max!"

Now.

Max pressed the trigger on the machine and felt them cough to life. Targeting the helicopter's rotors and engine housing, he bore down, ignoring the jungle canopy that rushed toward them at an impossible speed.

Ack-ack-ack-ack-ack!

The machine gun spit an endless stream of hot metal toward the unsuspecting chopper, and Max watched in macabre fascination as the engine housing was perforated and mangled. Sparks flew from the rotors and metal casings as the rounds made impact, making the craft look for a moment like it was being electrified.

"Pull up, Max!" Isabel shouted. "Pull up!"

It was good advice, but Max stayed on the trigger a bit longer, knowing that if he broke off the assault, and it hadn't been enough to bring the chopper down, then they were themselves dead.

Then the machine stopped firing on its own. Whether it was jammed, overheated, or out of ammo, Max did not know and had no time to investigate. He abandoned the weapon and put all of his strength into pulling the Camel out of the screaming dive. He could feel the aircraft straining, arguing with his decision, and at the outer limits of its endurance. The entire structure ground, and then a strut popped. A wire sang as it snapped and then flapped madly in the rushing wind, and Max sent up a silent prayer that it didn't somehow wrap itself around the props.

"Max! You have killed us!"

"No … I … have … not!"

Max's muscles were about to give out. He hadn't ever considered the sheer physical stress of aerial combat, but now he knew that a WWI flying ace was essentially a world class athlete as well, performing in the most dangerous sport of its day. Still he kept up the pressure, willing the craft to perform beyond anything it was ever designed to do, even as he thanked his lucky stars that he'd never had to arm wrestle the Red Baron.

At last, with excruciating slowness, the plane dragged itself from the dive, just feet above the jungle cover. As they skimmed along the tops of the trees, still traveling at a blistering pace, Max risked a glance over his shoulder, just in time to see the helicopter spinning out of control, headed toward a certain crash landing into the jungle.

The glance was a risk he should not have taken. As he looked back through the front of the canopy, his vision had only a split second to register a shadow on the right side of his peripheral vision.

"Max!"

The shadow—which was in reality a tree whose ambition had outstripped most of its siblings—just caught a strut that had taken most of the strain during the lunatic attack dive on the chopper. It ripped loose, banging against the side of the Camel as it sucked past, caught in the slipstream.

"Uh oh." Max felt the plane begin straining against the controls, trying to roll and yaw in ways that made no sense whatsoever. He spoke into the comms: "Hey, Isabel?"

"Sí?"

"How mad would Uncle Philo be if we didn't return the plane to him?"

"He would be angry."

"And your boss?"

"Angry as well."

"Well ... er ... how angry?"

"Very angry."

"M'kay."

"We are going to crash?"

"We are going to crash."

"And die?"

The conversation was held in an absurdly calm manner, given the nature of their current predicament, but Max would have expected nothing else. He was growing to enjoy their unconventional relationship, even if he wasn't exactly sure of its true nature. Whatever it was, he did know one thing: he was not ready for it to end in a fiery pile of crumpled metal and canvas on the jungle floor.

With this in mind, new determination flooded his chest. He took a quick, assessing look at the right wing, which appeared ready to rip off at any moment, and pointed ahead.

"There—a river. If we can make it that far, I might be able to set us down without fireworks. No chance, otherwise—the tree cover is just too dang thick."

"Then you will make, Max. I have belief you will. That stupid Billy Bumpkin has nothing on you!"

Max knew she was speaking nonsense for the sole purpose of lifting his spirits, but he didn't care. Her words had their intended effect, and he put the new determination he'd felt into action by gripping the controls with rejuvenated strength and fixing a steely gaze on the river ahead.

While they had seemed to be moving at the speed of light moments ago, that same speed now felt like a slug race. The river crept ever nearer, the wing and plane structure rattled and groaned, and every now and then a profanity would rip from between gritted teeth—although Max wasn't sure who was saying the words.

At last, without a minute to spare, they flew over the bank of the river, and Max brought the plane to as slow a speed as he could before it made contact with the water's surface, and then cut the engine.

It was not a pilot's textbook smooth landing. The landing gear broke the water's surface tension, causing the plane to take a sudden, nose-first dive into the water. The brown river water began immediately seeping into the cockpit, coming in from the floorboard and the canopy seams.

"Cheap piece of junk," Max muttered. "Even my watch is waterproof up to 30 meters." He ripped the comms headset off his head and yelled to Isabel, even though he didn't need to, now that the engine wasn't making its infernal racket. "You free of your harness? Once I open this canopy, we'll be underwater in seconds."

She gave him a silent thumbs up, and he turned to fiddling with the canopy latches.

20

Max dragged himself out of the water and lay panting on the riverbank. While he'd tried hard not to allow any of the dank water into his eyes and nose, it had been impossible to completely avoid, and he imagined a billion microscopic organisms even now racing to infect his brain tissue. In fact, his head did feel a little tight, like it was constricting. He lay, spitting into the muck along the river, as Isabel crawled up beside him.

"Bad news," she gasped.

Max gagged as a trickle of death water tried to sneak down his throat. "More?" He looked over and was annoyed to see Isabel grinning at him. Normally, seeing her plump lips set in that happy expression would set his pulse throbbing erratically, but right now he was not in the mood. "Fine, get it over with. What's wrong now?"

"I think the plane is a goner."

Max looked out at the river, just in time to see the Camel's vertical stabilizer disappear under the surface.

"Hump is always last part of Camel to go," Isabel said, laughing.

Max glared at her. "Why the hell are you in such a good mood?"

"We are alive!" Isabel threw her arms wide, which drew Max's attention to the fact that her shirt was sticking extremely tightly to her very appealing curves. "If that is not something to be happy about, Mr. Grump, then you are just... how do they say? A cause that is lost."

"I'm just realistic," Max protested. "We're in the middle of the jungle, many miles from anywhere, with no supplies. And I'm pretty sure I'm dying."

"What?"

"My head is all tight and weird feeling. I think I have a brain-eating amoeba."

If Max was feeling annoyed with his traveling companion before, her sudden outburst of raucous laughter only increased his frustration. It took a full two minutes before she was able to control herself enough to even try to speak.

"I am so happy my impending death is so hilarious," Max pouted.

"Max, you are silly idiot."

"You won't say that when I'm eating through a straw, days from death."

"It takes days for symptoms to begin, you goose. Your head is tight because you put back on that silly leather helmet, which is now wet and probably shrinking."

Max stood up and felt around his head, realizing that, yes, he had decided that wearing the "silly leather helmet" might somehow improve his chances of survival. He yanked it off and was both relieved and chagrined when the uncomfortable sensation immediately disappeared.

"Ah," he said, clearing his throat. "I had, er, completely forgotten about that. A little distracted by saving our lives, you know."

Isabel's smile softened, as she apparently made the decision to allow Max to retain a shred of dignity.

"Of course," she said. "You are quite the hero."

Max bowed slightly and affected a horrific British accent. "It was but nothing, milady."

Isabel kept smiling as she stood up to join him.

Together, they turned on the riverbank and looked into the treeline, into jungle so deep that they could only see a few feet into it, made even darker by the fading light.

"I am hoping," Isabel said, her smile audibly fading, "that you have more heroics, how do they say, up your arm."

"Sleeve," Max muttered. "Up your sleeve."

THE SUN SET TOO QUICKLY for Max and Isabel to make camp, and the two bedraggled wretches passed a horrific night beset with aggressive insects and chills. While it never reached a truly cold temperature, the milder range at night could bring vast discomfort to someone without shelter and sitting in damp clothing.

As soon as the light turned gray with the earliest hints of morning, Max was up and looking for firewood, rubbing his hands together for warmth. There had been a part of him that had thought spending a cold night with Isabel would not be all that bad. They could, for example, share body warmth and perhaps rubbing one another's extremities to encourage the circulation. This, of course, had been a total pipe dream. While they had indeed huddled together throughout the long night, dozing on and off between frantic battles with biting insects, the conditions had been far too miserable for even Max to indulge in thoughts of romance. His fantasies had instead taken the form of a warm bed and hot cup of coffee.

Now, however, the first order of business was to get their clothes good and dry, and—hopefully—discover some manner of sustenance to give them strength during what promised to be the worst hiking experience of his life. Based on how long they'd been flying, he knew it would take them days to find their way back on foot, assuming they ever did. Max had no illusions; he had enough jungle experience to know that none of the time was going to be enjoyable.

"Watch out for snakes!" Isabel called after him.

"Don't worry about it," Max called back. "I'm basically a survival expert."

She did not reply, but Max knew she was rolling her eyes, even though he couldn't see her from where he'd wandered. He could practically hear it.

"I heard that!" he shouted, his eyes trained on the jungle floor, in search of proper firewood.

"What?"

"Your eyeballs. You rolled them, didn't you?"

"Never you mind, Señor Expert. Just find the wood. I want to dry my underwear. It is sticking to places I do not want it to stick."

"Intriguing!" Max shouted.

Isabel did not reply, although he knew another eyeroll had ensued. But that one was on her. She couldn't seriously think she could make a comment like that and have it go un-remarked-upon, could she?

After a few moments of silent searching, Max channeled his inner Bembe and shouted, "You mad, brah?"

Isabel's voice wafted to him through the trees. "You will find the wood."

Yep, she's mad.

Never one to be able to resist poking the bear, Max said, "You know, you could make yourself useful as well. It's going to take two of us to make it out of here alive and in one piece."

There was no response.

She is very *mad.* For some reason, Max found this amusing, and he chuckled to himself. There was something about engaging in time-honored domestic sparring in such ridiculous surroundings that was hilariously incongruous.

Spotting some prime firewood, Max bent down to retrieve it.

"There we go," he muttered, picking up the wood. "That should be enough to—"

He choked back a startled yelp. There, staring at him from where he'd just removed the wood, was a coiled reptile. Considering how much time he'd spent in the wild, Max had seen a surprisingly low number of snakes. While they were certainly plentiful in the jungle, the sneaky reptiles preferred to avoid contact unless one happened to be a delicious small rodent. For the most part they preferred live and let live. But now Max, likely because he'd been distracted with his oddly titillating back and forth with his stunning strand-mate, had essentially removed the snake's cover from directly over top of it.

And it was not pleased.

Max took stock of the creature in just a matter of moments. It was currently coiled, making it impossible to accurately estimate the length—but it was certainly either full-grown or close to it. Its thick body seemed to undulate under his gaze, and it's wide, triangular head lifted slowly. Beady eyes, centered by narrow, vertical pupils, held Max's gaze captive, and a tongue flicked out once, twice, and then three times.

It was a cantil snake, one of the most feared venomous reptiles of the region, its venom able to kill within hours of injection.

As Max watched, the viper lifted the last few inches of its tail and vibrated that section wildly, the impacts against its own body and the surrounding foliage creating a loud, percussive whipping sound.

It was going to strike. Max knew it. He also knew that he had no time to move. He instinctively glanced around for a weapon, but again knew that he'd never be able to grab something and use it, before the snake had its fangs sunk deep in his flesh.

He closed his eyes.

There was a single step behind him, then a voice hissed,

"Max! Don't move!"

The cantil flinched, as if to fulfill its strike.

Thwang!

The viper jerked, caught in mid-strike. It seemed to hang in the air for a moment in suspended animation, then fell forward and down, landing over the top of Max's right boot with a sickening *thump*.

He looked down at the clearly dead reptile and now noticed a length of sharpened stick protruding through the animal's body, just below its head. Then he slowly turned around.

Isabel stood there, still staring at the snake with residual horror on her face.

"How—?" Max began.

Wordlessly, Isabel held up a crude bow.

"What—?"

"I ... " Isabel sounded breathless. She was clearly affected by the close call as well, a reality that Max found comforting to a surprising degree. "I began to work on this right after you left to gather the wood. It is just a green piece of branch, a vine, and a straight, sharpened stick."

"Just? It darn well saved my life."

Isabel shrugged, appearing to regain her composure a bit. "Well, as you say, Señor Expert, it is going to take two of us to make it out of here alive and in one piece."

Max cringed inwardly and then, because he thought she deserved it, cringed outwardly as well. "Yeah ... sorry about that. I was just having a little fun."

Isabel smiled, and Max instantly felt better. "This I know," she said. "But I still like to have some of my own fun at your expensive."

"At my expense," he corrected weakly.

"What?"

"Nothing." Max began walking away. "Come on, let's make a fire and finish drying out your ... delicates."

"How's your snake?" Max asked, looking at Isabel across the fire.

Isabel looked back, gamely chewing on her piece of cooked snake. Max had to admit, it did take some chewing.

"I have had better," Isabel said.

"Yeah." Max held the twisted, greyish meat away from his mouth and gave it a good stare. "It's not great. But it might get us through the day if we ration it."

"I do not think rationing this food will be a problem," Isabel said, grimacing. "But I am more upset that you ruined my bow trying to start this fire."

"Sorry about that. I'll make you a new one. But, hey! Your underwear looks pretty dry."

Isabel looked toward the hanging garments and nodded. She rose and retrieved them from their place near the fire. She squinted at the panties. "Why are these so dirty?"

Max shifted uncomfortably. "Yeah ... sorry, I used those to filter some water from the river before I boiled it. The water was full of sediment."

Isabel huffed. "I would like to be mad at you, but I did enjoy the nice water, especially watching you boil it by placing the hot stones in the hollow log. Very nice trick." She sniffed at the underwear. "Smells like smoke, but they are dry and warm. I will put them on now." She walked a few steps away and behind Max. "No peeking. I know how men are."

"Pfft," Max said, waving a hand dismissively. "You don't know me."

But when he heard the rustling of clothing, the urge to sneak a quick look was almost overwhelming—almost.

Then Isabel was walking back to her place by the fire. "Good work, Señor Expert! I am impressed by your self-control."

"I hate myself for not looking."

"But I would have been so disappointed."

"It would probably have been worth it."

"But also painful." Isabel playfully smacked one fist into the palm of her opposing hand and grinned at him.

"Now I *really* wish I had looked."

Isabel laughed. "You are such a stupid, Max. But I am coming to not hate you ... as much. Come on—let us put out the fire and begin our journey out of here, okay?"

"I wish we could take the rest of our water with us. We are not likely to run across any safe water and may not have the opportunity to boil."

Max grinned. "I thought of that," he said, holding up the leather flying helmet. "I cut off the chin straps and tied them together into one long piece. Now I can gather the sides of the helmet together and secure them with the strap, like a leather pouch. It's not entirely watertight and won't hold much, but it should help."

Isabel smiled broadly and clapped her hands. "You have impressed me, Max. I was certain you would be useless in jungle, but you have redeemed yourself from embarrassing snake incident." Laughing, Isabel kicked the fire out and turned to walk away, leaving Max standing there, leather helmet/flask dangling from his hand.

"Hey!" he shouted after her. "What do you mean, 'embarrassing snake incident'? Anyone can get surprised by a cantil, ya know!"

21

Using the map that Isabel had from the plane—she had shoved it into her pocket after huffily refolding it during the flight—they mapped out a reasonably accurate path back to civilization. However, just because it was reasonably plotted did not mean it would be an easy trek. In fact, they had an absurdly difficult task ahead. Miles of thick jungle, no supplies (other than the map), and very few people knew of their location—perhaps none who would care enough to send a search team.

They'd been pushing through the brush for half the day, both avoiding conversation in deference to simply sweating and then sweating some more, so when Isabel suddenly spoke to him directly, he almost jumped.

"Max," she huffed, "there is something you should know. Something I have not been honest about."

"I've stopped being surprised—or offended—by that," Max said, being mostly honest himself. "What now? Are you actually married to Philo or something?"

Isabel smacked the back of Max's head. "Don't be ridiculous," she said. "Uncle Philo is a nice man, but he is—how do they say—not sexy."

"Don't let Belinda hear you say that."

"And he is not my real uncle."

"Shocking."

"You shut up now and listen. Everything I am doing—the pointing of the gun—all of this is because I have orders from my employer."

Max sighed. "I already know that. And I must say that—"

"And you know who that employer is."

"I do?"

"Sí. Because he is your employer, as well as mine."

Max stopped swatting at low-hanging branches and slowly turned to look at Isabel. "As well as ... you're working for Myron Crabtree?"

"I am. He is the Emcee I mentioned before."

Max felt like slapping himself in the face. Emcee ... M.C. ... how dense could he be? And then another thought struck him. If Crabtree was Isabel's boss ... and Isabel worked for a secret organization ... then Crabtree was up to a lot more than just collecting a few artifacts.

And then Max started to get mad.

"It appears that our dear Mr. Crabtree has been playing his contractors against one another."

"In a way, yes," Isabel said. "And in a way no. Emcee has always been one to... how do they say, hedge bets. He wants very badly to beat Estrada to the crystal, and he probably decided two teams would be better than one."

"But then his teams ended up together."

"That is right. But it also meant that he had no one to inform him of Estrada's movements."

"Then why'd you come with us? You could have stayed there and kept spying for Emcee."

"No," Isabel said. "It was becoming dangerous for me at the compound. I was being increasingly watched and suspicions were rising. Perhaps not with Estrada, but yes with his men. Some of them did not trust me from the beginning. Once I was caught communicating with Emcee, and I had to kill the man who discovered me."

"Raul?"

"Sí. I tried to make his death appear as an accident, but I do not think many were fooled."

"Ahh ... the empty chair."

"*Sí.*"

Max recalled Estrada's sad expression and the glint in his eye. Isabel was most likely correct that her safety had been very much in question.

"I think Estrada would have arrived at the same conclusion as his men, if he hadn't already," he said. "There was certainly something going on inside that head of his, but I didn't have enough information at the time to put things together."

"Estrada is many things," Isabel said, "but not a stupid man."

"Most inconvenient, that," Max said, breaking out his terrible British accent.

Isabel's lip curled up, as if she'd just heard something disgusting.

"Well," Max went on, abandoning the accent, "I appreciate you telling me. And now I'm going to have to kill you."

Isabel burst out laughing. "My dear Max, you know you could never do that."

"Why, because you are too beautiful?"

"Because I would kill you first."

"Ah."

They grinned at each other for a moment that stretched on long enough to become awkward.

"Anyway," Isabel said, "I do not defend my actions, but I hope that you can know my reasons and are not too mad at me."

"Mad?" Max assumed a wise, long-suffering expression. "No, Isabel, I'm not mad. Disappointed, yes, but not mad."

"Good," she said. "As long as you're not mad."

Another long, weird moment ensued, and Max had no earthly idea how to break the silence with any sense of dignity. Isabel appeared no better off and ... was that a hint of a blush? Isabel could be embarrassed? Max felt his head begin to whirl with this new information. His cool, confident, gorgeous Isabel had actual human feelings!

This epiphany, which would likely have led to Max saying all sorts of things he would have regretted, was mercifully interrupted by a small plane flying overhead at low altitude. The craft's passing caused a rush of air through the trees, and both Max and Isabel watched as it disappeared beyond their line of sight.

"Well, that's interesting," Max said.

"Estrada?"

"It certainly could be. Maybe he ran out of helicopters."

"And I noticed something else," Isabel said.

"And that would be?"

"The plane was equipped with pontoons."

"Ah ... so you think they are intending to land on water."

Isabel nodded and pulled the map from her pocket. "There is a small lake not too far from here. Ahrum is reported to have been surrounded by water, but that most of same dried up."

Max walked back to look at the map for himself. "Yes, I've heard that as well. In fact, the lake you're talking about has long been thought to be what remained of the water that surrounded the city. Of course, Ahrum has stayed so well hidden that no one's ever been able to prove it."

They looked at each other for a moment, and then Max nodded in understanding.

"You think that pontoon plane is headed for the lake ... and that it's someone looking for Ahrum."

"It is possible?"

"Very possible. Perhaps even likely, given what's been going on lately. The dominoes feel like they are starting to fall."

"Why would dominoes fall?"

"It's a game that ... never mind. But listen—you know what this means, right?"

"That you do not understand the game of dominoes?"

"No!" Max tapped annoyingly on the map with a forefinger. "Look, the lake where that plane may have been heading is miles closer than trying to get back to some sort of civilization. And we're not even guaranteed of making it out alive anyway, given our current plan. I say we head for that lake and find out who flew that plane and, if they're friendly, we ask for a lift out of here. If they're Estrada's men, we swipe the plane and give ourselves a lift out of here."

Isabel's forehead wrinkled. "The lake is in the opposite direction of our path out of the jungle."

"True."

"And if the plane is no one? Maybe just sightseers who have no intention of ever landing and exploring?"

"Well, then we've made our job a whole lot harder," Max admitted. "But I think it's a risk worth taking."

Isabel was silent for a moment, and Max could see her mind working furiously, calculating the odds.

"If you want to keep on going, I'll do it," Max said softly. "You decide."

Isabel considered for another brief stretch, then nodded abruptly. "You are right." She thought for another moment then added. "For once. Let us head for lake." They both turned to begin, but then Isabel stopped short and glared at Max. "But if you are wrong ... then I will for sure kill you."

Max grinned. "Babe, if I'm wrong, you won't have to kill me. The jungle will probably do that for you."

THEY MADE it most of the way to the lake before nightfall, but they lost the race against the sun and had to stop for the night. Traveling the jungle was treacherous enough when one could see where one was going; Max wasn't about to try it after dark. He wouldn't even try it with a torch, knowing that although it would help him see, it pointed out their position at the same time.

They halted in time to get a good fire going and then to spend a while gathering edible plants and insects for supper. It was a pitiful meal, but they both ate without complaint, hoping the nutrition would keep them going long enough to reach the lake once the sun rose.

After the sad repast, they shared the last drops of water from the leather flying helmet/flask, said goodnight, and then set about trying to fall asleep ... just as the distant snarl of a jaguar wafted through the darkened jungle.

22

Max and Isabel broke camp early and didn't bother trying to find breakfast. They were close to the lake and, if luck smiled upon them, a ticket back to civilization. Eagerly, they set off into the jungle, keeping their eyes and ears attuned to everything around them. Several times, Max halted as he sensed himself losing focus in his haste to reach their destination. Even though they'd had some sustenance, it hadn't been enough and while hunger was not yet a real problem beyond mere discomfort, thirst was. The small portion he'd managed to bring on the journey yesterday had certainly been a lifesaver, but they had struggled mightily through the jungle and needed far more hydration than they had received. Now, in the growing heat of the morning, dehydration was becoming a major issue. The exertion, together with the heat, was sapping their bodies even faster than normal, and Max could practically hear his cells screaming for water. And it was this inner cacophony that was robbing him of focus.

The lake had to be close.

He glanced over at Isabel, who had remained doggedly silent all morning. "How are you doing?" he asked, shocked when his voice came out sounding weird and gravelly.

"Thirsty as have ever been," she bit out, making it clear she did not wish to converse.

Max merely nodded. *The lake is probably dried up,* Paranoia said. *You think you're thirsty now? Wait till tomorrow. And the next day. And the next ... oh, wait, you'll be dead by then if you don't find water.*

"Shut your mouth," Max growled out.

"I just said I was thirsty," Isabel said.

Max flinched, realizing he'd answered his inner demon aloud. "Sorry," he muttered. "Wasn't talking to you."

In pretty much any other circumstance, Isabel would likely have pressed him on the issue, but neither of them had it in them to carry out one of their semi-friendly arguments.

He wasn't *really* in the mood to argue with Paranoia, but it had been obnoxious lately, and the opportunity to tell anyone to shut up, even if it was a shadow-toned mind-creation, felt pretty good. Still, they needed to find some water, and a legendary lake full of it would fit the bill nicely.

Max thought of the plane, however. Isabel was probably right on the money about it being no one of consequence. But the more he pondered it, the more the possibility of it being Estrada or his men or a combination of the two increased.

This part of the jungle, aside from being courted by treasure hunters and scientists alike as the approximate location of Ahrum, did not attract a lot of casual visitors. Mr. and Mrs. Anderson from Alabama weren't soaring in for a weekend of fly fishing.

"Good thing too," Max said aloud, knowing that sort of thing worked a lot better in a river than a stagnant ex-moat, or whatever the water had been.

"Talking to yourself more?" Isabel asked, her voice becoming progressively rough as well.

Max didn't bother to respond.

One of the unwelcome family members that comes along with dehydration is the gradual decline of mental processing, but they weren't there yet. That meant they'd remembered to move cautiously, quietly. Jungles aren't really designed for stealth, but they'd both been in more than enough arboreal situations to know it was possible, and they'd not been shot thus far today, so fingers crossed.

Just then they heard a loud voice through the trees. Max judged it was still rather far off, but he instinctively turned to Isabel with his finger placed over his mouth in a "shush" manner ... only to see her doing the same to him. The more they worked together the more he saw evidence that she was another version of him, only with—to his eye—a much more attractive body. They began to creep in the direction of the sound, altering their course several times.

One of the fun games the jungle likes to play is Where Is That Sound Coming From? In general, sounds that could be heard from far enough away tended to be made by animals for whom consuming a human was no moral dilemma. Also, in general, you wanted to move in the opposite direction of those.

But this had been a man, young sounding, who was swearing in Spanish about having to land a plane in the "tank of a toilet," or something to that effect. In different circumstances, he would have asked Isabel to explain, but right now he wanted to find the source. He wanted to find the water. Or, at least, the toilet tank.

"There," Isabel whispered, pointing.

They were behind a thick stand of brush, and Max squatted even lower, then peeked in the direction his companion was indicating.

There was indeed a lake. There was indeed a plane with pontoon landing gear. And there were indeed men moving around the shore.

"Is Estrada's men," Isabel whispered, her brow furrowing.

"Yep. Looks like three. Kind of unfair." He'd intended to bring a little wise cracking back into the conversation, but Isabel beat him to it.

"*Sí.* For them."

Max smiled in spite of himself and surveyed the situation further. The lake was indeed small, far from how he would have imagined something designed as a defense against an invading force, but he also knew that it was most likely a mere shadow of its former self. Still, there was more than enough surface for an experienced pilot to touch down safely upon it. The men on the shore appeared more than competent and heavily armed, Max noted with annoyance, and were dressed similarly to the fighters that he'd seen in Estrada's compound.

Max continued to survey the situation, attempting to come up with a plan of attack which overcame all the natural advantages the men had: the lake between them, a modern aircraft, and angry-looking automatic weapons.

Isabel pressed her mouth close to his ear. "You go left," she whispered. "It takes you around the lake while keeping out of sight."

Max nodded. "And you?"

She looked at him like he was the dumbest man on the planet. "I will go the other way, of course," she hissed. "You will shut up now and go."

Max grinned. What was it about this woman that made smiling so easy? And then that question was answered as she leaned even closer and, to his great surprise, planted the lightest of kisses upon his cheek.

"In case you are stupid and die," she said.

And then she was gone, moving quietly into the brush.

Max began moving in his assigned direction. Three against two legitimately felt like an advantageous ratio, but only if he moved into position. He paused to arm himself with a length of green, pliable vine—which he had to chew on to break—and then began creeping slowly toward the character he'd already dubbed Bad Guy #3.

He was closing in when he heard a man scream from the other direction. Max growled low in annoyance—killing them *quietly* would have been preferable, because the chilling sound had alerted his own target, whose head snapped in that direction.

Although Max much preferred to explore ancient places, and the wondrous artifacts he found there—some of which were still awaiting a more complete understanding—he'd had to learn several other ... *peripheral* skills along the way. He relied on one of those now, simultaneously pad footing up behind Estrada's mercenary and readying the length of vine.

The man heard the approach just as the make-shift garrote went over his head and, after a brief struggle that resulted in much wheezing and eye-bulging, was eliminated from the list that, had it actually existed, would have been titled "PROBLEMS."

As Max allowed the lifeless ex-problem to drop to the sand, he heard another man's voice coming from Isabel's direction. This voice was screaming as well, but it was screaming threats and instructions.

"*¡Suelta el arma!*" he called. "*¡Quédate donde estás!*"

Despite the situation, Max emitted a brief chuckle. Telling Isabel to throw down her weapon and stay where she was? Not likely.

He bent to retrieve the man's weapon—an MP9 similar to the one he'd taken from the guard at the Jeep in the city—and then straightened, waiting. A moment later, he heard the voice scream again, although this time it lasted a considerably shorter time and sounded all too similar to the first man. Less than twenty seconds later, Isabel emerged from the trees, holding her mom's knife and grinning like a mischievous child.

The two assassins walked toward each other and, upon joining up, gave each other an irreverent high-five.

"You really enjoy sticking that knife into people, don't you?" Max asked her.

Still smiling she replied, "You want to find out? First fist?"

He pondered that one for just a second before saying, "*First-hand.* The expression is firsthand." He squinted at her suspiciously. "You're starting to get things wrong on purpose, aren't you?"

Isabel scowled and brandished the knife.

With an involuntary gulp, Max nodded. "Never mind." He felt it was probably the best response to a woman covered in blood and holding a hunting knife.

"Good," Isabel said, "because it would be a shame to almost die of thirst, only to get gutted on the shores of a lake."

Max nodded again. "You make an excellent point. Should I start making a fire to boil some of this gross water?"

Instead of answering, Isabel walked past him toward the airplane. She took a few steps into the water and pulled open the cabin door. With a happy exclamation, she pulled out a pair of canteens. Shaking them, she found they were both at least nearly full, and tossed one to Max.

As much as he wanted to examine the aircraft, superior in every way to the Sopwith, including being *on* the water as opposed to *under* it, getting that same substance into his body was his top priority. He drank long but slow, then took a break to allow his body to adjust to not dying. While he waited, he looked inside the plane. Then he turned to Isabel, who was still guzzling from the metal container.

"You're going to puke."

"What?"

"The water. It'll make you puke."

"You shut up now," Isabel said, still drinking.

Max shrugged and gestured around the interior of the airplane. "This should work quite nicely when we're ready to leave."

"When we're ready?" Isabel paused in her fluid consumption. "For leaving here I was born ready."

Max grimaced. "Not to make you all stabby or anything, but don't you think it would be a little foolish to be this close to a possible site of Ahrum ... and not check it out?"

Isabel huffed.

"Remember who you work for," Max said, keeping one eye on Isabel's knife hand.

"That damn Emcee," she muttered.

"My sentiments exactly," Max said, "but my point holds. Plus, what explorer could resist that?" He pointed in a direction neither of them had yet examined. Most people would not have noticed, but to the experienced eye, there was a definite trailhead that appeared to lead into the depths of the jungle.

"A path," Max said. "Not super well maintained, but too obvious to be only a game trail or to be easily explained."

"It could be nothing."

"It could. But it could also be something."

The two looked at one another for a long moment. Then, at the exact moment, their faces broke into smiles.

Max felt almost giddy. "This seems to be the lake that was part of the natural boundary of Ahrum. We might be here!"

Isabel cast one mournful glance at the plane, then at the trail, and finally back to Max. She nodded.

"Okay," she said. "I stay a little longer."

Max pumped his fist like a grade schooler.

"But one thing first," Isabel said, her cheeks puffing and her eyes watering.

"And that is?"

"I am going to puke."

Max moved quickly toward the shore, not wishing to witness.

23

"This is definitely no game trail," Max said.

And indeed, the path had not only quickly revealed itself to be human in origin, but it also had a sense of purpose. It was difficult for Max to explain, but once one had traveled as many byways, back alleys, and wilderness trails as he had, one developed a sixth sense about both the utility and futility of pathways. This sixth sense was not always correct, but it was accurate enough to consider.

Wherever this path was leading, however, it was in no hurry to get them there. After several hours, they came upon a small rise in terrain, almost enough to be a hill, and Isabel suddenly gave a shout of glee as she realized it led to another section of the lake. Without warning—Max was learning that no notice was her specialty—she happily slid down the slope into the water, landing with a splash. She was almost immediately up to her neck, as the lake bottom dropped off abruptly. Just as quickly, she was splashing madly to shore, screeching loudly. She made the shore and began stripping off her clothing with reckless abandon. Max was on the verge of pinching himself to make sure he wasn't having some lecherous dream, when he saw the reason for the display. As she bared yet more skin, he saw she was covered in leeches. Max had never seen a woman try to jump up and down while disrobing before, and he wasn't entirely sure how he felt about it. Not to mention that the sexiness of the display was dampened by the nasty, slimy creatures flapping from the otherwise gorgeous body.

At that moment, Isabel caught sight of Max as he just stood mutely on the hill, staring down at her as if frozen in time.

"You! Dirty boy! You get down here and help!"

She pulled viciously at the creatures, but there were some on her back that she'd never be able to reach. Max forced his legs into action and stumbled down the hill to the lakeshore.

As he approached, Isabel scowled. "*Sanguijuelas*," she said once more reverting to Spanish for the truly unbearable surprises.

"I can see that. You want me to—"

"Get them off my back, you dumb! Now!"

Max obliged, flinging the horrid things away into the water. He looked at the little rivulets of blood trickling down from where the leeches had attached.

"We should have looked for a first aid kit in the plane. I'd like to disinfect these. And I don't think splashing this lake water on the wounds is likely to help."

Isabel made a face. "This lake is death water."

Max nodded and reached for his canteen. He unscrewed the metal lid and then poured some of the clean water over the bite marks. "Not much, maybe it'll help."

"But that was your drinking water," Isabel said, her tone unusually gentle.

Max shrugged. "I still have some left. Enough to get back to the plane." He grinned. "Worst case, I boil leech water." He gestured to Isabel's wet clothing. "We'll likely need a fire anyway, because I guess you'll have to dry your underwear again, huh?"

She shot him a look, the fleeting gentleness having disappeared.

"You shut up now."

"Okay."

"I must get dressed."

"Okay."

"Without you looking."

"Okay."

"WITHOUT YOU LOOKING!"

"Sorry." Max jumped at the sheer volume of the yelling, and then dutifully turned away, his face reddening. This woman made him crazy. It was like his IQ dropped fifty points (or more) when she was around.

"I am ready," Isabel said finally.

Max turned around but avoided looking at her.

"Did I miss any?"

He looked up and saw her peeking down the neck of her wet shirt.

"Ah ... I wouldn't know."

Isabel shrugged. "Oh well—if so, we will have it for dinner."

Max gagged. "Give me cantil any day."

Together, they climbed back up the short hill and walked deeper into the jungle.

"I really wish we'd been able to secure a guide," Max said, for no other reason than to make conversation.

Isabel snorted "Who knows their way around the jungle?"

"Well, me and Axel," Max replied without thinking. His heart contracted painfully. He would never see Axel again.

In another moment of uncharacteristic empathy, Isabel let the moment linger, as if sensing Max needed the time to grapple inwardly. Finally, she said, "We do not know what happened. And besides, you want to hire a guide, not be one. In any case, I believe this trail is its own guide."

"Some guide! You'd hope it would bring us ... someplace by now."

She placed a hand lightly on his arm and smiled. "It did. To the leeches."

Again abandoning the moment of levity almost as quickly as it had begun, Isabel pointed into the distance.

"What do you think of that?"

She'd singled out a tree with an obvious notch, likely macheted into it. It was a good catch. As much as Max expected something of the cut's nature to appear of recent creation, it had in fact turned brown, almost the same shade of fawn as the bark itself. The sort of way an *old* slash would look. They walked to it and Max touched it lightly with his finger.

"I can tell you two things right away. This is very old ..." he looked again, "... almost too old. And it feels to me like it was cut by someone moving in that direction." Now he pointed down the path the way they'd come.

"I don't understand."

"Well, I could certainly be wrong—"

"Proven already," Isabel injected.

"—but it feels like it was notched by someone running away from ... wherever we're headed."

"But why?"

"To find his way back, later?" he offered, clearly sounding more questioning than explanatory.

"Perhaps."

They walked for a couple more hours before the exhaustion of all they'd done and been through began to set in. At last, Isabel let out a moan.

"Oh, Max. I waited for you to cry first, but now I confess. I can go no more."

With a sigh that admitted his own tiredness far more than he'd intended, Max said, "No shame. I'm beat too."

He looked ahead in the growing gloom and saw a place where the trail bent off to the left, which it had done several times. Generally, this indicated nothing more than a course adjustment, but this time it seemed as though it had been widened in a way that provided them a place to rest for the night, build a fire even.

"How about there?" he asked, pointing.

"*Sí.* We rest. Fire?"

Max grinned. "*Sí,*" he grinned as he began looking for suitable kindling. Isabel did the same and soon they had enough to start a reasonably sized but comfortable blaze, as well as some pieces to throw on to keep it burning.

Isabel noted that there were places where the grass-like ground cover grew in a way that might make lying upon it, if not comfortable, at least not traumatic. Settling into one she let out a contented sigh.

"Every jungle needs this!"

Max had finished getting the small fire going and looked around. Another such patch was evident, although it was easily fifteen feet from where Isabel lay and was considerably smaller. He headed to it and sat.

The beautiful, and now almost dry, woman looked at him, her eyes catching the light of the flames.

"Max, that is dog bed. You come share this space." She scooted right and patted the ground to indicate there was room here and that he was welcome to it.

His first instinct was to decline, but his memory pulled up the sight of her in the water. Covered in leeches, yes, but still lovely. So, he pushed himself upward—no small task, given his exhaustion, and walked gratefully to the place she'd offered.

MAX JERKED AWAKE, eyes immediately wide as his mind whirled in an attempt to pinpoint the cause of its sudden alarm. The jungle could be a noisy place at night and this night was no exception, with the constant hum and chorus of insects and frogs, and the occasional howl of a primate or other unsavory animal. But despite the din—which Max had come to consider comforting white noise, or off-white at worst, akin to sleeping in a room with a running fan that clunked at little—there had been something else. Something that had been incongruous to the time and location—a sound, perhaps?

And then he heard the sound again.

A movement in the brush ... but not the slow and stealthy rustle of an animal on the hunt, but the sudden shuffle of something pulling back quickly into concealment. The way a human might when afraid of being seen.

The hairs on the back of Max's neck rose and he felt his forehead prickle as cold sweat prepared to bead. He held perfectly still, allowing only his eyes to move as they surveyed the shadows, probing the darker splotches for any evidence of danger.

Another movement ... a shifting in the darkness. Almost too slight to notice, it was as much a sensation as a physical manifestation. But it was definitely there.

As concerned as he was about revealing his own state of vigilance, he knew that rousing Isabel was a top priority. She was currently engaged in heavy, slow breathing, somehow managing to drop into a deep sleep despite the less-than-five-star accommodations.

Slowly, carefully, Max reached over and gently shook her shoulder. No response. He shook again, hard this time.

Isabel's eyes cracked open. To her credit, she came awake in full control of her faculties. As if instinctively aware that something was amiss, there were no gasps of surprise or sudden attempts to sit up.

"What is it?" she whispered.

Max gave a little shake of his head, probably too quick and brief to even be seen in the gloom. "Not sure," he muttered. "Something is out there."

"Animal?"

"No."

"Human, then?"

Max said nothing.

And then they both leapt to their feet as the night air was ripped asunder by the piercing shriek of a voice. The horrifying sound rose in pitch and volume, echoing through the jungle, bouncing off the trees, and seeming to come from every direction at once. It raked saw's teeth of horror over every nerve until at last, reaching its apex of sound, it began tapering off in a gut-wrenching, quavering sound, until that too ended in a deep, guttural choking sob.

And then silence.

Max's entire body felt ice-cold. Droplets of sweat trickled down the length of his frame and his knees felt like putty. His breath came in short, halting gasps, and his heart thudded in a powerful but irregular rhythm.

They waited there for several long minutes, silent and unmoving, but heard and saw nothing further. Slowly, they sank back down together onto the patch of grass and stared at each through the darkness.

"What ... was ... that?" Isabel breathed.

Max swallowed hard. "I ... have no idea. But it was the worst sound I have ever heard in my life."

"It made me feel ... " Isabel broke off, unable to put her feelings into words. And this time it was not due to any sort of language barrier, for Max was at a loss as well. The sound had pierced deep inside his soul. It had been a sound of distilled terror and agony and rage, all wrapped into one horrific reverberation that belonged nowhere but the deepest circle of hell.

Or deeper.

Finally, painfully, they gathered their wits about them and began to breathe normally once more.

"Should we ... ?" Isabel gestured vaguely and weakly off into the jungle.

"No," Max said immediately. "Whatever made that noise is not something I want to tangle with in the dark. I mean, never, but certainly not in the dark. We'd never find it in the dark anyway."

Isabel did not argue, no doubt seeing the wisdom in the words. As unpleasant as it seemed, they had no choice but to remain where they were until morning.

"We'll stoke the fire," Max said. "Whatever is out there likely knows our location anyway, if my earlier experience is at all related to what we just heard, *and* if it's an animal, the flames might help keep it at a distance."

Together, they revived the still-glowing coals of their evening fire and fed it fuel until they had a healthy blaze. Just that small amenity provided some comfort and, while they were still massively disturbed by what they'd heard, they were coming to grips with the fact that they had several hours of darkness still ahead, no matter what.

Isabel moved nearer the fire and looked at Max. "You go to sleep," she said. "I have slept well already, and one of us should remain awake to watch."

Max considered arguing, but knew she was right; she'd definitely been sleeping harder than he'd been, and for a longer time. So, after resisting for just long enough to shore up his pride, he settled back down on his side of the patch of grass.

"Wake me up in an hour or so, and I'll take watch," he said.

Isabel smiled and nodded, and then Max fell into a surprisingly restful slumber.

24

Max jerked himself awake and looked around, feeling confused and out-of-place. The night had faded, replaced by the damp greyness of dawn. He sat up to see Isabel pulling several small bundles from under the coals of the fire.

"You didn't wake me," he accused, the tone of judgment tainted by a massive yawn.

She smiled at him. "You were sleeping," she said, stating the obvious. "And I have decided I like you better when you are sleeping."

"Aww. Because I'm cute when I'm sleeping, right?"

"Because you are *quiet* when sleeping."

"Ah." Max pointed to the bundles of what appeared to be rolled up leaves. "Please tell me you found a pig wandering the jungle and that's some good old American bacon."

Isabel laughed. "I would not say bacon. But it is food and energy."

She passed him a bundle, which was exactly as advertised—

rolled up leaves. He took it as well as a canteen, which she offered him next.

Max paused before unwrapping the leaves. "I'm not going to like this, am I?"

"Crying baby."

He slowly opened the bundle and there, in a neat little row, were several curled up ... things. Whitish in color, with scorch marks along the sides.

"Yeah ... this isn't bacon."

"It is bacon of the jungle," Isabel said. "Grubs. I found them in a rotten log."

"Yummy."

"Eat up."

Max sighed, but this wouldn't be the first time he'd dined on this particular delicacy. And he'd eaten much worse.

Truthfully, it was largely a matter of the mind. The creatures didn't taste horrible, if fully cooked, and they were certainly nutritious—but he could never get over the *pop!* they made when bit into. These, at least, had been cooking long enough that the outer flesh had crisped, and this created a not-unpleasant crunch to complement the nauseating pop.

With their breakfast complete, the two adventurers fully doused the fire and began a systematic search of their surroundings, slowly moving outward in a circular motion, looking for any evidence of the late-night intruder. But there was nothing unusual to be found. There were scattered signs of life throughout the area, but that was to be expected in a biome teeming with same. There was simply nothing to suggest that anything—or anyone—untoward had lain in wait or intended them immediate harm. Still, Max knew that he had not imagined the experience under the dark canopy earlier. Newcomers to the jungle often had the same sort of reaction to spending the night in the wild, seeing and hearing phantoms about their camps, but Max had long gotten over that natural and largely unhelpful tendency. He knew something had been there—and that it had not been a friendly presence.

Even if he had imagined the sound and movement around the camp, however, there was no denying—or forgetting—that scream.

Max shook his head to rid it of the memory, if only temporarily.

"We've wasted enough time here. You ready to get moving?"

Isabel nodded. "Let us do it."

And off they went, following the trail deeper into the jungle, moving toward God knew what. Max was a master second-guesser, and Paranoia was hot on his heels this morning.

You're leading the woman to her death, you idiot. And even if you turned around now, you'd probably die in the jungle from whatever's been following you.

"A little late now," Max said.

"What?"

"Nothing," he said to Isabel, who'd spoken to him from where she brought up the rear. *I have got to stop arguing with my madness out loud. It's making me look ... well, nuts.*

You are *nuts,* Paranoia piped up. *You've been nuts for years. Only before, you only endangered yourself. Now you're harming other people.*

We're not dead, so shut up, Max replied, this time silently. *And we've got a mechanically sound plane to return to. I can fly Isabel out of here any time we want to leave.*

Who said I was talking about Isabel, Paranoia said.

Max gritted his teeth. *Leave Axel out of this.*

You don't seem to be overly distraught over his demise. Especially since you're the one who left him at that airport.

Max felt his insides twist and thought for a moment he was going to vomit. The sickness in his stomach had nothing to do with the grubs for breakfast, — it was because for once, Paranoia might just have a point. He had not properly grieved for Axel. He knew that was true. But he also knew there were reasons for it. Solid reasons, he thought.

First, he was not entirely willing to admit that Axel was dead. He had not seen bodies at the airport, had not heard a casualty report, had heard nothing whatsoever. Of course, if Axel was alive, would he not have tried to contact Max to let him know all was well?

Beyond that, however, Max did not feel prepared to mourn the loss of his friend, even if Axel had indeed met his end at the airfield. He knew that if he went down that road now, he'd never finish his current task. Once he allowed himself to begin grappling with a post-Axel life, he'd be down and out for a very, very long time ... and he just could not do that right now. Too much depended on him staying on his feet. Add to that the fact that Max knew that Axel would not have wanted him to stop. He could almost hear his friend now, saying, "Dude, I just died trying to finish this job. The least you could do is not waste my effort. Geez!"

Despite himself, Max felt a smile tug at the corners of his mouth, and with that smile came a glimmer of hope. He'd felt certain yesterday that he'd never see Axel again ... but maybe that was not the case. Perhaps his friend still walked the earth, (stomped the earth if he'd been drinking), and perhaps there was a completely rational explanation for his silence.

Max was so deep in thought that he'd been ignoring one of the cardinal rules of wilderness trekking: "Always look where you're going." And it was only Isabel's warning scream that stopped him from walking straight into one of the most terrible things that Max had ever seen.

He might have argued that she could have screamed a little sooner. He'd stopped, true enough ... inches from the tattered face of a man. At least he thought it was a man. In any case, whatever it had been, it was clearly dead.

And skinless.

"Thanks, pal," he managed to gasp out, intended for Isabel but projected directly toward ... the thing.

"Who that is?" Isabel asked Max in a voice that would have sounded equally at home coming from a frightened teen.

As foolish a question as he felt it had been, it was exactly what he needed. Max took a single backwards step then turned to face her. He spoke to her in a voice so calm and mechanical that it was blood-curdling.

"I'm sorry, Isabel. I do not know the identity of this individual. I have not actually had sufficient time to determine *anything*, except, quite clearly, that his—or her—skin has been removed. Punitively, I would propose."

She stared at him for several seconds.

"What in the Devil's mudroom—"

"Wait! No one has ever said that," Max interrupted, raising a hand in protest.

"My point is we should not be wasting our energy talking."

"We – bah – wasting? Isabel, you asked me!"

After another moment of glaring at Max, she let out a disgusted and unassailably dismissive sigh, then pushed her way past him.

Max watched her as she began to carefully examine the ...

man, he determined with another cursory glance. But there was no way to deny that most of his attention was drawn by Isabel. Nor could he fault her for what was a very effective, though more than a little passively aggressive, method of avoiding his tirade.

And it was prudent to examine the body. No brainer.

It was indeed a man, with strong vines tied to the areas formerly known as wrists and ankles, and a trunk devoid of the outer layers of its bark.

"You are right," Isabel said. "He has been skinned." She took another look. "And you are also right that it was done as punishment."

"I'd hate to meet the person who would do this merely for fun," Max agreed.

Isabel's mouth twisted in disgust. "You *have* met him."

"Who would ... Estrada?"

"How do you think I can stomach the sight of a human with no skin?"

"Because you've seen it before."

It was not a question, and so Isabel did not answer.

Max stood silently for a moment. Then, "Quite the imagination the man has."

"*Sí.* Although, he did not come up with this all on his own. The indigenous peoples of this area had their own history of brutality. Many different techniques, often used during human sacrifice, were designed for being as painful as possible."

"You think whoever did this is copying ancient sacrificial methods?"

Isabel nodded. "I am not a student of the time, as you are, but it does seem to bear some of the marks."

Now completely over his initial shock at, first, coming face-to-face with the creature and, second, Isabel's unnervingly calm examination of the same, Max made his own detailed analysis. And she was right. He could make out some of the cutting marks, obviously made with a sharp but non-metal blade

Obsidian, perhaps, Max thought.

After taking a few more mental notes—the depth and angle of the slicing, the patterns cut into the body below the skin—Max gratefully stepped away from the carcass. "Yeah," he said, "whoever did this is clearly copying the old methods, right down to the tools they used. Which leaves us the obvious question ... it was probably Estrada or one of his people but if not...who did it?"

"They would have to know much about the history of the originals."

"Okay, let's start there. One: the original originals are dead."

"Or two," Isabel interrupted, "it *is* Estrada's men, and *that* is bad news, because it means there are more than just the three we put in freezer."

"Er ... huh?"

"You know," Isabel said. "Gangster talk."

Max started laughing, partly because of what she'd said and partly because this whole scenario was beginning to make him a tad hysterical.

"You mean 'iced.' The three men that we iced."

Isabel scowled prettily. "Whatever. That is not the point. Right now, it is about the math. There could have been more on the plane?"

With a slight wince he nodded. "Besides a two-person flight crew there was room for three passengers. So, if they transported in a full house, there are two more to deal with."

"And Estrada would definitely send in a full house, with stakes so high."

Max frowned. "Explain."

Isabel's prior scowl had since turned into a grin, which now widened with excitement. "Think, Max—if we are near to, you know ... the place ... then the stakes could not be higher!"

Max literally slapped his own forehead. "So you think this show of force is evidence that ... we really are on the right track?"

Isabel nodded excitedly. "*Sí.* And evidence they want scaring us off."

"I don't scare off easily," Max said almost absently.

"I know," the woman returned with a smile.

A deeper analysis would have revealed that this should not be seen as a major revelation, but it hit Max like a ton of bricks. Certainly, they had come out here with the intention of searching for Ahrum and had even taken this trail with the inkling of the same idea. But the events of the past few days had lent his existence an almost palpable air of surreality, as if he was living on borrowed time—to put it most charitably. There was part of his brain, since Axel's presumed death, that had shut down thinking the possibility that this mission would end in success. He had proceeded as though it could, but his faith had been at an all-time low. Now, with a blinding flash of insight, that faith returned, and he felt as if some manner of emotional scales had dropped from his eyes. Those same eyes widened, and he stared at his traveling companion.

"We might actually be on the doorstep ... of Ahrum."

"Yes! And Estrada is desperate to stop us now."

"But ... but last night. Why were we not just killed? Why—" he motioned to the skinned carcass, "—all of this?"

Isabel shrugged. "I do not have all answers ... but do feel something in the air." She lifted her nose and sniffed, as if she could smell their destination. "You don't sense, Max?"

He took stock of those very senses and, yes, he thought that he could. Of course, it could all be his mind playing tricks, or perhaps this was all part of his internal mechanism for dealing with the loss of his best friend. But either way, Max took hold of this glimmer of hope with both hands and held on tight.

"Yes," he said firmly. "I do." He took a final look at the body. While he had no proof it had been this person's screams they'd heard it seemed unlikely there had been any other. That piece of the puzzle was not what was bothering him. "Still, if this was the work of Estrada's men, why such an authentic Maya style? It's not like we're going to blame anything on them." He shrugged. "Well, we should go. There's not really anything more we can do here."

Isabel hesitated and gestured toward the corpse. "Maybe we should bury him?"

Max shook his head and started walking. "We've already lingered too long." He started walking and she stepped behind him. "Come on, let's find out if our combined senses can find this place at last."

25

They made their way along the trail with increasing care. They had taken to walking each side of the path, ready to move into deeper foliage at a moment's notice.

They kept conversation to a minimum, using their attention to watch, listen ... and think. Of course, thinking was not always a good thing where Max was concerned, especially if there was even the slightest opportunity for self-flagellation. Still, he kept his eyes, and at least a portion of his mind, on survival. Even if conversation had been initiated, Max wouldn't have known what to say. While he certainly possessed the requisite vocabulary, too many self-belittling words were plodding through his mind, jumbled and angry.

Of course, the words, at least in this forum, didn't matter. It was about themes—one in particular.

How could he have been so blindly optimistic as to think that Estrada would send only three men in a five-seat plane?

There are people ... there are KILLERS ... everywhere.

He heard those words. He heard them plainly, although he

could no longer be certain whether they were his or had been whispered by Paranoia. So, when his frustration finally bubbled over and escaped his lips, he said only one word. And that word was directed toward only himself, and it was not complimentary.

"No, you are not ... that!" Isabel hissed, speaking in a ragged stage whisper. "There is no time for beating yourself now. And you will not have to later, because I will do it for you."

Max looked over, making a finger to the lips gesture with a pleading face. He didn't want them to be heard obviously, but he also wasn't in the mood to hear it himself. Of course—and he was quickly learning this lesson—asking Isabel not to do, well, *anything...* was just a waste of time. Like now. She didn't appreciatively quiet down, and she definitely did not slow one bit.

"Everybody's enemy is own worst, but sometimes you put on pause for the ... the greater good."

With a low-lying grin, Max looked at her again. He knew that this was her best pep talk, in her best English, and it was for his benefit. After all, she could have as easily gone with, "You shut up now."

"So, you're saying I'm cute *and* I hold the operation together."

He couldn't mistake the glare in her eye as she replied.

"You shut up now."

THEY INDEPENDENTLY HAD COME to one like conclusion: this was the longest, most spiteful trail they'd ever walked. Hours passed by uncounted as one kept their ears and eyes tuned into the environment, and before either of them had the time or inclination to consider it, the horizon would be bathed in the day's last color by now ... if they could actually see a horizon in any direction.

Max figured they could make some more ground before it got dark, but as he was about to run this by Isabel, they heard a sound behind them.

They both instinctively whipped around but had no time for either flight or defense before they saw a sight *possibly* more hideous than the dangling flayed man.

It was another man, this one living, but as best they could tell he wore only a blood-spattered loin cloth—under the very suit of flesh that had been removed from the victim. The person moved quickly from one side of the path to the other, emerging from and disappearing into the thick forest. He shouted in a mumbled burst. Max thought he detected Maya, although he only knew the second word which meant, "filthy."

And then the man was gone.

"He thinks you are 'filthy pig,'" Isabel said.

"How do you know he was talking to me?"

She turned to him. With a game show-like sweep of her hand she indicated her own body, one eyebrow raised as if to say, "Seriously?"

Max nodded, conceding her point.

They pushed on, but not as far as Max had hoped. The path now was taking frequent and sharp turns, making it not only more challenging to traverse, but also more difficult to watch for threats—a difficulty that grew more daunting as the sky darkened.

One of the oddly angled turns struck them both as a good place to break for the night. Whether by design or through hubris it appeared that this turn, at least, was not laid down with vision as its major consideration.

Max quickly gathered wood and started yet another small fire, and they sat down to enjoy its limited comfort when they heard the distant trading of gunfire.

"Kill the fire!" Max followed his own instruction, dousing the still infant flames within moments.

Isabel groaned aloud. "This will be a longer night than usual."

"It will," Max agreed, grimacing. "But we can't risk someone seeing the light." He considered for a moment. "That also means a third party, because Estrada's men wouldn't fire on themselves."

Perhaps the skin-wearer was not on Estrada's side after all, he thought. *Isabel hadn't recognized him, after all. Perhaps there is another player in this game.*

But the night was now heavy, and so they rested as best they could. The jungle did not become an icebox at night, but neither did it hold its swelter, and both Max and Isabel were spoiled by the climate.

They also conversed quietly, and, despite the criticality of their current status quo, it devolved into cautious small talk.

Then, though neither would boast that they'd done more than lightly doze, they fell silent.

The jungle, in all honesty, was saying more than enough for both of them.

THE NEXT MORNING, exhausted and irritable, they pressed on. They'd traveled little more than a quarter mile when they reached the crest of a small hill, the top of which was largely devoid of cover. Max stood at the crest, his chest heaving from the exertion. The incline had not been steep, but his stamina was heavily depleted. He was not so tired, however, that he did not notice something wonderful ahead. Something that could just be seen beneath the distant tree canopy

"Isabel! I—"

Schwap!

Something snapped the air past his ear, and he instinctively dropped to the ground, pulling Isabel with him. As they hit the dirt, the sound of a gunshot cracked the morning air.

"Was that—?" Isabel tried to raise her head to look, but Max pressed her face into the dirt.

"Yep," Max said. "Someone tried to snipe me. My own fault, I suppose, for giving them such a wonderful silhouette target."

"Oh, yes." Isabel rolled her eyes. "How dare you stand right in front of gun sights."

"I know, right? Remind me to apologize while I'm beating the crap out of whoever that was. First, though, we need to crawl off this hilltop as if our lives depend on it."

Thwaaaap!

Dirt kicked up between them and another shot rang out.

"Which they actually do."

Together, they performed their best serpent impressions and were soon far enough down the far side of the hill to risk standing up and sprinting the rest of the way.

At the bottom, they took a moment to rest in the relative safety of the heavier jungle cover. Gasping, Isabel looked over at Max, who was bent almost double, bracing his hands on his knees.

"You ... were about to ... tell me something?" she said. "When you were ... on the hill?"

Max nodded and held up a finger to ask her to wait a minute. Slowly, he gathered himself and stood upright.

"Yeah," he said, his breathing slowly regulating. "It was ... it was Ahrum."

"What?"

Max nodded again. "Couldn't make out ... much. But it was definitely stone ruins. Underneath the jungle canopy. That's why you can't see it from the air. That hill is probably the only vantage point where you can see it unless you just stumbled right into it."

Despite her obvious exhaustion, Isabel gave a little leap into the air. She rushed forward and grabbed Max, tumbling them both to the ground. Straddling his waist, she playfully pummeled his chest.

Max started to yell for her to get off, that he couldn't breathe, but then decided he enjoyed the current situation enough to risk asphyxiation.

"We did it!" Isabel whooped. "We did it, Max!"

Finally, she rolled off him, and Max sat up, back to gasping for air. But he grinned happily and nodded.

"Stinking right, we did." He got to his feet, digging deep for any remaining reserves of strength. "Now ... let's finish this."

26

They came upon it suddenly. The looming remains of the Mesoamerican pyramid seemed to materialize in the greenish gloom of the thick jungle cover. They both stopped in their tracks and just stood for a few moments, looking up at the crumbling structure as if they could not believe their eyes. And, considering all they'd been through, it did seem almost like a dream.

From the limited historical records, Max knew that in its heyday, Ahrum had been surrounded by open fields used for agriculture, but those had long since been obliterated by the creeping jungle. Now the trees and growth reached to the very edges of the pyramid, and vines climbed up the sides, as if nature's tentacles were trying to pull the entire thing to the ground.

Even now, however, Max could clearly make out steps leading upward toward an opening near the top of the structure, and his adventurer's heart tugged hard toward them. He nudged Isabel and pointed.

"Look—steps."

"We go up."

"We go up."

They had taken but a few steps forward when shots rang from the jungle and bullets spattered the heavy growth around them.

"We go faster?" Isabel said.

Max nodded enthusiastically. "We go faster."

They sprinted toward the pyramid, bending low to provide as small of a target as possible. Max would normally have zigged and zagged, but the creeping vines littered the jungle floor and all he needed was to trip and fall at this moment—that would surely be a death sentence.

And then they were taking the crumbling stairs two and three at a time. Twice, the stone lips of the steps gave way and they stumbled, but quickly regained their balance and continued onward, upward, with bullets smacking around them, sending up shards of rock to sting their faces and arms.

"Go!" Max surged ahead, Isabel's hand in his own, as they reached the final step and charged onto a shallow platform at the top. Ahead was the door, partially draped with more vines and foliage, and they pushed headlong through it.

Almost immediately, the gloom of the thick jungle turned to blackness, and they stopped short, feeling their way in the dark to find the marginally safer places on the sides of the walls, waiting for their eyes to adjust.

The targets now under cover, the shooting from outside stopped, and the duo took their temporary blindness as an opportunity to heave some deep breaths.

"That was ... fun," Max said at last. His eyes were adjusting, and he unslung the MP9, readying himself for a possible frontal assault on their position.

Isabel, just visible in the dim list, grinned at him and waggled the pistol she'd taken from the guard at the lake. "I think the fun is only now beginning."

"You think a gun will be as satisfying as a knife kill?"

She shrugged. "We will see."

Max grinned back. It wasn't her bloodthirstiness that got him going—not really. It was the sheer badness of it, the attitude, the swagger. At the same time, he knew there was a soft core somewhere under that tough exterior, and he very much hoped to have the opportunity to begin peeling away those layers.

Blinking hard, both to reset his wandering mind and to test his vision, Max discovered that he could now see well enough to make out the beginnings of a passage. In fact, he could almost see that better than his closer surroundings, which seemed odd until he realized that a low-level, greenish glow tinged the walls of the passage. Initially, he assumed there was an opening to the jungle outside, which was letting in that foliage-filtered sunlight. But after staring for several seconds, he noticed the light source was variable, growing stronger and weaker at regular intervals.

"You seeing that?" he asked.

Isabel hummed softly. "I am seeing that. Not natural light."

"Wouldn't seem so. I say we proceed with caution and weapons at the ready. There are definitely bad guys outside, but there may be some in here as well."

As one, they moved forward, taking short steps, and testing each move with the toes of their feet before putting full weight on the floor. The risk of boobytraps in archaeological sites was overdone in books and movies, but they did exist, and the way their adventure had gone thus far, Max was not willing to take any chances.

In fact, Max thought, it had kinda sucked right from the beginning... the night Bembe had told him the story of the failed ritual, coinciding with a full invasion of Spaniards. Not fun.

But it was not only the contents of the tale, which if true were frankly life-changing on their own. Rather it was the way the skater had told the tale, not like he was repeating an age-old saga from the oral history of the Maya but rather as if it was being brought up into his mind, that he was sharing his *memories* of it.

Ridiculous, he knew, but man.

And in the days since their first return from the jungle to La Libertad every interaction he'd had with the young man had really done nothing to clear up the story in his own mind. Bembe never indicated that he'd been anywhere near the city of Ahrum, yet his details were too good to be casually included in an old wives' tale. Unless he was just a master storyteller.

Or had been there.

Moving deeper into the passageway, the greenish hue began steadily growing brighter. They crept along, keeping their hands on the walls to steady themselves.

Abruptly, the passage ended, and they found themselves at the opening to a surprisingly spacious room.

"Well, that explains the light," Max said, pointing.

27

In the center of the room, nestled atop a stone pedestal, was a large, green crystal that glowed brightly. The room itself was bathed in the greenish light emanating, making Max feel as if he was looking through a pair of night vision goggles, something he'd done more than once in his life. He lifted his hand to his head and half-expected to feel the equipment in question but instead his palm rested on his forehead. Isabel looked at him.

"You have a headache?"

Max shook his head mutely. He didn't feel like speaking because his mind was spinning. First, there was the room—a *temple* room, from all appearances. Aside from the randomly distributed objects which resolved themselves, eventually, into treasures, the room looked perfect for the conducting of Mayan rituals, especially one with the gravity and ramifications of that which Bembe had described – that of the Crystal of Ahrum.

And therein lay the source of his unease. Bembe, again, never said he'd been to the city, yet he described this part so exactly that it was if he'd been studying a hi-res photograph as he told the story.

Isabel had stopped her forward progress upon seeing the chamber, and had Max not done the same, at precisely the same moment, he'd have left her behind. Instead, he turned to her and beckoned for her to stand beside him.

"This is the Temple of Ahrum," he said to her, speaking quietly, reverentially.

"No shirts, Sherlock," she replied.

"That's wrong."

Instead of actually telling him to shut up, she held aloft a single authoritative forefinger. It had the same effect. But after only a second, he spoke again.

"The thing that's feeling weird to me is how perfectly this matched the scene Bembe described that first night when I found him getting the snot kicked out of him. And look, do you see?"

Isabel turned in the direction that he was pointing.

"The treasure?" she asked. "Yes, is pretty..."

"It *is* pretty," Max replied, nodding. "But it's not all native. At least not to my eye. Some ... several of these look ... European?"

"*Sí,* and some will fetch good price. But are we not looking for that?" Now she pointed to the left of where they'd been examining the baubles—if one can call a gold conquistador's helmet a "bauble." She pointed back to the pedestal and the glowing that issued from it.

Max looked back now too. She was right. The gold was not walking out under its own power. But that glow! It *was* the goal and any time spent talking about, well *anything*, was wasted time.

Continuing to carefully test each footstep, he made his way toward the altar and the shining podium. Isabel followed closely behind, alternately glad for the human shield in front of her and wishing she would brush past Max, getting to the source of the light first, before him. *Instead* of him. Old habits, she knew.

But as she looked at the outline of his form in the green radiance, her heart, which was usually... no, *always* very prone to becoming mission-centered during times such as this, she realized that one-upping Max did not hold the grinning excitement this sort of thing usually... no, *always* did. Sharing it, co-discovery ... that felt somehow more appropriate. Both more respectful and more respected.

Max reached the first of the steps that led up to the altar, to the podium, to the crystal. He paused, placing a fraction of his weight on the base and waiting for something bad to happen. When his head was not pierced by a formerly hidden arrow nor severed by a swinging razor-sharp pendulum, he took a full step before again pausing. Still nothing happened, and he made his way more than a little nervously forward.

Before he'd fully reached the podium, Max got an unhappy feeling that something was awry with the crystal itself. He turned to Isabel, but she'd momentarily halted on the last step and was scanning the area closest to them. As he waited, she turned to him and stepped forward.

They arrived at the podium together, side-by-side.

"Is that it?" Isabel said. "It is ... smaller than I expected."

Max had to admit to similar feelings. He felt around the artifact, turning it in his hands. "It's weird ... smooth on some sides, but jagged and rough on others."

"It is broken?"

"Possible. No way for us to know."

Max again did a quick mental inventory. Here was the crystal, such as it was. The passage they'd taken from the outside was not that intimidating. They had access, Max hoped, to Estrada's plane back on the water. It felt like time to grab up the crystal and high tail.

And as he did, the green light—the shimmer that had been their only connection to sight in this place—vanished.

"Well, *that's* not good," Max said, still speaking quietly. "But not to worry. I have my trusty flashlight ... or torch? Which is the one you guys prefer?"

"I prefer you turn it on," she replied, worrying less, perhaps, about her own volume level.

Max reached to his belt and found the light to pull it free. Unfortunately, he also found a rather substantial gouge that had been shot out of it, forcing him to momentarily deal with how close they'd come to being victims themselves. He pulled it free and tested it, but didn't linger long on the experiment.

"No good. Estrada's goons shot it."

Isabel could not see him in the dark, but she gave the direction from which his voice came an angry scowl.

"Brave Max Barnes fears no ancient Mayan traps but doesn't bother to look at anything but gold and so *he* didn't see a box with candles. Probably."

"It wasn't just the gold that held my attention..."

"Oh, *sí?* What else, great explorer?"

Max stood in the dark and pictured the curves of her body, the tight arcs of her rugged pants.

"Ahh, tell you later?"

With her best sigh yet, she stopped talking and moved carefully back in the direction she'd just come, and down the steps, backwards on all fours—a truth that made her glad Max couldn't see either. However, as soon as she reached the floor level, she stopped and remembered the mental picture she'd taken when cresting the altar. There had been a wooden crate less than five steps away containing something that had looked far too much like candles, albeit old, probably beeswax ones, to be anything else.

When she found them, she grabbed several.

"Do you have lighter? Or did crack sniper kill that too?"

"Matches," Max called back.

"Sexy," Isabel whispered as she made her way back to him. This time she was very conscious of her volume.

She gave him one of the candles, holding another herself. Three others were pushed into her various pockets. A moment later Max struck a match, which briefly seemed to shine brighter than the sun—a very small sun—before igniting the two candles.

Now it was Barnes' multiple adventurer's pockets which came into play as he quickly and securely pressed the crystal sections in three safe locations. With a candlestick apiece, they turned to walk back down and get out the way they came.

Max wondered at the candles, clearly very ancient, and the ease with which they lit and burned. He was a little disappointed with the brightness, seeing that they did not cast much in the way of luminosity. But they quickly found their way to the passage leading out.

The way to freedom.

Ha, you fool, Paranoia said. *The way to freedom is rarely clear and freedom is rarely free.*

And this time, Paranoia had hit the pessimistic nail on the head. For as soon as they began to walk into the passageway, they found themselves surrounded by what amounted to five men. Some of them were familiar from Estrada's headquarters. They were all armed, and each had his weapon trained directly on Max and Isabel.

28

More than once in what now seemed to him a miserable failure of a short life, Max had begged off the tough topics by saying he was not a rocket scientist, and therefore had no answers. This, however, seemed to be a case where the slide-rule brain of said scientist was not required. He knew that they were both in it up to their calves.

Though the two were likewise carrying weapons, there was no consideration of trying to use them now. They'd be dead before they'd wrapped a hand ... before they got a *finger* around them.

There were five of them altogether, meaning when you subtracted the gentlemen they'd removed from the equation, there had either been more planes than the one they'd left floating on the lake, or the puddle-hopper had been here more than once. Max recognized the face of the man closest to him. It wasn't the sort you forgot. It was Colón.

Head clean-shaven, wearing a thin black shirt matched with black everything else, the man had a scar across his face that was, at least in Max's case, the first thing one noticed about him.

Whoever had done this to him was probably not on his Holiday Card list. He was probably not on *anyone's* list for anything anymore ... except perhaps the person who pays attention to the names of the corpses and where they end up.

Max cursed quietly and just a little. He was telling himself off for getting that distracted in what was surely a moment that called for all his attention.

Or did it?

Axel was dead, Rosita with him. And how could Bembe not also have been lost in the airstrip firestorm? His boss, he was learning, was something of a many-layered jerk, and his father... well he just had fewer layers. Isabel was beautiful, and he had a growing suspicion—or perhaps the hope—that she was sweet as well, at least on him. But she was standing to his right, grabbing the sleeve of his shirt, most likely thinking her own final thoughts.

So, when it came to the cards he was holding, as some people insisted on saying, they added up to "garbage." Why worry about dying now, as opposed to many years from now surrounded by a bevy of women who were probably nurses and more than likely not really there even though they all looked like Pamela Anderson?

"*Hola,* Colón. Are you in charge here, or were you just the first guy to get this far without falling down?" Isabel asked the scarred man.

The tone of her voice was moderately sassy and defiant, but there was no denying it held the frail bones of her own mortality.

In that moment, Max made peace with his own death. He'd gotten close, although no one would ever know. He might have righted the ship. But in the timeless words of the Beatles, "Let it Be," he thought, *I am done.*

"GET BACK!" came a voice from the dark passage, far beyond the reach of any lights.

Max thought two things. One was there might be too many Beatles fans in the temple. The second occurred an instant later, when the five heads of the men his wandering mind had dubbed "The Five Stooges" all turned as one to the direction of the new voice. Isabel saw the updated dynamic as well. While the thugs were turning in the wrong direction, looking for the wrong hazard, they both reached for and acquired their own weapons.

And just about the time the quickest of their enemies began to turn back, they fired off enough rounds to eliminate the Stooges. Before any one of them really had time to do much of anything, they were all dead. Even Colón, who had impressed Max as Estrada's right hand.

He was nobody's hand now.

What a fitting ode to life itself! Max thought, beating Paranoia to the punch for once.

Now the pair, suddenly feeling something perhaps distantly related to hope, nonetheless held their firearms on the ready. There was no way to be certain that whoever had sent that ridiculously prescient warning was here on a mission of mercy.

"Show yourself!" Max commanded, his voice imitating the strong strands of heavy metals he didn't think he'd possessed for a long time now.

From the distant shadows they heard a laugh.

"Why do you always get so excited when I show up, brah?"

As Max and Isabel had dropped their candles in favor of firing guns, it was the beam of the strike team's fallen and abandoned flashlight—*or was it torch?* Max realized he'd never learned—that revealed the hidden terror.

It was Bembe.

"Bembe?" they both called at the same instant, running toward him. He grinned broadly as they approached. The pair reached him and there was a quick and awkward group hug.

But as Max stepped back, he noticed that Bembe's unassuming skaters' outfit was gone, left behind in favor of ... something quite different.

Barnes recognized it at once. He'd seen enough drawings. He'd gained access to enough codices. Bembe was dressed like a neophyte shaman as one would have looked when Ahrum was an active, bustling center of humanity.

"You look a little cattywhumpused, Maxxy. I'm guessing you've got questions."

Max's mind whirled. He was having immense trouble distilling this brain chaos down into the form of an actual query. At last, he managed, "How did you get here?"

Bembe looked over the five motionless former annoyances splayed out across the floor, making sure none of them were just goofing about the whole "being dead" thing. He spoke as he did.

"Walked."

"From ... where?"

"From not here, Maxwell. Got any *good* questions?"

"How did you get away from the airstrip?"

"Jeep."

"You drove out of horror show?" Isabel asked, her voice seeming to return for the first time since she'd spoken to Colón, whom she'd always been convinced took more than his share of dessert at the compound in addition to his general grumpiness.

Bembe turned and gave her his grin. "Not me personally. I was just cargo."

"Who drove?" Max asked, suddenly allowing far more desperation to manifest itself in his voice. He put a hand on each of

Bembe's arms and looked directly into his eyes. "Who drove the Jeep, Bembe?"

As if the dark hallway's only purpose was to be the setting for dramatic introductions, another voice appeared from the ebony ether.

"Did you keep your promise and not sacrifice them?"

Wait, Max thought. The voice was deep, with the influence of several languages: Mayan, Spanish, English. And, as always, it was at least slightly irreverently toned.

It was Axel.

A moment later he appeared, and an instant after that came Rosita.

Max was not currently paying much attention to how he felt, but later he would not be able to describe it effectively. It was as if his entire body froze solid, then became flush with heat, before re-freezing in a continuous cycle of extremes. His mind, a confused whirl before, now just stopped working altogether.

"Ax?" His voice sounded like it had gone through a woodchipper. "How ... why ... I ..."

"No time for emotional reunions," Bembe said, placing a hand on the backs of Max and Isabel. "Let's move back into the temple, dudes." After only a few steps, however, a series of patently unpleasant noises—a shaking rumble—began coming from that direction. "Um... let's move back the opposite way, dudes."

"What's all that?" Axel asked as the group reunited.

"Nothing good," said Bembe. He turned to Max as they picked up speed. "You didn't happen to come across that crystal, did you? You know – that whacky one I told you about that first night? During the job interview? And if so, did you, oh, I don't know, maybe take it?"

"Well ... yeah. A little," Max confessed.

"Oops. Yeah, we're not running fast enough. Not nearly." As he spoke the words, he began sprinting. "Don't look back. Just run as fast as you can this way," he called over his shoulder.

Everyone took him at his word without debate and started their own version of the Passageway Dash. But even as they ran, the floor and walls began to tremble. Silt left by the centuries began trickling down from overhead, as ancient blocks of stone shifted against one another.

Max looked ahead and could see the outside light—they were close. But the low frequency rumble was increasing by the moment, reaching a crescendo that could not possibly result in anything positive.

Then there was a sudden *whump!* and the light from the opening went dark. All the adventurers came to a screeching halt, a couple of them literally. A flashlight beam played across their destination, revealing an enormous stone slab that had fallen across the opening.

Axel, who was the one with the flashlight, yelled an impressive string of obscenities, but Max was prevented from praising him by a piercing scream from behind. They all whirled. The flashlight beam, following their progress, played shakily over Rosita, who was standing stock still. It was difficult to make out exactly what was happening, even with the illumination from the flashlight, as the air was thick with floating dust particles.

The rumbling had ceased now, replaced by an eerie silence.

"Rosita?" Axel asked, taking a step forward.

"Axel, don't—" she squeaked.

And then Max saw there was someone behind Rosita, someone holding the shiny object—a knife, he now saw. And then, the someone spoke in a voice old and creaking.

"It is as the prophecies have, er ... prophesied," it said.

Despite the seriousness of the situation, Max felt a bubble of laughter deep inside at this person's awkward attempt at dramatic intonation.

The character continued speaking, admirably rallying from this less-than-stellar opening line.

"You have been led here by tradition and the inevitable march of ... "

"Tradition? Again?" Max offered.

"Exactly. Now, all of you drop your weapons onto the floor."

They all did so, and then the character shifted into better view. Max saw it was an old man, so old that it was impossible to even hazard a guess as to specific age. The man was dressed similarly to Bembe, although in grander fashion.

A shaman of higher rank, Max thought.

"Well, you have the advantage, then," he said. "We didn't know we were fulfilling anything, except maybe a sketchy contract put out by an even sketchier client."

"The prophecies move in mysterious ways," the old man said. "Sometimes it is difficult to divine their exact methods."

"Because they're mysterious," Max said.

"Exactly," the man said, apparently not realizing he was being mocked.

"Okay ... so what's up with the knife?"

"Ah! The knife. It too is part of the prophecy and tradition, as you will all soon see."

"I don't follow," Max said.

"But you will," the old man replied. "Well, actually, I will follow you. And you will walk that way." He pointed with the knife, briefly removing it from Rosita's neck. In that moment, Max wished it was Isabel being held, for he had no doubt that she would have taken the opportunity to escape the old man's grip—

but Rosita still appeared rendered helpless by fear. Max could scarcely blame her. This was a far cry from dressmaking, which he had to assume was a good deal less dangerous as a rule, discounting errant needle pricks.

And then the knife was back at her throat, and the opportunity was lost.

Max and the others looked to where the old man had gestured. As the stone slab had fallen, it had apparently counter-weighted another slab, which had risen into the ceiling, revealing a flight of stairs heading upward.

"There," the old man creaked. "Up the stairs, toward your destinies."

"To fulfill the prophecies?" Max asked.

"Exactly."

"Just checking."

As one, the group moved toward the stairs. Axel's face was a study in rage, and Max knew that the only thing keeping him from charging in a fury of death punches was the knife blade that even now pressed hard into Rosita's neck, the steady pressure a matter of real concern. It wouldn't take much ...

Up they went, slowly, their movements echoing about the stairway. After a few minutes, Max saw another glow of outside light, but this time it seemed less inviting than before. As if in explanation, he heard a rumble in the distance. At first, he thought it was more ancient architecture showing off and his heart quickened, but then he recognized it for what it was: thunder.

Mere minutes later, the group exited onto a flat surface atop the pyramid. Max looked around and was shocked to see how well-kempt and maintained the area was, especially considering the rubbled appearance of the rest of the structure. This part could almost have been built yesterday. The stone carvings were in good repair and sharp relief, not worn by hundreds of years of weather. The floor was clear of debris and vines, and the altar stood even and imposing.

Wait ... altar?

Nothing good ever happens with ancient altars, Paranoia hissed, and this time Max whole-heartedly agreed.

"You are absolutely correct," he said.

"Of course, I am," the old man replied. "The prophecies never lie."

"Actually, no, I was talking to ... never mind."

Max looked at their captor. The man was old, yes, but did not look frail. He also looked crazy, but not completely stupid—a dangerous combination. The old man's head was completely shaved, and a misshapen patch of skin on his forehead told of some past wound—quite a bad one, from the look of the scar.

Max sighed. "Okay, look—why don't you just tell us—"

"In good time," the old man interrupted. "First, we must secure your friends, there." He nodded his head to Axel and Isabel. "You will find good rope atop the altar. Use it to bind them."

"Is that in the prophecy?" Max asked. "Because I can't do it unless it's in the—"

"Tie them up, or I shall slice this woman's throat!"

"As you wish." Max hurried over, retrieved the rope, and then walked over to his friends. "Don't worry," he whispered. "I'll make the knots loose."

"And don't even think about making the knots loose," the old man called out. "I will be checking them, and if they are shoddily tied, I shall slice this woman's throat!"

"Darn!" Max said.

However, while the old man may have been bonkers, Max didn't believe he was bluffing. He was just crazy enough to actually slice Rosita's throat, and that could not be allowed to happen. And so, he did a reasonable job of knot-tying. Not his best work, but good enough to pass inspection by an ancient shaman.

"There," he said, looking at Axel. "Knots as snug as a bug. Just like when we were kids."

He stood up afterward and glared at the old man.

"Okay, now what? It's been a hot minute since I read the prophecies."

"Bembe," the old man said. "Bembe must climb up and lay upon the altar."

Max's eyes widened. "How ... how do you know his name?" He looked over at the skater punk, who was having a difficult time meeting anyone's gaze.

"Bembe," the old man repeated. "You must climb upon the altar."

Max reached over and gripped the young man's arm. "Bembe? What is going on?"

Bembe at last met Max's stare, and his eyes were filled with tears. "Sorry, bruh. I should have told you everything. I thought I could work it out—"

"Bembe, now!" shouted the old man.

Bembe nodded sadly. "Yes, Horado."

"H-H-Horado?" Max stammered. "You know this guy?"

Max let his hand fall away and, without answering the question, Bembe walked slowly to the altar. Just as slowly, he climbed on top and lay down on his back. As he did, another rolling clap of thunder sounded, and the sky darkened as black clouds began scuttling over the sun.

"And now," the old man said, "the ceremony may begin."

"Should I tie myself up?" Max asked helpfully.

The old man, Horado, frowned. "You would do well to take this more seriously, young man. It is really quite a privilege. You have the opportunity to bring about a new world order. A role to play."

"Great," Max said tonelessly. "Just what I always wanted."

"Exactly," Horado said, apparently missing the sarcasm.

Max looked around. "What's next? Is Estrada going to come waltzing out to take all the credit?"

Horado's face twisted suddenly and became dark with rage. "Estrada!" He practically spit out the name. "The evil man defeated us once at Ahrum, but this time the tables have turned." He calmed slightly, and then said, "And I do appreciate your help in removing his forces from the temple. Had they reached the crystal first, this all might have gone differently."

"Well, yeah, we wouldn't be stuck on top of an ancient temple with you, for one thing."

"The enemy of your enemy is not always your friend," Horado said. "Do not think Estrada's men would have let you live, even if they had reached the crystal first."

"So, you're basically saying we were doomed either way," Max accused.

"Doomed? Who said anything about being doomed?"

"I just assumed from the ropes, knives, and altar that things were headed in a sort of doom-ish direction."

"I have no intention of killing all of you," Horado said. "Bembe is the only one I need. The rest of you simply must be restrained so as not to interfere with the fulfillment of the prophecies."

"Oh, well, if you only want to kill Bembe— hey, wait a minute!"

Horado laughed. "You are getting ahead of things, my friend. Since you are unfamiliar with these prophecies, I shall overlook it. But first, we need to secure our final spectator."

With that, Horado shoved Rosita toward Max. She stumbled forward into his arms, throwing him off balance for long enough that he had no opportunity to attack Horado before the old man had shifted the knife to Bembe's throat instead. While it did seem that Bembe might be a lost cause anyway, Max was determined to stretch out the scenario as long as possible, hoping beyond hope that a solution would find time to present itself.

"Tie her!" Horado shouted, his voice cracking in concert with another peal of thunder.

Max led her over to where he'd tied Axel and Isabel, adding Rosita to the growing line of captives. He stood up and turned, only to find Horado securing Bembe to the altar with thick leather straps.

"Bembe!"

The young Maya looked at Max with forlorn eyes. "It's too late, bruh. Look—" he motioned upward with a nod of his head. "—the storm."

"What about the storm? It's just ... a storm! It doesn't mean anything!"

Bembe shook his head. "Nah, man. It means it's too late."

Max wanted to scream. His was a rational mind and, while he'd seen enough during this adventure to make him question many things, he did not believe in the inevitability of things: fate, predestination, providence ... these were things that suggested individual helplessness. Max knew his rejection of these made him somewhat traditional, but he doggedly clung to the power of the individual, free will, the ability to make one's own choices and take responsibility for the results—for better or worse. For him, life was not worth living otherwise.

And this was a perfect example.

The oncoming storm was, no doubt, spoken of in the prophecies that Horado was continuing to harp about. And Bembe, apparently being at least somewhat familiar with these prophecies, was taking the freak display of weather as proof that it was all meant to be. That's why he wasn't struggling. That's why he looked to despondent and resigned.

Confound it! Max thought. *Why doesn't he fight?*

He started forward, fire in his eyes, but Horado saw the look and brought the knife down to Bembe's throat with terrifying speed and force. The blade pressed deeply, and Bembe choked a little. Max came to a halt as a tiny trickle of blood ran down the side of the little man's neck. He growled low and looked at Horado with seething rage. It was all foolishness, he knew, but for now he still needed to play the game.

"All right," he said, his voice low and steady. "You said I had a role to play. What is it?"

Horado reached below the altar with one hand and came up with a golden goblet, ornately engraved and encrusted with gemstones. He held it out toward Max.

"As the prophecies describe, a witness must drink from the sacred goblet to signify the consumption of the old order, in order for the new order to assert itself."

"Uh, I'm not drinking blood."

Horado's creaking laugh cut its way through the rumbling thunder overhead. "Ha! It is not blood—what do you think we are, savages?"

We? Max thought.

Horado waggled the goblet, which irritated Max even more. He stepped forward and took it from the old man. He looked into it, smelled it, and then glanced back up.

"Wine?"

Horado nodded. "Exactly. Only wine. It is simply a symbolic thing you do."

"But you just said that it was required to—"

"THE PROPHECIES MUST BE FULFILLED!" Horado shrieked, so loud that Max's ears rang. He might have even stamped his foot like a toddler, but Max couldn't be certain, because a flash of lightning distracted him at just that moment.

"Geez! Fine! I am rather thirsty."

"Very good," Horado said, calming himself. "Then drink, my young catalyst, drink it all ... "

Max held the goblet and looked deep into its contents. He then looked at Bembe and saw that the knife was still pressed hard, depressing the skin of the neck to a distressing degree. He then looked over at Axel ... who winked.

Time, Max thought. *We just need time.*

As he brought the goblet to his lips, he felt the first scattered drops of rain hit his head and shoulders. They were big, heavy drops, and they felt good.

He put his head back and drank.

As he did, Horado began spouting a long string of nonsense, indecipherable rhythmic incantations that made Max queasy. Or was that the wine that was making him queasy? The wine had been delicious, but perhaps ... it ...

Dizziness settled into Max's head, accompanied by the floating idea that he'd felt exactly this way before ... when had it been? At the compound, yes ... he ... it was ...

Max knew he was falling, but there wasn't a damn thing he could do about it.

29

Max awoke to a low rumbling sound.

The storm, he thought. *It's still storming. At least that means I wasn't out for too long.*

He wondered if it was still raining. He sort of hoped so, because his skin felt flush, as with a fever, and the cool water would feel good pelting his body.

He groaned and tried to roll over.

"He's awake!"

Isabel?

Max struggled to open his eyes, succeeded, and then immediately regretted it. Sunlight was in far too great a supply. He groaned again and put his hand over his face to block the offending rays. *Whatever happened to that nice, black, stormy sky?*

"And I think he is grumpy boy," the voice said again, definitely Isabel's.

"What's happening," Max moaned. "Why is everything bright and people are cheerful? Aren't we all about to die? Wait—did we all die? Is this ... "

"No one has died," Isabel said. "Well, except for maybe that one old man."

"Horado?"

"*Sí*, yes."

Someone else chuckled, the deep voice betraying its owner. "At least, we *think* he's dead," Axel said. "When I charged him, he jumped off the side of the pyramid and disappeared into the undergrowth. We didn't take the time to search for his body, but I can't imagine anyone surviving that kind of fall."

A smile slowly grew across Max's face. "So you got free. You remembered." He opened his eyes to see Axel grinning back at him from the cockpit of a plane. *So that's what the rumble is. Not thunder, but the engine of the plane!*

"Of course I remembered. We spent weeks inventing that knot as kids. We called it the Maxel Slip. Looks and feels tight, but if you pull two different pieces of the rope at the same time, it pops right open. Horado, or whatever the heck his name was, figured we were out of the way. With you unconscious from that little concoction in the wine and Bembe strapped down, he felt safe. But once he took the knife from Bembe's throat and backed up enough to finish his little ceremony, I rushed him."

"And instead of facing you, he jumped off the pyramid," Max finished.

"That's about the size of it."

Max groaned again. "I have so many questions."

"Yeah, I can probably help out with some of those," Bembe said, coughing awkwardly.

Max looked over and saw the little Maya had his throat bandaged up. The knife had cut a little deeper than he'd thought, he realized. It had been an extremely close call.

"First, I should apologize to all you folks. I thought we'd be able to stop it from getting this far, ya know?"

"Can you make this short and sweet?" Max said. "My head is starting to throb. Maybe you can start with why the stuff in the goblet didn't kill me. I'm pretty sure it's the same as what I got at Estrada's compound."

"Yep, that's right, brah. And good thing it was because your body had built up a resistance to it. So instead of killing you, it just knocked you out for a while."

"Okay, with you so far."

"That crystal you took in the temple—that's the same one I told you about that first night. The one that the shamans were trying to use to save their gods when the Spaniards attacked. And you remember how I told you about that young guy who tried to complete the ritual?"

Max nodded.

"Well, it must've worked, because the crystal seems to be the key to resetting the world order. Both Horado and Estrada want it for its encapsulated power."

"Problem is," Bembe said, grimacing. "The crystal is broken."

Max groaned. "I was afraid of that when I felt how it was rough on some sides but smooth on others. Were there others shards around? Did Isabel and I miss anything?"

"You didn't miss anything," Axel cut in. "We double checked on our way back down from the top of the temple. There is just a piece—or pieces—missing."

"So ... what does that mean?" Max's head was really starting to throb.

Axel sighed. "Well, we've been talking about that while you were having your beauty sleep. Based on Bembe's recollections and knowledge, and what we can deduce from everything that's happened, the search for Ahrum wasn't anyone's final goal. It was just step one. It isn't just grabbing that one crystal and being done with it, it's—"

"Putting the crystal back together ... reuniting the pieces," Max breathed.

"Bingo," Bembe said. "And that's why Horado didn't just perform the crystal ceremony. He couldn't because he didn't have all the pieces. He was performing a ceremony to find out where the rest of the pieces are located."

Max heaved a deep breath. Then he looked at Bembe. "Hey ... what happened to your lederhosen or whatever?"

Bembe grinned. "You're too much, dude. It was ancient Mayan garb, and I got it from the shaman quarters in the temple, before I came out and screamed at those jerks who were gonna shoot you."

"It fits you perfectly."

"That's cuz it was made for me, bruh. I mean, you've probably kinda figured this out, but I'm a lot older than I look. In fact, I was there when the Spaniards attacked Ahrum. I was the young shaman who cut his hand to try to complete the ritual." As he spoke these words, Bembe held up his hand to show off the scar that Max had noticed that first night, the night that now seemed so long ago. "I wore the same outfit on that day."

"It held up well," Max said drily.

"Yep, more evidence that I actually succeeded. The magic kept everything pristine that would be needed for the final ceremony."

"And Horado?"

"He was there too. Remember the senior shaman who was shot through the head?"

Max nodded and then immediately regretted it.

"Well, that's him. You probably saw the scar."

"So let me guess," Max said. "Estrada's the conquistador, isn't he?"

Bembe grinned. "You're gettin' it, brah! Yeah, he must've got a whiff of whatever happened in that chamber with the crystal after I got knocked out."

"This all makes a sort of weird, bizarre sense," Max said, "and I am getting very sleepy. But one more thing before I drop off into a non-poison-induced slumber. What happened at the airport? I saw the flaming wreckage on TV!"

"Ah, yes, flaming wreckage," Axel said. "You can thank that toothless little jerk Manuel for that. One of Estrada's men. That 'lidar' he installed was actually a bomb. It was supposed to go off when we reached cruising altitude, but he messed up the timing. It went off while he was doing the final pre-flight check."

"And where were all of you?"

"Rosita and I were out with Bembe, trying out his rigged-up skateboard. He'd pilfered some old plane parts and tried to make it usable."

"Did it work?"

Bembe shook his head sadly. "Not even a little." He brightened. "But it looked cool!"

"So anyway, all of our stuff was gone. I'd even put my phone and wallet in my backpack and tossed that into the cockpit. After the explosion, we didn't know exactly what was happening and assumed we were under attack. We grabbed a Jeep and got the heck outta there, but by the time we reached where we thought you and Isabel were ... you weren't. We did some detective work and figured you were headed here."

"How'd you find it? Isabel and I benefited from some good luck on that score."

Axel jerked a thumb at Bembe. "It was him, mostly."

"Wait a minute," Max said. "If you knew where it was, why didn't you take us there in the first place?"

Bembe shrugged. "Mostly a timing thing, bruh. You don't think I tried returning home a dozen times? The magic had it locked down. It was like a moving target. All the elements had to align, one of which was the return of Horado to the temple."

All the events hurled through Max's mind at dizzying speed, including the skinned man (no doubt one of Estrada's) and the man wearing the skin suit (no doubt Horado returning to Ahrum, wearing the flesh of his enemies). It all made a sort of horrible sense, although more questions were even now piling atop one another in his mind.

However, all that could wait, he decided, as both his body and mind, tapped completely dry from recent events, began turning off all on their own.

"I think our intrepid adventurer is falling asleep now," Isabel said.

And that was the last thing Max heard before drifting away, lulled by the rumble and gentle shake of the plane.

ALSO BY CRAIG A. HART

The Shelby Alexander Thriller Series

Serenity

Serenity Stalked

Serenity Avenged

Serenity Submerged

Serenity Engulfed

Serenity Betrayed

Serenity Reborn

Serenity Possessed

The Maxwell Barnes Adventure Thriller Series

Mayan Shadows

The SpyCo Novella Series

Assignment: Athens

Assignment: Paris

Assignment: Istanbul

Assignment: Sydney

Assignment: Alaska

Assignment: Dublin

Assignment: London

The Cleanup Crew Thriller Series

The Demon of Denver

The Simon Wolfe Mystery Series

Night at Key West

Collections

The Shelby Alexander Collection, Books 1-4

Assignment: Adventure, SpyCo Books 1-3

Assignment: Danger, SpyCo Books 4-6

A Cleanup Crew Collection, Books 1-4

ALSO BY S.J. VARENGO

The Cleanup Crew Thriller Series

The Beauty of Bucharest

The Count of Carolina

The Terror of Tijuana

The Demon of Denver

The Maxwell Barnes Adventure Thriller Series

Mayan Shadows

The Cerah of Quadar Fantasy Series

A Dark Clock

Many Hidden Rooms

A Single Candle

The Shelby Alexander Thriller Series

Serenity Reborn

Serenity Possessed

The SpyCo Novella Series

Assignment: Paris

Assignment: Istanbul

Assignment: Sydney

Assignment: Dublin

Assignment: London

Collections

Assignment: Adventure, SpyCo Books 1-3

Assignment: Danger, SpyCo Books 4-6

A Cleanup Crew Collection, Books 1-4

Standalone Novels

Jelly Jars

A NOTE ABOUT REVIEWS

If you enjoyed this book, a review would mean the world. Reviews are so important to authors and are essential to being able to market books effectively.

Just a line or two makes a huge difference!

Thank you!

ABOUT THE AUTHOR

Craig A. Hart is the stay-at-home father of twin boys, an author, and audiobook narrator. A native of Grand Rapids, Michigan, Craig lives in Iowa City, Iowa with his wife, sons, insane dog, and anti-social cat.

He is the author of the Shelby Alexander Thriller Series, the historical mystery *Night at Key West,* and co-author of the Maxwell Barnes Adventure Thriller series.

For up-to-date info on new releases, follow Craig on BookBub at: bookbub.com/profile/craig-a-hart

ABOUT THE AUTHOR

S.J. Varengo is a married father of two adult children. He lives in Upstate New York despite dire warnings. His published works include a volume of short fiction (*Welcome Home*), the Cerah of Quadar fantasy series, the Cleanup Crew thriller series, and the Maxwell Barnes Adventure Thriller series, which he co-writes author Craig A. Hart.

facebook.com/sjvarengo

twitter.com/PapaV

bookbub.com/authors/s-j-varengo

amazon.com/S.-J.-Varengo/e/B06XBCL1KR

Printed in Great Britain
by Amazon

30799548R00169